the universes await ...

Discover all of the Balky Point Adventures!

The Universes Inside the Lighthouse
The Secret of the Dark Galaxy Stone
The Planet of the Memory Thieves

the Planet of the Memory Thieves

a Balky Point adventure

Books by Pam Stucky

FICTION

The Balky Point Adventures (Middle Grade/YA sci-fi)

The Universes Inside the Lighthouse

The Secret of the Dark Galaxy Stone

The Planet of the Memory Thieves

Mystery

Death at Glacier Lake

Final Chapter (A Megan Montaigne Mystery)

The Wishing Rock series (contemporary fiction)
(novels with recipes)

Letters from Wishing Rock

The Wishing Rock Theory of Life

The Tides of Wishing Rock

NONFICTION

the Pam on the Map travel series

Iceland

Seattle Day Trips

Retrospective: Switzerland

Retrospective: Ireland

From the Wishing Rock Kitchens: Recipes from the Series

www.pamstucky.com

twitter.com/pamstucky

facebook.com/pamstuckyauthor

pinterest.com/pamstucky

The Planet *of the* Memory Thieves

a Balky Point adventure

Pam Stucky

This book is a work of fiction. Names, characters, places, and incidents either are products of the author's imagination, or are used fictitiously. Any resemblance to actual events or locales or persons, living or dead, is entirely coincidental.

Published in the United States by Wishing Rock Press.

Cover design and artwork by Jim Tierney jimtierneyart.com

ISBN-13: 978-1-940800-18-9 (paperback)
ISBN-13: 978-1-940800-19-6 (ebook)

wishingrockpress.com

for Paula and Dean

"A human being is a part of the whole
called by us *universe*, a part limited in time and
space. He experiences himself, his thoughts and
feelings as something separated from the rest,
a kind of optical delusion of his consciousness.
This delusion is a kind of prison for us, restricting
us to our personal desires and to affection for a
few persons nearest to us. Our task must be to free
ourselves from this prison by widening our circle
of compassion to embrace all living creatures and
the whole of nature in its beauty."

~ *Albert Einstein*

chapter one

"Déjà vu," said Emma as she set up her tent. She looked around, puzzled. She felt like she'd been in this moment before. Something about the landscape was familiar, though she knew she'd never been there. Not this place, not this planet. Had she? In a dream, maybe? No, she was sure. Wasn't she?

"What?" said Ree.

"I feel like we've done this before. You, me, Charlie, Chuck. I remember us setting up our tent, and Charlie and Chuck setting up their tent, and then they stay here while you and I go back to the Hub for ..." she stopped.

"For what?" asked Ree.

"I don't know," said Emma. "It's gone. Déjà vu over."

chapter two

"Everybody smile! And one, two …" Dr. Waldo counted, smiling broadly himself but with a hint of confusion as he looked through the unfamiliar phone and tried to take a picture. Dr. Waldo was a brilliant scientist on his planet Lero, and was well respected both there and here in the Hub, a place where all the multiple universes overlapped, and also a place where truly everything was possible. But Emma Nelson's iPhone baffled him.

"Oh!" he said, laughing gleefully after snapping the photo. "Why, I've taken a picture of myself!" He turned the phone so the others could see.

Emma jumped up from the couch where she'd been posing with her twin brother, Charlie, and several of their friends. She took the device from Dr. Waldo and tapped on the screen. "Sorry, I left it on selfie mode," she said. "But don't delete that picture. I want to keep it." She handed the phone back to Dr. Waldo. "Just tap there," she directed, then returned to the couch.

Shaking his head, Dr. Waldo held the phone up once more and this time took the picture correctly. He handed the phone back to Emma, who nodded her satisfaction.

"Why you use this primitive camera is beyond me," Dr. Waldo said. "I have a camera that will take a 360-degree image that you can project into space! It's like you're there again!" Without another word he ran off.

"Is he going to get his camera?" said Eve with an amused smile. Eve was also from Lero, the same planet as Dr. Waldo, and had been working with him for a good while, even though she was still only a teenager, by Earth years. About the same age as Emma and Charlie, they'd calculated, somewhere near seventeen. Emma and Charlie were from Earth, but had become good friends with Eve through many previous adventures.

Also on the couch were Emma and Charlie's counterparts, another Emma and another Charlie from a parallel Earth in a parallel universe, whom they'd also met on earlier journeys throughout time and space. To avoid confusion, they'd decided to call the Charlie from a parallel universe Chuck. The parallel Emma had only recently started hanging out with the group more, and had told them all to call her by her middle name, Ree.

Emma smiled softly to herself as she looked at the picture. Aside from her parents, these were the people she treasured most in life. There was Eve, sweet Eve. Emma tilted her head. This was the first picture she'd actually taken of Eve. Of course Eve looked like herself in the picture—that is, like a person from Lero. Her neck was slightly longer than human necks. Her skin, more translucent and quite pale. Her eyes, slightly larger. All the friends had bracelets they wore when they explored the universes—bracelets with stones that carried special powers, almost magical properties, though of course they believed in science, not magic. One of the stones made its wearer look like the observer's species; that is, to humans, if Eve was wearing a bracelet, Eve looked human. Other stones made the atmosphere of a planet safe to breathe, or translated languages seamlessly. Even in the Hub, where the air was good to breathe and the friends all felt safe with each other, they still wore the bracelets so the translation stone would work. This was much easier than learning a whole new alien language. So Emma was used to Eve looking like a human. She knew she'd have to be careful with this photo. No one else could see it. No one outside their circle, anyway.

Rounding out the subjects of the photo was another young man named Ben. Ben was also from Earth—Emma and Charlie's Earth, rather than Chuck and Ree's Earth—and, along with Eve, was now working almost full time in the Hub with Dr. Waldo and the other scientists.

Ben leaned over Emma's shoulder to check out the photo. Emma felt her heart skip a beat. She'd had a mild crush on Ben since she and Charlie first met him, and while neither of them had done much to further that attraction, she still felt a twinge of excitement at having him so near.

"Great picture," Ben said with a smile. He absentmindedly ran his fingers through his dark hair. "Send that to me?"

"Me too," said Ree, who had joined them to look at the image. "It's so weird," she said to Emma. "I'm used to having a twin, but not yet used to looking at another me. Seeing both of us in that picture is weird."

"Do you think you could pick out which of us is Chuck and which of us is Charlie, if you didn't know?" asked Chuck, Ree's twin.

"Of course," said Emma, but she hesitated. She studied the photo, zooming in for a closer look at Chuck and Charlie. To be honest, she admitted to herself, even in real life sometimes she had to do a double take before she knew who was who. The Earth that Chuck and Ree came from had been so similar to her own when they had first met. Sure, there were a few differences, but the major facts had been more or less the same. However, as time went on it seemed the parallel earths were diverging more and more. Chuck and Ree's grandfather, their mother's father, had just died, for example, whereas Emma and Charlie's grandfather was still alive and well. Dr. Waldo had explained that this was how it worked with parallel universes: often they started out the same, but then took different paths as time went on. These paths could be spurred by a single different choice, a single moment that made all the difference, literally, in the world.

Charlie saw Emma's face and knew she was bluffing. "We're going to test you," he said, nudging Chuck, who had also joined them. "Same clothes, series of pictures. I'll bet you won't be able to guess."

"Of course I will," said Emma defiantly. "You underestimate me. I know you very well, Charles Rainier Nelson."

"But that's just it," said Chuck. "I'm Charles Rainier Nelson, too."

Emma frowned. He was right. Would she know?

"All this is great speculation," said Eve, "but what I want to know is, Chuck and Charlie, are you ready for your exploration? Packed and ready to go?" She saw their gear in packs next to the couch and gave them two thumbs up.

Since discovering that they could travel all over the universes via an "elevator" inside the lighthouse at Balky Point, on Dogwinkle Island, Charlie and Chuck had been trying to figure out how they could make some money off of it. Originally, their idea had been to sell travel packages in which people could have an adventure inside the Hub, but Dr. Waldo had immediately vetoed the idea.

"Impossible!" the scientist had said. "Everything is possible in the Hub!" As it turned out, in a strange quirk of the multiverse, anything that was possible in any of the universes was therefore possible in the Hub. With infinite universes and infinite possibilities, that meant within the Hub, everything was possible.

"Yes?" Chuck had replied, his one raised eyebrow revealing his confusion. "Isn't that the point?" To Chuck and Charlie, this seemed like an exceptional selling point for their travel company. "People can come here and do things they've only dreamed of," Chuck had continued. "Fly. Breathe underwater. Talk to animals. Anything they can imagine."

"Yes, yes, yes," Dr. Waldo had said in his breathless way, as though his thoughts were flying so fast he had to catch them before he could talk. "But don't you see, *everything is possible.* You can't have people coming in here without security clearance! What if someone were to come in and start tampering with my scientific equipment?" Dr. Waldo had spent years creating his dream lab inside the Hub, imagining things into existence through the power of intention and then adjusting over time as he had new ideas and new questions. And then, in a flash, the wrong person got in and it had all been destroyed. He'd had to start over from scratch. The Hub—at least, this one, as there were many Hubs in the multiverse—this Hub was his treasure, and he couldn't imagine having to start over again.

Emma had jumped in at this point. "They'll come up with something else, Dr. Waldo, don't worry," she'd said, and had steered the boys away from the conversation. She'd decided that was not the time to point out that none of *them* had ever gotten security clearance.

After much discussion, Chuck and Charlie came up with a new idea: they would act as travel guides to other reasonably hospitable planets. They would explore the universes on their own at first to find prime travel destinations, each tailored to a certain demographic. With all the universes and all the planets to pick from, they'd surmised, surely there would be places both ordinary and extraordinary where they could lead people of all levels of adventurousness. For people who merely wanted a nice vacation away from crowds, they would find planets with pristine beaches, for example, or some nice bucolic lakes. But for others who liked a bit more risk, they might lead excursions to a planet they'd discovered previously, a planet where dinosaur-like creatures called plassensnares still roamed freely.

Emma and Ree were still trying to convince their twins that the latter was not, perhaps, the best idea, but Chuck and Charlie were determined.

For now, however, the boys were busy plotting their destinations and putting together their Travel Adventure Packs. Interuniversal travel had its dangers and challenges, of course, and it took multiple brains to try to anticipate every possibility. All of them—Emma, Ree, Eve, Ben, and even Dr. Waldo—had gotten involved in helping with that effort. The challenge, the Charlies had learned early on, was that things that worked in the Hub did not necessarily work out "in the field," or outside the Hub. While everything was possible in the Hub, not everything was possible outside of the Hub. Much testing had been done, and much more testing remained.

As far as taking paying customers along was concerned, the logistics were still being worked out. In the meantime, the Charlies were having a blast discovering interesting locations for their future customers. Sometimes with Ben's help and sometimes without, they'd pinpointed a few planets that showed great promise. At the moment Chuck and Charlie were almost packed and ready to go check out one of their prospective locales. Emma and Ree had agreed to go along for a day or two. Eve and Ben were needed for their work at the Hub, but promised to come along on another excursion soon.

"Did you check the weather for this planet?" Charlie said to Chuck, as he lifted his large pack onto his back.

Chuck looked sheepishly at Ben. "Uh … no. Ben, did you happen to …?"

Ben smiled. "Clear and dry, at least at the landing point, as far as I can tell. There was some electrical disturbance, but I'll work that out. I haven't perfected weather forecasting on other planets just yet."

"They haven't perfected weather forecasting on *this* planet just yet," said Emma reassuringly. "We'll take what we get. I'm packed and ready," she told the group, and nodded at her backpack leaning against the couch.

"Me too," said Ree. She smiled broadly at Ben. Emma noticed an unusual twinkle in Ree's eyes. Ree was normally rather quiet, but with Ben, she seemed to glow.

"I wish we could come with you," said Eve, but her smile never wavered. "Next time."

Just then, Dr. Waldo returned carrying a metal ball in his hands. "Is that a new kind of pigeon?" said Chuck. Pigeons were devices that would transport a person or people back to one specific pre-determined place. Dr. Waldo had named them after homing pigeons, a wild pigeon on Earth that was always able to find its way home, even from long distances.

"No, no, no," said Dr. Waldo. He held the tiny ball up to eye level and stared intently into it, as though he could see a whole world inside. "This," he said, "is my camera. A real camera, not like that phone! Shall we?"

The others looked around uncertainly. "What do you want us to do?" said Eve, beaming at the mad scientist she loved so well.

"Smile for the camera!" said Dr. Waldo, as though this should have been obvious. The teens all grinned; Chuck and Charlie struck dramatic poses. "Click!" said Dr. Waldo. Then, "There, it's done!"

"You say 'click' and it takes a picture?" said Charlie doubtfully.

"That is exactly right, son, exactly right, exactly right," said Dr. Waldo. "Now come with me!" He rushed away toward the Experimental Building without looking to see if the others were following. But of course, they were.

The Experimental Building was one of Emma's favorite parts of the Hub. Simply put, it was a building in which Dr. Waldo (and other select scientists, if they were lucky) conducted some experiments. But it was much more than that. The exterior wavered in and out of view—an early quirk that Dr. Waldo had kept because he enjoyed the illusion, even though he'd long since figured out what was causing the visual disruptions. The building was much larger inside than one expected from the outside; this being the Hub, of course, everything was possible.

Dr. Waldo rushed the group into the building and past their favorite familiar rooms: "Thought," with its giant maze; the Secret Garden, where people planted their secrets; and more.

"This room," Emma said as they passed a door with a placard above it that said, simply, KNOWLEDGE. "What is this? Is this new?" She felt an almost physical pull to go inside. How could a person resist a room of knowledge? "Is it a library?" she asked.

"Ah!" said Dr. Waldo, as he stopped to admire the door as though it were knowledge itself. "No, not exactly," he said. "You see, you see, every planet has *two* worlds. There is the *physical* world, of course, what we see, hear, touch, smell, all these things. But on advanced planets, planets with advanced civilizations, there is a world of *information*. Wisdom. Knowledge. Many of these planets have developed systems similar to your internet. In this room," he said, pausing briefly for dramatic effect. "In this room, I am working to find a way to access all the civilizations' internets."

Charlie and Chuck exchanged a meaningful look. "No!" they said in unison. "Seriously?" said Charlie. "That … that is amazing."

"And *useful*," added Chuck. Charlie nodded in agreement.

"Now, now, children," said Dr. Waldo. "It's still a work in progress. Don't get too excited." He moved on along the hallway, but the others moved more slowly, contemplating the ramifications of a room that held all the knowledge in the multiverse.

"Dr. Waldo," said Emma, as she jogged to catch up with the older man. "Dr. Waldo," she repeated, "I remember something you once told us. I remember it almost word for word, actually. You said: 'The universes reveal secrets in their own time and in their own way. Sometimes it's a matter of whether you're ready to see it. There's a room in this building, for example, that you can only see if you're ready to see it. Otherwise you wouldn't know it even exists.'"

Dr. Waldo turned, a sparkle in his eye. "Yes?" he said.

"So, what room is it?" said Emma impatiently. "Is it Knowledge?"

"One day you will know, Emma," he said. "One day. But for now," he stopped at a room that had no placard over it. "For now, we are at our destination."

"What is this room?" asked Ree, looking around for any clues.

"It is an empty room," said Dr. Waldo.

"Yes," said Charlie, "but what does it *do*?"

"It is just an empty room," said Dr. Waldo, holding his hands wide. "Sometimes you simply need an empty room. Well, mostly empty," he said. He opened the door to reveal a large room with tall white walls and a thin pillar at the center, about three feet high. He led the teens inside and pulled the small metal ball from the front pocket on his lab coat. After ceremoniously placing the spherical camera on top of the pillar, he stepped back. "Display photo," he said to the device, enunciating carefully.

Suddenly, the room was filled with the image the camera had taken minutes before. But it wasn't just a flat image on a wall; this was, instead, more like a hologram that they could walk through.

Emma stepped around the image of herself and examined herself from the back. She could see that she hadn't gotten the part in her shoulder-length auburn hair quite straight that morning, and she subconsciously reached for that part on her own head.

"Crazy," said Charlie, his mouth agape in awe. "How many pictures does that ball hold?" Already he had visions of ways he and Chuck could monetize this tiny camera and offer it up to clients on their travel adventures. He and Chuck exchanged another knowing glance and nodded simultaneously.

"Oh, not that many," said Dr. Waldo. "It's just a prototype, based on technology commonly available. Maybe a few hundred," he said. "But it will last forever, and you don't have to print out the images, unlike your phone camera, where the pictures will be lost within a year or two when the phone technology becomes obsolete and you forget to transfer the photographs," he said wistfully. "Alas, I've lost pictures to technology before, and to the ravages of time on paper. This," he said, his hand held out to the metal ball, "this will last forever."

Ree, too, was navigating her way through the three-dimensional image that filled the room, her hand instinctively reaching out to touch objects that weren't actually there. "Can I have this one?" she asked. "I mean, we can make copies, right?" she said. "I don't want to take the only copy."

"It's yours," said Dr. Waldo. "Close display," he said to the camera, and the image disappeared, leaving behind an almost eerie, empty space again. He picked up the ball and handed it to Ree. "Yours forever."

"Amazing," said Chuck. He looked at Charlie. "But we've got to get going. That *planet* won't be around forever," he said.

"You guys sure you don't want to come along?" Charlie said to Eve and Ben. "We'd love your company."

"'Want to' is not the same as 'can,'" said Eve. "I'd love to. But I've got this big project and my boss is very demanding," she said, smiling at Dr. Waldo.

"No, no, no," said Dr. Waldo. "If you want—"

"Not at all, Dr. Waldo," said Ben. "We can't go running off every time Chuck and Charlie have a new brilliant idea. We'd never get any work done!"

"That is true," said Chuck with mock humility.

"Off we go, then!" said Charlie. "We'll be back soon! Don't wait up!"

chapter three

The universes held many mysteries, Dr. Waldo liked to say, and revealed the answers to their secrets in their own time and way. No one knew for sure, and likely no one would ever know, all the ways a person could travel from one place or time to another. But so far, Dr. Waldo and his scientists had discovered a handful of methods.

The easiest, and likely the first that most civilizations discovered, was the elevators. The concept of elevators, while rather unbelievable at first, was actually quite simple. The group had come to think of the infinite universes as layers, similar to the layers of batting in a quilt, all stacked on top of one another. At certain points within the universes—such as the Balky Point Lighthouse on Earth, near where Ben and Emma and Charlie now lived—one could travel from universe to universe simply by stepping into a small room and entering another universe's coordinates into a control panel on the wall. Evidence suggested that not all universes were connected to all elevators. On Earth, every elevator was inside a lighthouse, but not every lighthouse held an elevator. On other planets, an elevator could be just about anywhere.

As indicated by the power of certain rocks, such as the ones on the bracelets they wore, it was clear that rocks in the universes—at least some rocks—were powerful. Recently, Eve's mother, Kata, had discovered yet another way to travel within universes that seemed to confound the metaphor of universes layered on top of each other. By accident, she had come across a place in Australia where, by holding in her hand a magnet and a black opal, multiple universes suddenly opened up in front of her, like a life-sized slide show where she only had to jump through to the other side. Her hypothesis, which she was now studying back at the Hub, was that while some universes were layered like batting in a blanket, others were interwoven. An atom, she pointed out, was about 99.999999999 percent empty space. But was it truly empty? Kata speculated that in fact, all that empty space was taken up by other universes. "If there are infinite universes," she liked to say, "They all have to fit in somewhere." Kata had inadvertently traveled to a few different universes this way, but at this point they only knew of the one spot on Earth where they could access other universes with this method. Part of what Eve was doing in her work in the Hub was helping her mother learn more.

A third, and quite unexpected, way they'd found to travel was unique to Emma, as far as they knew at this point. In an emergency, Emma had once discovered that she was able to transport herself and others through space and time simply using the power of her mind. Dr. Waldo was working with her to study this ability, and had advised her not to use it unless absolutely necessary, until they knew more. At first they'd seen evidence that this sort of travel shortened her telomeres, which were a part of her DNA. Shortened telomeres indicated shortened life span, which Dr. Waldo didn't have to tell Emma or anyone else was not a good thing. However, he now suspected the telomeres could be repaired, but more study was needed.

And so, generally, the group now relied on the fourth method of travel: the Dark MATTER sphere, which stood for Dark Multiverse And Time Travel Energy Redistributer, an acronym of which Dr. Waldo was quite proud. The Dark MATTER spheres could transport people almost anywhere, and it was one of these spheres that Charlie, Chuck, Emma, and Ree used to get to this new planet they were about to explore.

"Everyone ready?" Charlie said, and all the twins gathered around him, holding each other tight for the journey through the multiverse. Charlie swiped a tiny screen on the little sphere, and the teens disappeared from the Hub, their molecules instantly scattered to parts unknown. From their perspective, the feeling was next to indescribable. It was as if their bodies were suddenly a part of everything and nothing at the same time; like they'd been stirred in with the universes and any one exact thing was indistinguishable from any other. Then, within milliseconds, the process reversed, and they found themselves made whole again on completely unfamiliar terrain.

Traveling through space was always disorienting, and for the first several moments after they landed on their destination planet the teens lay on the ground in what the Charlies had started to call "recombobulation time." After all, they reasoned, if *discombobulated* was a word—and travel through space was most certainly discombobulating—then the time they spent letting the molecules of their bodies re-settle into their proper positions surely could be called recombobulation.

After a short while, Chuck was the first to sit up. "How many suns did you say this planet has?" he said, squinting up into the sky.

"And how many moons?" Ree chimed in, standing up and brushing the dirt off her clothes. She turned in a full circle, arms wide, gazing at the thrilling, exotic plane.

"One sun, three moons," said Charlie. He stood and looked around the landscape with great pride. This planet, whatever it might be called, if it even had a name, was his find. Ben had helped some, but Charlie had done most of the research on his own. "Stunning, am I right? Old Charlie came up with a winner, I'd say." He stood, arms akimbo, looking out on his new domain.

"It's beautiful," said Emma. She got up and put an arm around her brother. "Nice find, Charlie." While they would need to do some tests to ensure the atmosphere was amenable to humans—and others—the air seemed sweet and fresh. A light breeze swept faint floral scents to her nose, maybe something like roses, Emma thought, ignoring the fact that beyond roses she didn't recognize many floral scents. Under their feet grew something akin to grass, its long green blades poking up through the dirt, interspersed with a small flowering ground cover. The land was mostly flat where they had landed, with a few hills nearby. There were no trees in the immediate area; only bushes. The teens could see far into the distance, out as far as some majestic mountains very far away, or maybe hills; their tops were bare, with no visible snow cover.

The sky glowed a faint yellow, a dim that made the teens want to blink to clear their eyes to see better. Whether this was sunset or the natural color of the sky, it was impossible to tell at this point. By morning they would know.

"What sort of day and night do they have here?" Emma asked, looking around the sky to find the sun. She finally found it, low on the horizon.

Charlie looked at his iPert, a watch/phone/device that Dr. Waldo had created that somehow worked through all the multiverse. They could even call each other on it, most of the time, even from one universe to another. Among its many features was an app that calculated a planet's day/night cycle. "Looks like we're either at an equinox or that's just the way it is all the time. Fifteen hours of light, fifteen hours of dark. And we're just nearing sunset." He looked in the direction Emma was looking, toward the sun as it dipped nearer and nearer the horizon.

"You know," said Emma, "you may have to figure out some way for your clients to deal with jet lag. A fifteen hour day followed by a fifteen hour night, that might mess up some people's body clocks." Emma knew that details were not always her brother's strong point. She wanted to help.

But Charlie saw it otherwise. "Seriously, Emma. Do you need to always ruin everyone's fun? It's a vacation. They'll deal with it for a few days." He huffed and walked away.

Emma was taken aback. What had she said wrong? She turned to Ree, who just shrugged.

"Come on," Charlie called back to the others. "If it's nearly sunset we need to find a good place to set up the tents." He looked at his iPert. "Supposedly there's a small lake over this way." He continued walking, knowing the others would follow. He looked from his iPert off into the distance and back again. "There should be a beach farther out. I'm looking at this planet as a potential beachy destination for our beach-loving clients. If the beach is good."

"So you're saying there's a beach?" asked Chuck.

"I'm saying there should be a beach," confirmed Charlie. "But let's check out the lake first."

After not too long, they found the lake that the iPert had promised would be there. Chuck and Charlie scouted out a reasonably level spot a safe distance away from the water, and started setting up.

"Will there be mosquitoes this close to the water, do you think?" said Emma. "I hate bugs." She shuddered softly. Camping was not really her thing. Her idea of the perfect campsite was s'mores roasted in the oven at home.

"You can always transport yourself home if it's too inconvenient," Charlie sneered. He turned his back on her and pulled a tent out of his pack.

Emma held her tongue. Clearly something was bothering Charlie; he wasn't normally so short with her. She would talk with him about it later.

"I'm starving. What's for dinner?" said Ree. She started digging into her backpack and came up with a protein bar she'd packed.

The Charlies looked at each other, eyes wide.

"What?" said Emma, starting to get annoyed herself. "Did you not plan any food? You're our travel guides. We assumed you were in charge of that."

Her exasperated, superior tone sparked Charlie's anger. "We're not travel guides *yet*. This is a group trip. You were welcome to come along but you should have known to be responsible for yourself," he snapped.

Emma shook her head. "Okay, sure. So what did you bring for *yourselves* to eat? If you were being so responsible?"

Charlie said nothing.

"Did you even bring food for *you*?" Emma challenged, but she already knew the answer. She looked at Chuck; clearly he, too, had forgotten about food. How the two of them, growing teenage boys who ate almost nonstop, could have forgotten to bring food was beyond her. "You've been so caught up in the idea of making money that you forgot we need to eat!" she said, waving her hands uselessly in the air. The travel through space had left her feeling tired and on edge, and finding out there was no dinner to be had put her over the top.

"Emma, I have an extra protein bar," said Ree, reaching for her bag.

"No, no," said Emma. "I have some protein bars, too. I just didn't think I'd have to think of everything, but I guess I was wrong." She grabbed the tent she and Ree were to share and walked off to set it up.

"We can't all be The Chosen One, Emma," Charlie called after her, his words dripping with insult. The unexpected words stung Emma deeply. She set up the tent while hiding her face so the others wouldn't see her tears.

No one went to bed completely hungry. Ree, having predicted that the boys might not remember everything, had brought more than enough protein bars for everyone. She had discreetly distributed them to Chuck and Charlie when Emma wasn't looking, then had given one to Emma, too. The original plan had been to set up a campfire, tell ghost stories, and gaze at the unfamiliar constellations late into the long night, but after Emma and Charlie's fight, no one was in the mood. Chuck and Charlie retreated to their tent to plot the future and to sleep, and Emma and Ree tucked themselves into the tent Emma had set up.

They didn't go to sleep immediately, but rather sat up talking, cozily wrapped in extra-thin but ultra-warm blankets the scientists in the Hub had created. The night was cool but not cold, and the sky was clear. The tents were designed to be airtight, with an oxygen generator built in to give the people inside the air they needed. But there was a wide flap at the top that could be opened for stargazing, and the girls had it open now.

"These tents really are pretty nice," said Emma. Charlie and Chuck had spent a good amount of time with some designers from Lero working on them. She had to admit, they'd come up with some great features. Because they'd been able to use extremely lightweight material, they were able to make the tents quite spacious without adding extra weight to what people would have to carry.

And besides, Chuck had pointed out, people wouldn't really have to carry them far. They'd basically transport themselves directly to the spot where they were going to camp. No one would have to carry anything very far at all.

The light of billions of stars that few people from her own universe had ever seen shined down through the open window in the tent, glowing bright in the night sky. One moon watched over them in the distance; the other two must have been below the horizon. Emma stared at it a while, trying to decide if this moon looked smaller or bigger than her own Earth's moon. Smaller, she finally decided, but maybe brighter. She wondered briefly how long the moons took to orbit this planet; how long this planet took to orbit its sun. The travel excursions were really a great idea, Emma thought, though she'd been too busy ribbing Charlie and Chuck about just wanting to make money to tell them. It wouldn't only be partying holiday-goers in search of pristine beach who would want to take these trips. She could easily imagine eager scientists and curious travelers from all over the world. If she weren't already traveling the multiverse, certainly she herself would be saving up pennies for such an unbelievable adventure. And the boys had been taking the endeavor very seriously, she had to admit. Emma had meant to tell the Charlies how nice the tent was, but after Charlie had put on such an attitude, she didn't feel so charitable.

She turned under her blanket to look toward Ree. Ree's eyes were aglow with the reflected light of the stars, and Emma knew she, too, was lost in the wonder of it.

"What do you think Charlie meant," Emma said softly. "'We can't all be The Chosen One.' What does that mean?" In the pit of her stomach, she suspected she knew the answer, but she hoped she was wrong.

Ree looked away from the swath of stars and turned to Emma. "He's jealous. He feels like you have powers and he doesn't and that makes him nothing," she said.

"Do you think so?" said Emma. "That can't be right. Charlie wouldn't be jealous of me. He knows I didn't ask for that. He knows how hard it is on me."

"And he also is mad at himself that he couldn't save you. That you had to save yourself that time. He wanted to be your hero and instead he was just ... your inferior twin," Ree said.

"My inferior twin! What are you talking about? Do you really think that's what he thinks?" said Emma. She saw a falling star skate across the sky and she remembered: that's how this whole adventure began, months ago. Her and Charlie, sitting in the back of a truck, watching the stars and thinking they had seen UFOs.

"That's what he told Charlie—my Charlie—Chuck. That's what Charlie told Chuck."

Emma paused, stunned. "Charlie told Chuck," she said.

"Yes," said Ree. Her eyes were watching the stars again, but Emma knew Ree's mind was watching her.

"And Chuck told you," said Emma.

"Yes," said Ree.

"But no one told me," said Emma.

"I'm telling you now," said Ree.

Emma was quiet for a bit, thinking back to the times she'd traveled through space and time using only the power of her mind, sometimes bringing other people along with her. She'd never told anyone, but in some ways it felt like a window into her own death. Dr. Waldo had tried explaining time to them before. His belief was that all of time existed at once. If that was the case, then brushing through time meant rubbing shoulders with herself at birth and at death, and with the vast field of time in which she didn't exist at all.

She'd only traveled through space a few times, and had gone forward or backward in time a few days at most. It was scary. To be honest, she didn't love doing it. That was the problem, she realized. Charlie would have given his right leg to be able to travel through space with his mind. He was fearless and brave. He would have been off to all corners of all universes every day. The Charlie and Chuck travel company would have taken on a whole new dimension. Literally. As far as he was concerned, she was wasting her talents.

She noticed the night was getting a bit cool, and remembered that Chuck and Charlie had designed the tents with a heating and cooling system that pushed warm or cool air out through the molecules of the fabric to create an almost perfect atmosphere. "I know how you hate sweaty tents," Charlie had told her. "In our tents it'll be just like being at home. So you can come with us more." And the airtight feature, he'd mentioned that he'd thought of her when they designed that, too. "So creepy alien bugs can't get in," he'd said.

She wanted to protest to Ree that she couldn't believe Charlie had told Chuck about his feelings but not her, but she already knew why he'd done that. Chuck and Ree were separate people, yes, but talking to them was almost like talking to versions of themselves. The fear of being judged for her thoughts was almost abolished, because Emma knew it was likely whatever she thought, Ree thought something along the same lines. Charlie would have told Chuck something that he wouldn't tell Emma, only if he thought it would make Emma mad. In the darkness, her face flushed with heat at embarrassment and shame over the fact Charlie had felt he couldn't come to her and tell her what he'd been thinking.

"It's just not fair that Charlie thinks I think I'm special because I managed to travel through space without a pigeon or anything. I didn't do it because I'm special. I did it to save us. All of us," Emma said.

"That's just it," said Ree. "Charlie feels like he let you down."

"But he didn't," said Emma forcefully, tears filling her eyes. "He didn't. I know he would have done everything and anything he could to save me. And maybe if he tried, he could do it, too. I don't think it's some trick the universes gave only to me. I really think anyone could do it, if they had the right motivation."

Now Ree was quiet for a minute. Emma could tell Ree was thinking, and so she let the silence fill the tent until Ree was ready to speak.

Ree turned in her sleeping bag and took a deep breath. "I haven't told anyone else this," she said, and she paused. "Not even Charlie—Chuck. Not even Chuck."

Emma's attention was piqued. "What?"

"Since you … well, since you seemed to be The Chosen One, and you and I are sort of the same person, I wondered if I could do the same thing. If I could travel through space with my mind, like you can."

Emma sat up and looked at the shadowy shape of her parallel self, sitting in the dark on the other side of the tent. "And? Can you?"

"Not exactly," said Ree. "I can't travel through space."

The hesitation at the end of her sentence told Emma there was more to what she was saying. Emma waited impatiently.

"I can't travel through space," Ree repeated finally, "but I can travel through time. All of it. From the beginning to the end."

chapter four

"Tent lights: on," commanded Emma, and small, bright lights along the seams of the tent lit up, illuminating the interior of their cozy space. Emma looked at Ree incredulously. "You can travel through *time*? From the beginning of time to the end of time?" Her jaw dropped in disbelief.

"Well," Ree said, "maybe I exaggerated. You can't really tell if it's the beginning or the end. There aren't clocks there." She smiled.

Emma sat, stunned. "When?" she whispered, wondering whether the boys could hear them from their own tent, only a few yards away. "With your *mind*? When did you go? How did you go without our knowing?" Her brain was swirling with questions as she thought back the past few months. Had Ree really been able to travel without the rest of them catching on? Then again, if she could travel through time, did it matter how long she was gone?

"When you guys went off without me, you know, to find Eve's mom," Ree said casually, looking up at the sky through the open window above them. With the tents light on, the stars were impossible to see, but she stared at them intently nonetheless.

Emma sighed with understanding. If the others had all gone off without her, she would have felt sad, too. She wouldn't have said anything, but she would have felt left out. Emma kicked herself mentally for having been so caught up in the adventure of it all that she forgot to think about Ree. About herself, in a way.

"But I thought you didn't want to go that time. You could have come!" Emma paused. "Okay. Back up," she said. "We were gone. And you … what? You just … willed yourself through time?" She knew Dr. Waldo could take them through time with his devices, and she herself had traveled backward and forward in time a few hours, or a few days. But this seemed bigger.

Ree shuffled in her sleeping bag and pulled it up over her shoulders. "So, first, I was just wishing a lot. I was wishing that I could go back in time and … you know, say something. I wished I'd told you guys I wanted to come along. I wished I hadn't just been quiet. I wished I could go back and change things." She paused, constructing the sentences in her mind before speaking them, a habit Emma recognized as she did it herself. "I remembered Charlie—Chuck—telling me about when you were on the ghost planet, in the ghost universe. He told me how you'd talked to Eve's dead great aunt."

"Great Aunt Doethine," Emma nodded. She remembered it quite well. Great Aunt Doethine, in her infinite calm and wisdom, had guided Emma to see deep within herself.

"Yes. He told me that Eve's aunt told you that you had the power inside you. That you'd had it inside you all along. And I started to think about that. I mean, you know, you and I are pretty much alike. A few differences, but mostly you're me and I'm you. So I thought, if you had those abilities in you, maybe I had them in me, too." She grasped the edge of the midnight-blue sleeping bag and started to unconsciously roll the fabric between her fingers before continuing to recount her tale. "I tried really hard. I mean, I didn't know exactly what Doethine had told you so I had to just imagine, to pretend that I believed I had the power inside me all along. I thought I remembered Chuck saying that one time you thought really hard about Charlie, and that enabled you to go to where he was. So I thought really hard about Chuck. I thought as hard as I could about how much I wanted to see him again, because I missed you guys and I wanted to be off in Australia or wherever you were at the time, traveling with you and exploring your Earth and all that. I thought it so hard I could almost feel it, physically; I felt like I could almost imagine myself with you, under the heat of that Australian sun." She put the sleeping bag down and smoothed out the fabric. "But it didn't do anything. So then I started just wishing so hard that I could go back in time. Back in time to when it all started, so I could do things differently. And next thing I knew, I did. I was in my room, and then, *poof*, I was still in my room but things were slightly different. It took me a minute before I realized I was in my room but I was *watching myself sleep*. I was there, back in time, with myself. I went back in time to when Charlie was at our house on our Earth, and the rest of you were off who knows where. It scared me so bad that I flipped back to my own time almost instantly. But after that, I tried again and again. I couldn't do it again for the longest time. I think I was too afraid. Then, one day, I was out at the lighthouse on my Earth, and I traveled back in time again to when you guys first showed up on our Earth. I hid so you wouldn't see me, and I followed you home." She looked at Emma. "After that, I just kept doing it. It turns out I can't travel in space at all." She laughed a small laugh. "Wherever I am, that's where I'm stuck. But within that point in space, I can travel through all of time."

Emma was speechless. Even Dr. Waldo hadn't traveled backward or forward in time more than a few years, to the best of her knowledge. Or had he? Dr. Waldo was a man of many secrets, she realized. There was no telling how much he wasn't telling them. But Dr. Waldo had been so adamant in his warnings about the dangers to her own life that she hadn't done much experimenting at all. She felt a sudden pang of envy. Her own travels had been to get herself and others out of danger; she'd traveled out of fear and to save the universes. But Ree had been able to travel for pleasure. For play. Emma wanted that. She wanted to grab Ree and for the two of them to just start traveling the universes and forget about everything …

"Oh no!" said Emma. "I just remembered, your telomeres!"

"Yeah, I know," said Ree. "I've thought about that. But it can't be shortening my life all that much, can it? And didn't Dr. Waldo say he had a method to … you know, to regrow your telomeres?"

"He can only regrow them if he knows you're shortening them," Emma reprimanded. "We need to get you to the Hub for him to test you, right away!"

Ree's shoulders drooped. Everyone knew how much of Dr. Waldo's testing Emma had undergone, and how much more there was ahead. "I don't want to be another lab rat," she said.

Emma bristled. "I'm not a lab rat," she said. "I'm helping with scientific knowledge. And you can, too. And besides, if you're going to be traveling like that, we need to make sure you're safe. We don't know everything about how space travel affects a human being, and we most definitely don't know much about how time travel affects you." She paused. "Wait, you said the first time you went back in time, you were back in your room and you were watching yourself sleep?"

"Yes," said Ree. "That's right."

"But I thought a person couldn't travel back within their own timeline and see themselves? I thought that messed with the time-space continuum and potentially … I don't know, like it could make you never be born or something?"

Ree shrugged. "I don't know. I've seen myself a lot and nothing seems to have happened. Nothing bad, anyway."

"Okay, you've seen yourself, but you've been hiding, right?" said Emma. "The other you didn't know you were there?"

Ree's cheeks grew red. "Well, no," she admitted. "I've … I've talked to myself."

"You've *talked* to yourself?" Emma said, flabbergasted. "In the future or in the past?"

"Both," Ree said. She picked up the edge of the sleeping bag and started rolling it between her fingers again.

"Oh my gosh," said Emma, the ramifications of Ree's time travels running far beyond her ability to speculate. "We need to get you to Dr. Waldo." She looked at her iPert. "It's the middle of the night in the Hub. Although I suppose that doesn't matter if you can travel through time," Emma said.

"Well, I'd have to be inside the Hub to time travel inside the Hub," Ree pointed out. "That's how it works."

"Have you done that?" Emma's eyes went wide. "Have you time traveled inside the Hub?"

Ree blushed again. "Just once … or twice. But not a lot. There are too many people around all the time and … it's hard to get privacy."

Emma suspected that maybe Ree had done so more than she was admitting, but she let it pass. "Okay," she said. "Well, regardless, we need to tell Dr. Waldo. I think he should know." She thought about her own relationship with Charlie. "And you should tell Chuck. Chuck would want to know."

Ree met Emma's eyes. "You're right. I'll tell him in the morning, and then we'll go."

Charlie lay awake in the tent he was sharing with Chuck, a few yards away from the girls' tent. He and Chuck had also opened the flap at the top of the tent so they could watch the stars, but Chuck had managed to fall asleep quickly and Charlie was left alone with this thoughts. Those thoughts ranged from the trivial to the painful. On the trivial end, he was thinking about what they would call the tent flap. "Sun window" seemed inaccurate. "Flap" was dull. Maybe "star window," he thought. He imagined himself describing it to clients: "Your tent also has this mind-blowing feature, a *star window* through which you can gaze out on the stars in other universes. You can lie in your tent and conjure up names for constellations no human has ever seen." Yes, he thought, star window. That might be it.

And, he contemplated jet lag. It hadn't occurred to him until tonight that if they were going to visit planets with completely different lengths of days and nights, he and Chuck were going to have to figure out how to get people to sleep. Considering what their clients would be paying for these Exclusive and Incomparable Experiences (he capitalized the words in his mind), they definitely would not want to sleep away the days and lie awake all night long, as he himself was now doing. He and Chuck would need to talk with the scientists about some remedies for sleeplessness. And then, maybe once they'd done that, they could use it on Earth, too. People on Earth needed help sleeping sometimes, just as much as people traveling on Exclusive and Incomparable Experiences to other universes did.

Emma had probably managed to fall asleep, he thought. Emma could do anything.

His mind flitted around the painful thoughts a little more delicately. He regretted having called Emma The Chosen One. He knew it had hurt her. She thought she'd hid her tears when she was setting up the tent, but he'd seen her crying and he felt awful. Still, he hated it that she was special and he wasn't. Oh, he knew she'd tell him he was special in his own way, but there had to be something mighty special about a person that the universes would pick her to be able to travel anywhere—absolutely anywhere.

He'd tried to travel with the power of his mind, too. He'd tried a lot. *A lot*. He'd even tried with Dr. Waldo's help, but when he failed, he'd asked the scientist not to tell anyone. He didn't want them all to know he was a failure. Just the brother of The Chosen One. He couldn't even save her when she needed to be saved. She'd had to save herself. He was supposed to protect her and keep the world—all the worlds—safe for her, and he'd done nothing.

He felt like a nobody.

Now with this new business adventure with Chuck, at least he felt like he was doing something. He may not be special in the way Emma was special, but he was going to make some money and he didn't need her anyway. Sure, they were twins, and sure, they'd been inseparable before, but there came a time in a man's life when he had to leave behind the things that were comfortable to make room for the impossible. Right?

Chuck snored lightly next to Charlie, and Charlie started wondering if Dr. Waldo might have a cure for snoring. If they could travel to the ends of the multiverse, surely they could stop that annoying sound that was emanating from Chuck.

Late into the fifteen-hour night, Charlie finally fell asleep.

When he awoke, hours later, the sun was only starting to rise but Chuck was already awake and milling around outside the tent. Charlie pulled on a sweatshirt and jeans and went out to meet him.

Chuck greeted him with a smile. "This planet is perfect for teens. Fifteen hours of sleep! Best sleep I've had in ages, and no Mom yelling at me that it's time to get up!" He saw the dark circles under Charlie's eyes. "But maybe you didn't sleep so well?"

Charlie shrugged. "Eh. Not the best." He looked at the camp stove leaning against a nearby rock. "Wish we'd remembered to bring food to cook on that. Does Ree have any more protein bars? One of us will have to go back to the Hub and get some food today."

Chuck reached into his backpack and pulled out two protein bars. "She left all of them with us. Ree and Emma went back to the Hub. They have to talk to Dr. Waldo."

Something in the tone of Chuck's voice put Charlie on edge. "Why?" he said. "What do they need to talk to Dr. Waldo about?"

Chuck started rummaging through his bag again, avoiding Charlie's eyes. "Well, so, apparently Ree figured out she can travel through time with her mind." He looked up. "She can't travel through space, but she can travel through time. She says. Seems she figured it out when we all went off without her." He flinched. "And she's been practicing ever since."

Charlie felt like the wind had been knocked out of him. "So they're both The Chosen Ones," he said. "It figures, I guess. If we had a convention of Emmas, all the Emmas from all the parallel Earths, I bet every one of them would be The Chosen One in one way or another."

"I mean, I get it, dude," said Chuck, "but you can't let it bother you. We're doing this travel thing, and you know your Emma and my Emma could never do that. They don't have it in them. Different strokes for different folks or whatever the saying is."

"Whatever," said Charlie. He unwrapped a protein bar and started eating. What he wouldn't give for a big breakfast of eggs and bacon, he thought. The protein bar was gone in seconds and he was still starving. "I wonder if … I don't know, do you think we could find fish or something?"

"Would you know how to prepare a fish if we managed to catch one?" said Chuck.

Charlie shook his head. "I guess not. Okay, I'm going to go back to the Hub and get us some food."

"Charlie, I don't think—" Chuck started to protest, but before he could say more, Charlie had pulled a pigeon out of his pocket and whisked himself away, leaving his parallel self behind.

Charlie landed with a *whoosh* inside the infinite space of the Hub. The teens had worked for weeks to build their own gathering place off in one section of the Hub. It was there that they'd taken the photo earlier, and it was there that he landed now. They'd created a home of sorts, though without ceilings, because it never rained and they liked to look up at the open sky. Dr. Waldo had put the Hub on a sort of schedule that mimicked a regular day-and-night pattern, complete with sunshine during the day and stars at night. As they explored more universes, he liked to pattern the sky of the Hub after the skies of other universes, and various unfamiliar constellations were always rotating overhead.

Charlie had hoped—and expected—that he wouldn't meet up with Emma and Ree. He thought they would be off with Dr. Waldo, doing their Chosen One activities. But when he landed, they were right there in the living room of the house they'd all built, staring at him.

"Charlie?" said Emma. "What are you doing here?"

He blushed hard and turned away. "Well, as you know, I was too stupid to remember to bring food. So I came back to get food."

Ree looked around. "Where's Chuck?" she said. "Isn't he with you?" Since their early adventures, there was an unspoken agreement that no one should travel alone unless absolutely necessary. As hospitable as other planets might seem, all worlds were considered dangerous until proven otherwise.

Charlie squirmed. He hadn't exactly given Chuck a chance to come with him. "He's fine. I'm just grabbing some food and going right back. And if he's not fine, well, you can just take us back in time to before I left and fix everything."

Emma shot him a look that told him that wasn't fair. "Charlie," she said, "you know better than to leave someone behind." She glanced at Ree, who didn't appear overly worried, but at the same time did seem a little concerned. "Do you want to go with me back to the planet to make sure Chuck is okay?"

"Oh for heck's sake," said Charlie. "He's a grown man. He can be by himself for ten minutes. And you're just making it longer by arguing with me. He is fine! Nothing is going to happen to him!" Charlie huffed off to the kitchen. Emma and Ree followed behind, saying nothing. Charlie scrounged through the pantry and the refrigerator, grabbing random food as he found it: peanut butter, bread, cans of tuna and beans, crackers and cheese, and some yogurt. It wasn't a big deal, he told himself. This was all part of the planning and the figuring everything out. No paying clients had been starved. He and Chuck had been inconvenienced, that was all.

"If you take yogurt, you need to refrigerate it on the planet, and you don't have a cooler," Emma said.

Charlie glared at his sister, hating to admit that she was right. He closed his eyes and thought hard, imagining a cooler into existence. He shoved several yogurts into the cooler.

"But you don't know if the cooler will exist outside the Hub," Emma protested. Charlie bristled, and her stance softened. "Charlie," she said gently. "I'm sorry. Charlie, Ree told me ..." she looked at her parallel self. "Ree told me it bothers you that ... that I have powers that you … that you don't … yet."

Charlie noticed the word "yet." He knew Emma firmly believed everyone could travel through space as she had; what Emma didn't know, but what he knew, was how much the rest of them had tried. He and Chuck had talked about how great it would be, to be travel guides who were able to travel without a Dark MATTER sphere or an elevator or anything else. They'd spent hours in the Hub thinking until their brains hurt, trying to move one inch through space using the power of their minds. But none of them had managed it. No one but Emma. He looked down at the cooler and chewed on his words in his mind for a while. "I just think you're being selfish," he finally said. "We've always been a team, Em. And now you've got this ability and we could absolutely use it, and you won't. Think of it. We could go *anywhere*."

"You want me to take groups on trips, don't you?" she said. Charlie could see disbelief and even anger in her eyes. "You don't get it, do you? You know how hard it is on me. Remember? Remember how I almost died?"

"I would do it for you," said Charlie.

"Would you?" said Emma.

Charlie thought that he would, or at least, he would have. He hated this. He hated fighting with Emma. Most of the time, at least up until recently, they'd been like one person. But lately she'd been off with Dr. Waldo all the time, testing her magical abilities, and he'd felt left out. He'd started hanging out more with Chuck in part because of their business idea, but in part just to cover up the hole that Emma's absence left.

"I can't explain it, Charlie," continued Emma. "It's not some superpower I have. It's not mine. It's all of ours. The travel wasn't just my doing; it was all of us. A team effort. Like a safety box at the bank. I had a key, but you all had a key, too. I can't explain how

I know, but the universes don't just let me travel through space at will. There has to be a purpose behind it, something that increases the good in the multiverse, something that helps. Something important. Something that matters. I can't tell you how I know that but I do."

Charlie stood there, not saying anything but wishing he could fix everything. Instead, he hardened his heart and glared at her again. He was important, too. He would prove that he could be special, too. He pulled out another Dark MATTER sphere from his pocket. "Goodbye," he said, and, taking the cooler and backpack with him, he was gone.

He landed back on the planet where he'd left Chuck alone. For a moment, he was worried: what if Emma had been right? He *did* know better than to leave someone alone in the multiverse. It was, after all, infinite. If they lost one another, the chances of finding one another again were slim. Dr. Waldo was always working on tracking devices, and Ben could work miracles, it seemed. But Emma knew. Emma had been left alone on a ghost planet, once, and he remembered the terror he'd felt, worrying they might not get her back. She hadn't talked about it much, but he knew she'd been terrified, too. But she wouldn't have figured out that she was The Chosen One, he thought bitterly, if they hadn't left her behind, so maybe it was all for the best. A blush of shame rushed to his neck and face at the thought. Of course it wasn't for the best. He knew everything Emma had said was true. He shouldn't have left Chuck alone. She couldn't help it if she had powers that he didn't have. Still, he couldn't help but feel low.

Soon after his eyes and body had readjusted to the travel through space, Charlie saw Chuck crouched down behind a bush by the tent. The fabric of the tent was doing its job in somewhat camouflaging the structure, but Chuck had a strange look on his face. Was everything okay, after all? Had something happened?

"Chuck!" Charlie called out loudly. Chuck turned with a look of panic and quickly put a finger to his lips. "Shhhhh!" he mouthed wordlessly, then gestured for Charlie to join him.

Charlie crept over, making as little noise as he could. When he reached Chuck, he leaned in. "What's going on?" he asked. "Plassensnares?" Plassensnares were dinosaur-like creatures they'd encountered once before. If this planet had plassensnares, well, it might not be their top pick for carefree vacations. But it could still be a choice for risk-taking adventurers, he thought, and the possibilities started growing in his mind. Like Jurassic Park, he thought, but without having to recreate the dinosaurs first.

Chuck shook his head very slowly, and then pointed far across the plain where they'd set up camp.

"People," he whispered. "There's people."

chapter five

Dr. Waldo was in the middle of an experiment when the Emmas arrived. On hearing their explanation as to why they had returned early, he almost caused an explosion from excitement. Rumors were already circulating that for a brief moment, a new volcano had appeared in the Hub, and people suspected it had come forth from Dr. Waldo's mind before he'd regained composure and erased the volcano from existence.

While Dr. Waldo finished his work and cleaned up, Emma and Ree waited for him in the cottage the teens had built. That is where they were when Charlie found them. Once he'd left and Emma had forced herself to move on from all the drama, she realized how excited she was, how thrilled to have someone else who knew what it was like to travel using their mind. She suddenly felt far less alone.

Ree, however, was nervous. "But you *hate* all the testing," she protested. "Every time you come out of a test with Dr. Waldo, you look exhausted. I'm not so sure I want to go through all of that."

Emma's excitement could not be contained. "No, not at all! That's just because I'd rather be spending time with you guys. And sure, some of the tests are tiring, but it's also exciting to be a part of history. To be a part of discovery. To further the knowledge of humanity. And … uh … Lero-anity. Whatever people from Lero are called.

Are they called humans? I mean they're not Homo sapiens, but … I guess humans applies only to Earth? It's so much easier just to call all people and human-like creatures people…"

"But does it *hurt*?" Ree interrupted. "Do the tests hurt? Dr. Waldo said he wanted to do tests on my particles." She hugged herself protectively. None of this was sounding like a good idea.

"Not at all," Emma lied. The tests did hurt sometimes, but not in a way she could describe. The pain was sometimes physical, but more often it was … well, cellular, she thought. Smaller than cellular. And bigger. Traveling through space and time involved first becoming one with the universes, melding with everything known and unknown, and then separating again, extricating all her particles from all the other particles in the universes. Emma strongly suspected that each time she did this, a few of her particles were left behind, and what's more, each time she traveled, she picked up new particles from elsewhere, or from another time. Not a lot, but after a while, she wondered, would she still be herself?

"What's the difference between a particle and an atom, anyway?" said Ree. She pulled her knees to her chest and began rocking back and forth.

"Molecules are made up of atoms, and atoms are made up of particles," said Emma.

"I thought atoms were the smallest thing," said Ree, rubbing her chin against her knees.

"I did too," said Emma, "but particles are smaller. The thing is, atoms are matter and particles aren't matter. Particles are just the building blocks of atoms. They're not matter themselves. Protons and electrons, those are particles. Atoms are made of protons and electrons. That's why Dr. Waldo wants to study your particles. He wants to see how the travel has affected the charges, probably. To start with, anyway. There will be lots of tests, believe me." She paused. "Do you know, I was thinking, do you know what would be fun? We should have an Emma Convention. All Emmas. All the Emmas we can find. We could get Ben to help us find other parallel Earths, and we could go around and gather up all the Emmas and have a big party. Can you imagine? I wonder if all the other Emmas also have some ability, like we do, to travel through space or time or … or what? I bet if we found all the other Chosen Ones, we could discover a lot about the universes. I mean, what if each Emma has a different ability? What if each Emma has the ability to travel through a different dimension? Just imagine, we could be the key to discovering whole new dimensions!" Her eyes glowed with the possibilities.

But Ree did not seem as interested or as excited as Emma. She squinched her face in a combination of fear and apprehension. "But does the testing *hurt*?"

Luckily for Emma, Dr. Waldo appeared just then, with Ben by his side. As usual, Dr. Waldo was dressed in his pristine white lab coat. Ben wore a similar coat, and Emma noticed that his name had been embroidered on the left side: "Ben Stewart." Knowing how much he loved his job in the Hub, she felt a rush of happiness for him. Emma then saw Ree flash Ben the tiniest, quickest knowing smile, and then Ree seemed to remember herself and made her face neutral again. What was that about?

"Ben," Emma said, "a question. If we wanted to find other parallel Earths, could you do that? You're good at that sort of thing, right?"

Ben smiled at the compliment. "Well, actually, interesting that you say that. I've been studying universes, obviously." He glanced at Ree. Had he noticed the smile, too? "As it turns out, a useful analogy is to think of the signatures of universes, in some ways, like human DNA. The closer they are to one another—the more parallel, I guess you'd call it—the more alike their signatures are." He looked at Dr. Waldo, who was nodding intently with a giant smile of approval on his face. "I'm calling it UDNA for now," Ben continued. "Universe DNA. So the answer to your question is, yes, probably we could find other parallel Earths, if we tracked their UDNA."

Emma beamed. She was liking this idea more and more. Let the Charlies have their little travel company. She was going to have an Emma Convention that would lead to the greatest discoveries of all the past, present, and future. "Ben," she said, "you are going to be a famous scientist one day. I just know it."

Ree's eyes snapped open, and then she looked away.

"I don't know about famous," said Ben, "but I love what we're doing here." He looked at Ree. "Speaking of which, are you ready?"

Ree sighed. "Does this involve needles?" She rubbed her shoulder. "I hate shots."

"No, no," said Dr. Waldo. "Do not fear! Has our Emma been telling you tales? Nothing to worry about! Nothing at all!"

"So you promise it won't hurt?" said Ree.

"Uh … er … nothing to worry about! Nothing at all!" repeated Dr. Waldo. He winked at Emma.

"I saw that," said Ree, narrowing her eyes. "I can see right through you, Dr. Waldo. 'Nothing to worry about' is not the same as 'no it won't hurt.'" She sighed and stood. "Okay, let's get this over with."

"Don't worry," said Ben gently. "Today it's pretty easy. Just a few quick scans and then an assignment."

"Assignment?" said Emma, her ears perking up. This sounded interesting. "Do I get to be part of the assignment, too?"

Ben glanced at Dr. Waldo, who nodded. "Well, sure. But we'll have to do some baseline scans on you first, too, if you want to go along."

"Go along?" said Emma, her grin widening. This was going to be fun indeed. "Where are we going?"

Ben laughed. "First, to the lab. We'll get you guys scanned and then we'll let you loose."

The foursome took off toward a section of the Hub where Dr. Waldo and the other scientists had set up an enormous amount of medical equipment, including elaborate body scanning machines that, Emma had previously learned, could scan every bit of a person's body down to the level of the very particles she'd been discussing with Ree earlier.

"There's so much information in each scan, we had to create new hard drives to hold it all," Dr. Waldo said as Ben guided Ree onto the bed of a large, shiny, off-white machine.

"Five exabytes," said Ben. "That's a lot. That's one quintillion bytes. A thousand petabytes. A million terabytes." He carefully attached straps around Ree's body to hold her in place, and then put a helmet on her head that was attached to giant bolts, which would keep her from moving her head at all.

"What happens if I move?" said Ree nervously. "Does it electrocute me or something?"

Ben laughed. "No, don't worry! If you move, we just have to do it again. The scan wouldn't be accurate. But you'd be okay."

"But does this scan harm me? At a particle level?" If Ree had been able to move, she would have been trembling.

"Not at all," said Ben. He patted her hand reassuringly. "You'll be fine." He stepped to a panel at the side of the machine and hit a green button. With a steady hum, a transparent dome came out of the base of the bed, slowly encasing Ree inside. When it had settled into place with a satisfying click, Ben spoke into a microphone that would deliver his words to Ree inside the cocoon. "All good?" he said.

Ree tried to nod but was unable. "All … good," she said. "A little claustrophobic, though, so hurry up."

"Okay, now, close your eyes. Keep them relaxed so you are using as few muscles as possible. Just make your whole body relaxed. Relax your mouth, don't smile or frown, just be neutral."

"Easy for you to say," Ree said, but then she closed her eyes and let her mouth fall into a restful state.

"And … one, two, three." Ben pressed another button. Red, blue, green, and white lights fell in sheets across Ree from all angles and drew across her body from the top of her head to the tips of her toes. The machine hummed more loudly, making clicking noises now and then as the lights reversed and traveled the length of her body once more.

Finally, the lights and sounds stopped. Ben pushed another button and the clamshell dome opened up, returning to its resting place inside the base of the bed.

"You're done!" said Ben as he went to release Ree from all the bonds. A small tear had sprung to the corner of Ree's left eye. Ben wiped it away gently. "It's okay. You're done." He helped her sit up and get out of the machine. "See?" he said. "Painless."

"*This* one was," Ree said. She wiped her eyes and sat in a nearby chair.

Ben winked at her, then turned to Emma. "Next?"

After Emma was done with her own scan, Dr. Waldo sat them all down in chairs surrounding Ree's. "All right, then. Right. Now we are—oh me, oh my, right, learning to delegate, learning to delegate. I'd almost forgotten. Ben, would you like to do the honors?" He turned to the young man with pride. "As the young lady said, you may well be a famous scientist one day, certainly more famous than old Dr. Waldo!"

Ben blushed. "Well, I don't know about that. Anyway, what we want now is for you, Ree, to take yourself and Emma through time somewhere within twenty years of our own time code."

"Time code?" said Emma.

"Within twenty years of now," Ben said. "That's just technical talk." He turned back to Ree. "As I understand it, you can travel through time but not space, so we'd like you to start from your own Earth. Since that's home for you, it'll provide us with the best baseline."

"Okay," said Ree. "Any time I pick?"

"Within about twenty years," said Ben.

"And then?" said Ree.

Ben looked at Dr. Waldo. "Well," he said, "then return back to this time code."

Ree glanced at Emma. "But can we stay a while first, if I want to show Emma around?"

Emma's heart fluttered with excitement. "Oh yes! Say yes! I want to look around!"

Dr. Waldo laughed. "Of course," he said, "But come back soon!"

"'Soon' is relative," said Ree, raising an eyebrow in amusement. Emma was relieved to see Ree must be feeling relaxed again, if she was joking with Dr. Waldo.

"Time is tricky," said Emma, echoing one of Dr. Waldo's favorite sentiments.

"Time is of the essence," said Ben. He stood, trying to get everyone moving.

"Ah, take it easy, Ben," said Emma. "We've got all the time in the world! At least, Ree does." But, nonetheless, she followed him to the door that would take them to the elevator attached to the Hub, from where they would travel to Ree's Earth.

"Dr. Waldo," said Ree as they walked. "Now that you know about all this, I have questions."

"Yes, yes, yes," said Dr. Waldo. "Of course! Thinking about the mysteries of time brings more questions than answers, this is true!"

"So first, I was talking with Emma about this. We've always heard those stories about how you can't cross paths with yourself in a different timeline or everyone will die and all the worlds will be destroyed and whatnot."

"A bit dramatic, perhaps, but yes, I know the stories you're referring to," said Dr. Waldo, nodding enthusiastically.

"Well," said Ree, "the thing is, I've crossed paths with myself … a few times. I've seen myself. And … talked with myself." She looked slightly chagrined, as though she felt she'd broken some universal law. "And nothing seems to have happened. I mean, nothing bad."

"Hmmm," said Dr. Waldo, scratching at his chin and nodding more. "Well, you see, of course nothing *seems* to have happened because you don't know what would have happened otherwise. This is not to say that you disrupted anything that was not meant to be disrupted. What is, is. What is not, is not. What will be, will be. What was meant to be may not be meant to be after all."

Emma shook her head rapidly. "Ohhhhhhkay," she said. "That makes sense, sure."

They were by this point quite near the door to the elevator, so they stopped at a small cluster of chairs to continue the discussion before leaving.

"So this is my question," said Ree, settling into one of the couches. "Or one of my questions. Is the future set? Like, it's determined? I can't mess it up?"

Dr. Waldo took off his wire glasses and rubbed his eyes, then put them back on. "Yes. Well, young lady. This is all quite complicated but also quite simple. Let me see if I can explain it." He paused a moment, then continued. "Think of time like a river," he said. He waved a hand in the air, and an image of a river appeared in the air above them.

"Yes?" said Ree, watching the image. "Okay, time is a river."

"A river has a beginning and an end. Yes?" Dr. Waldo said. "It begins somewhere up in the mountains, say, and ends at the ocean. A definite beginning and a definite end. But at the same time, the entire river exists *all at once*. Beginning and end exist *at the same time*. It's not as though fifty drops of water start at the mountain and move down to the ocean, leaving a dry bed behind them and before them. The river is infinite, but yet in each moment it is distinct. In this way, time is like a river. It exists at all points, at all times. Even though a river is constantly moving, it's not as though the beginning of the river exists at one point in time, and then the end of the river exists at a later point in time. Imagine yourself as a molecule in the river. Right now, if you are a molecule, you exist at one single point in that river." He pointed at a spot in the river in the air, and then paused. "This is all hypothesis, by the way," he said. "An idea waiting to be proven true or false. Which," he said gleefully to Ree, "is part of where you come in. "Now. You are a molecule in that river. A future you is another molecule, existing at another point in that river." He pointed at a second spot in the image of the river. "Right now in a river, there are water molecules at every point. Let's say water molecule A is upstream, or in the past, and molecule B is you, where you are, in the present, and molecule C is in downstream, or in the future. Now, if you were to paddle upstream, or travel downstream, the river will still be there. But are the same molecules there with you?"

Ree looked confused and thought on this a while. "Um. No?" she said hesitantly. "Or, maybe some are but some aren't?"

Dr. Waldo looked pleased. "Exactly. Exactly! Maybe that's what time is like. And now, you ask, can you affect the future? Well, imagine now, what happens if you throw rocks into a river?"

"It causes ripples," said Emma, trying to keep up. "It changes things. It changes … it changes the river."

"Yes," said Dr. Waldo. "Yes! It changes things. The river still exists and is still the same river, but things are different. Those rocks," he said, "those rocks are your *choices*. The choices you make, make a difference in time. Your choices can disrupt what will happen in the future. Your choices have the power to both create and change your future."

"Ahhh," said Ben with a look of comprehension on his face. "I get it."

"I don't," said Ree. "I don't get it."

Dr. Waldo patted her knee. "Let me try again. You are molecule B, in the present. Correct?" He pointed at a spot in the middle of the river.

"Correct," said Ree.

"And at the same time, your past, molecule A, exists. And at the same time, your future, molecule C, exists." He pointed at a spot upstream in the river, and then a spot downstream.

"Okay," said Ree.

"This is why," said Dr. Waldo, waving his hands in the air as his excitement built, "this is why you can travel to the future and interact with yourself. Because both molecule B and molecule C exist. Molecule B is separate from molecule C."

"So, wait," said Ree. "You're saying that the future me is separate from the present me?"

"Yes," said Dr. Waldo, "it is separate at this moment. But in the future, farther down the river, when you, molecule B, have traveled through time, you will then still be molecule B; you'll just be farther down the river but you'll still be yourself."

"And," said Ben, snapping his fingers, "when you, molecule B, get down to where molecule C once was, you might not be in the exact same place molecule C was. Or even anywhere near it. Molecule C could have been near the bank of the river and you, molecule B, might be right in the middle."

"Everything exists at once!" said Emma. "All our past selves and all our future selves. But also, we are traveling through time. And everything is fluid. Even if everything already exists, nonetheless our choices now determine where we go." She high-fived Ben, thrilled that she seemed to understand.

"That's exactly it!" said Dr. Waldo. "At least, that is what I believe. And now, with our dear Ree's help, we may begin to learn more."

Ree took a deep breath. "Time," she said, "is very tricky indeed."

chapter six

"Do you think they've seen you?" Charlie whispered as he crouched behind a bush next to Chuck. In the distance, seabirds were soaring overhead, screeching and occasionally diving down toward what Charlie assumed was the beach he'd been planning to check out.

"I don't think so, no," said Chuck. "They just showed up a few minutes before you got back." He turned and looked at the tent behind them. "Do you think they'll see that? I know they'll think we look normal, because of the bracelets, but how will we explain the tent?"

Charlie scrutinized the tent, as well. "Huh," he said. "Never thought about that." Suddenly their travel business idea was taking on whole new complexities. He just wanted to take people to amazing places. They'd considered the idea of unfriendly beasts, like the plassensnares. But they hadn't thought about the fact that they might run into hostile natives.

"They're coming this way," said Chuck. "Maybe we should go out and meet them so they don't find our stuff?"

"Maybe," said Charlie. He squinted to try to see the people better. "Wish I'd thought to bring binoculars. Make a note of that, please, to tell the committee," he said, before he remembered that was a phrase he used with Emma, not Chuck.

Chuck smiled and reached into his bag, pulling out a pair of binoculars. "Wish I had, too. Luckily, Ree put these in here when I wasn't looking. It was on her list." Emma and Ree were notorious for their lists.

"Good job, Ree," said Charlie. Chuck handed him the binoculars and he raised them to his eyes. The sun had only come over the horizon an hour or so before, but already its heat was building. Charlie felt a warm breeze against his neck as he looked through the lenses at the creatures in the distance. His skin tingled with warmth. Sunscreen, he thought. Emma would have thought to bring sunscreen, too. For a moment, he wished she were there to help. Then, he pushed that idea aside. "We don't need her," he said out loud, to himself.

"What?" said Chuck softly. "They're getting closer." He shook his head. "Did Ben mention that this planet had inhabitants?"

Charlie looked straight ahead. "Ben didn't research this planet. I did." He paused. "I forgot to check. But maybe they're friendly aliens?"

"Technically, *we* are the aliens," said Chuck. "And sure, they probably are."

"The bracelets will make them think we're just like them," Charlie said again. He wondered momentarily whether the bracelets would ever let them down. He hoped they never found out. Lifting the binoculars again, he zoomed in for a closer look. "Meerkats," he said. "They're sort of like furless meerkats, but without the snouts. Did you see? Big eyes, big head, their ears toward the back of their heads." He adjusted the focus on the lenses and looked again. "And clothes. Thank goodness we haven't met naked aliens so far."

Chuck laughed. "Yeah, not sure I'm ready for naked aliens just yet."

"One, two …there are three of them," Charlie said. It was hard to determine the aliens' height. Charlie decided either they were shorter than average humans, or their heads were bigger in proportion to their bodies. Nothing on this planet was familiar, and so he had no sense of scale. They wouldn't know anything for sure until they were up close. "Well," he said, "I think you're right. We'd better go out to meet them." He rubbed his bracelet. "Don't fail us now, magic stones."

Chuck nodded. "You're right. And," he said, squinting in the direction of the aliens, "it looks like maybe they've seen us. Let's go."

The pair started walking toward the aliens, treading carefully on the unfamiliar terrain. Much of the ground was flat, and covered with something resembling a thick, hairy olive-green moss. A few tiny white and yellow flowers popped out of the moss here and there. The sparse bushes were about chest height, with tufts of soft, long needles like pine needles on an evergreen tree. In the growing breeze, a sweet scent wafted off the bushes into the air.

"Stop," said Chuck, putting up a hand. "They've seen us."

Standing and staring at the two Charlies, the three creatures resembled meerkats more than ever. Their oversized eyes were trained directly on the boys, and their ears seemed to be flattened back against their heads even more than before. They turned their heads from side to side, but kept their eyes on Charlie and Chuck. Two of them were sniffing the air.

"Do we wave?" said Charlie. "How do we let them know we're not hostile?"

"Should we smile?" said Chuck.

"Baring teeth is seen as threatening to many animals on Earth," said Charlie, "and to some people, as well." The instinct to smile was strong, however, and he had to fight to keep the corners of his mouth from turning up.

"Okay, what about open arms, hands out? Showing them we don't have any weapons?" said Chuck.

"Yeah, about that," said Charlie, hardly moving his lips. "Why did we not think to have some sort of weapon? Like a stun gun?"

"Because we are civilized people," said Chuck. "We don't just attack unprovoked." He paused. "But maybe get a pigeon ready just in case."

Charlie let out a soft grunt. "Mine are in my backpack," he said. "Do you have extra?"

"Yup," said Chuck. Then, "Here they come."

The three beings had started moving toward them again. Charlie and Chuck tried to make themselves look as neutral as possible, holding their palms up and out.

"Are you lost?" called out the being that was at the front of the group.

Charlie let out a sigh of relief. At the very least, the translator stone was working. He studied the face of the one who had spoken. In general, he and Chuck were pretty good at reading people's emotions—human emotions, anyway. But alien faces could be difficult. They'd once met up with a species that looked like nothing so much as octopuses, and their faces were almost impossible to find, much less read. But these creatures were more human-like. Charlie hoped he could trust his instincts, but he knew better than to make assumptions. The being seemed non-threatening, but Charlie knew it would be best to stay on guard.

"We are, yes," said Charlie, after a quick glance at Chuck confirmed that this was the story they'd go with.

"Where are you from?" said the one who was speaking.

Charlie gulped as a series of possible answered raced through his head. Washington state? Balky Point? Dogwinkle Island? What would raise the least suspicion? "We're from Earth," he finally said.

The three beings exchanged glances, small murmurs arising from their throats though none said anything. The one at front spoke again. "Where is Earth?"

Charlie started to point in the direction of the tents, but then he realized that was also, he believed, the direction of the water. Would that seem unlikely? Impossible? He decided maybe a location across the water might be the best choice. He pointed toward the beach.

"You came from one of the islands?" said the being in front, and more murmurs spread among the other two.

"Uh, yes," said Chuck. "And … our boat, it … sank. So we're, I guess we're stuck."

The one in front and one of the others exchanged a glance that Charlie couldn't read. He then lifted his nose to the air and sniffed. He looked again at his companion for several long moments that started to make Charlie nervous, then turned his large black eyes back to the boys. "A storm is coming. An early squall must have upset your boat. Do you have somewhere to stay?"

Chuck looked at Charlie, and Charlie thought it would have been wise for them to figure out a way to communicate with each other in code. Because of the translator stone, even if they spoke in Pig Latin, the aliens would understand every word they said.

"We don't," said Chuck, just as Charlie was about to say they did. Charlie flashed his parallel twin a look.

"You don't?" said the alien.

"Well, we could use a place to stay just through the storm," said Charlie, "if you think it will be bad."

All three of the meerkat-like creatures lifted their noses this time. Their skin was furless but nonetheless it was a sort of burnished mustard color; it gave the appearance of being quite thick. They were clothed in long shapeless shirts and pants, but the clothes looked threadbare, like they had been handed down several times. They wore simple boots, and no apparent jewelry or other adornments. Their hair grew in a strip along the top and back of their heads, much like a wide mohawk. The one in front had shorter hair; the hair of the other two was longer. As they sniffed the air, Charlie suspected they must have heightened senses of smell. Quite possibly they'd smelled the Charlies before they'd even seen them, he thought. It was a good thing they'd decided to come out of hiding.

"The storm will be fierce," said the alien in front. "Come with us."

"Thank you," said Chuck. The aliens moved past them and toward the water; toward the tents.

"Do you all—what are your names?" Charlie asked, trying to distract the aliens' attention. "I'm Charlie, and this is Chuck." He wondered if he and Chuck looked like twins to the aliens, but to be honest, he wasn't so sure he would be able to tell the aliens apart. Aside from the length of hair and the different clothes, they looked a lot alike to him. On closer scrutinization, he decided the hair of one of the two with longer hair was a darker shade of brown than that of the other one. They were different heights, as well. And their clothes were slightly different, but clothes would change. All of them were several inches shorter than him and Chuck; Charlie guessed they were maybe somewhere between five and five and a half feet tall. Their shoulders were narrow, but the one with shorter hair had wider shoulders than the others. Charlie decided he would need to pay attention, so as not to insult anyone by calling them by the wrong name.

The one in front, the tallest of the three, again spoke first. "I'm Leidar."

"Nice to meet you, Leidar," said Charlie. He held out his hand

and then realized that gesture might be meaningless to Leidar and the others. To his relief, Leidar looked curiously at Charlie's extended hand, but then reached out and grasped it with his own. Leidar then turned to Chuck and reached out his hand.

Chuck responded with a two-handed grasp and a wide smile. "Nice to meet you, Leidar," he said.

"I am Corala," said the one with the darker longer hair. Corala smiled and looked at her own hand, then reached out to Charlie. "Nice to meet you, Charlie," Corala said.

Charlie was sure there was a hint of amusement in Corala's eyes, and a bit more friendliness than he saw in Leidar, but he decided it would be best to keep an open mind.

The third one reached out a hand to Chuck. "Nice to meet you, Chuck. I am Akala."

"Nice to meet you, Akala," said Chuck, grasping Akala's hand. Akala quickly pulled her hand back to her chest, and didn't offer it to Charlie.

"You'll have to forgive Akala," said Leidar. "She is wary of strangers."

Akala seemed to frown, and Charlie noticed these beings didn't have eyebrows. "That's not true, Leidar," she said. She reached out her hand to Charlie. "He acts like we see strangers all the time. I only was not familiar with this grasping of hands."

This time, Leidar frowned. He exchanged a look with Corala, which seemed to include a hint of warning, Charlie thought. "You are the one who wanted to come with us," he said to Akala. "Maybe you were not ready to be away from Gleymara. I think next time Corala and I leave, you should stay at home."

"But—" Akala started to protest, but then she looked at Charlie and Chuck, and said nothing.

"Leidar and I often go out," Corala explained, "but it can be dangerous. Akala wanted to see what is beyond our home. I suspect it was not as exciting as she thought it might be," she said, looking directly at Akala.

Akala sniffed the air again. "The storm is close," she said. "We should hurry." She quickened her pace, leaving the others behind.

Charlie looked at the sky. "I don't see clouds," he said. "Are you sure there's a storm?" To him, the sun was bright; the day was beautiful. A storm was the last thing he would have expected.

Leidar squinted at Charlie, specifically at his nose. "Can you not smell it?" he said. "There is metal in the wind. The clouds will move in soon. An Electric is coming. Akala is correct, we should hurry." With a glance at Corala, he changed from a brisk walk to a jog, and soon he was far ahead of all of them. Corala followed suit, and with a shrug, Chuck started jogging as well. With a quick look behind him at the area where they'd left their tent, Charlie started running after the others, wondering if the tent, and everything in it, would survive.

The trail they followed was barely visible; either it was an old path, or one not taken often or by many people. They raced through the landscape, and it seemed to Charlie that they were getting ever closer to the ocean. He wasn't sure that heading toward the water during a storm was wise, but then, he thought, these people were the ones who could smell the storm, not him. On their planet, he would leave the survival instincts to them, at least for now.

After a while, the trail took them along a cliff overlooking the sea. Charlie wanted to stop and take in the view; he'd always been drawn to the power of the ocean, and this one was churning with wild ferocity. White-capped waves built up far from shore and grew in intensity in the dark waters until they crashed, dozens of feet high, against the cliff they were walking on. Charlie wondered if the sea was always this active, or if this was related to the storm. But there was no time to think on it; the others were pulling ahead of him and he didn't want to get lost. Dark clouds had started to move in quickly, and he had no doubts now that the aliens were right that a storm was coming.

Eventually, the path veered away from the cliff again and in toward what seemed like safer land. In the distance, short walls started to come into view, with a few tops of buildings poking up behind them. The group ran until they came to an enormous gate, made of intricately twisted and woven bars of some kind of metal.

"Um, it's an electric storm?" said Charlie, looking at the metal.

"Yes?" said Leidar, opening the gate and letting the others walk through before shutting it fast behind him.

"It just seems that … I mean, metal, electricity, you know …" He imagined a giant lightning bolt coming out of the sky and being attracted straight to this gate.

"We are not planning to stay by the gate," said Corala, the amusement once again shining in her eyes. She looked at Leidar and shook her head. "Strangers indeed," she said to him softly.

Akala grabbed Charlie's arm. "This way," she said, and she led him away. Chuck followed, while Corala and Leidar walked off, heads together, looking back over their shoulders at Chuck and Charlie, talking quietly. A few other beings were wandering around in the enclosure and looking at the strangers with curiosity, but they didn't approach.

"You are from Earth?" said Akala quietly as she led them through a door into a small building. "That is an island? I haven't heard of it. But then, we don't hear of much," she said. She glanced out the window as though checking whether anyone was listening. She held out her hands to the room. "This will be safe. Close the windows and doors. If you would like to sleep, you may." She pointed at a doorway, through which they could see a bed. "No one is using this home right now."

The home was small, with little in the way of furnishings. The front room, which they'd entered into, had a worn couch covered in a faded green fabric, a short coffee table in front of it, and two chairs framing a hole in the wall made of stone—possibly an old fireplace that hadn't been used in a while. Akala flipped a switch on the wall and overhead lights flickered on reluctantly. "No one knows how to fix that," she said wearily. "Anyway, everything should be clean. You are free to stay as long as you need." She sniffed the air. "The storm is very near. I should go to my home."

"Wait—" said Charlie, as Akala turned to leave. "Uh, well, you could stay here and talk to us?" he said. Chuck shot him a look. "How long will the storm last?"

"It's now half day," said Akala. "I'd guess the storm will be over before the evening meal. Not too long," she said. She rubbed her fingers together nervously and looked out the window again. "Maybe I could stay," she said.

"Stay and talk to us," Charlie said. "Please?"

Akala smiled and blinked. "All right," she said. "I will first get us some food to share." She ran off without another word.

Once she'd gone, Chuck turned to Charlie. "Do you think that's wise?" he said. "We don't know yet if these people are safe. You heard her. They don't seem to have a lot of interaction with strangers. Maybe that's because they *eat* strangers?"

"Don't be ridiculous," said Charlie. "If she was going to eat us, why would she go get food? We're right here!" He laughed. "Calm down. It's fine. I have a good sense about her. I admit, Leidar and Corala seem a bit odd, but Akala seems okay. I'd like to get to know her."

"Okay, she's not going to eat us. What if she's going to poison us? We don't know anything about the food on this planet. She could feed us something deadly and we'd never have a clue."

But before Charlie could reply, Akala was back, carrying a basket.

"Your home must be nearby," Chuck said.

"Just two houses down," said Akala. She walked through the front room to an adjoining room where a table and chairs were set up, and placed the basket on top of the table. "Hungry?" she said. She opened the basket and started pulling out containers of food.

chapter seven

Emma, Ree, Ben, and Dr. Waldo stood just outside the lighthouse at the remote, barely inhabited town of Balky Point, on north end of little Dogwinkle Island, in the waters of the northwestern part of Washington state, on the Earth that Ree and Chuck called home. No one would ever suspect that inside this lighthouse was a tiny room that was a portal to everywhere, or that on the other side of that room lay a space where everything was possible.

"It looks so normal," said Ree, gazing up at the striped tower. "You forget that it just looks like a plain old lighthouse."

"I still can't get used to the fact that this Earth, your Earth, isn't my Earth, too," said Emma. "It looks the same. Like, I know you're real, and I know I'm real, but the fact that your Earth and my Earth both exist and are the same except not quite the same … I don't know. It's hard to wrap my brain around. If I didn't know it was true, I wouldn't believe it."

"The universes hold many mysteries," said Dr. Waldo with glee. "Many, many mysteries indeed."

"All right," said Ben. "Where … I mean, *when*. When are you going? So that we can track you and find you if we need to." He was acting unconcerned but his furrowed brow betrayed him as he looked from Ree to Emma and back. "We don't want to lose you," he said.

"Don't worry," said Ree. "It's just time travel. Nothing exciting like space travel. We'll be right here the whole time. Well, near here anyway. I'm taking Emma about a dozen years into the future. Not far at all."

"'It's just time travel,'" Emma repeated, laughing. "'Nothing exciting.' Ha!" She remembered Ree's comment that she'd been to both the beginning and the end of time, but they hadn't had the chance to delve into that yet. Emma wanted to go, too. To the beginning of time, and to the end of time. She wanted to see it. If she was honest, a dozen years into the future didn't seem exciting at all. But it was a start.

"Okay," said Ben, tapping on his tablet. It was his job to record the experiment as best he could from the present time. "How does this work? Is it … does it feel the same as when we travel in the elevator or with the pigeon or Dark MATTER?"

Emma looked at Ben and suddenly realized, he wanted to go, too. She understood. If she hadn't been going, she would have been bursting at the seams. Watching others go on adventures but not going herself would have been torture. "Maybe you can come along next time, Ben," she said.

"Ah, no worries," said Ben, but he gave her a smile of gratitude.

"So," said Ree, "to be honest, a lot of the time … well, a lot of the time I just travel and see when I end up. I've gotten pretty precise, though. Most of the time I end up exactly when I want to be."

A chill ran through Emma's spine. "Most of the time? You mean, I mean this is fine, but you're not entirely sure where … *when* we'll end up?" She blinked. "And … this is the first time you've taken someone else along?"

Ree blushed. "Well, yes, you're the first person I've brought along. But I'm sure it'll work. Just hang on to me tight. And really, I've gotten pretty good at pinpointing the time I want. I only miss occasionally. Like if I get distracted just before I go, or if I sneeze. There was that time ..." Ree started to laugh, but then stopped. "Oh, never mind."

Emma looked at Dr. Waldo. "Instead of bringing a human along, should she first try bringing something inanimate or a mouse? ... No, never mind. I'm good. Okay. Let's do this." She shook her head to dispel the fears. "I believe in you, Ree," she said, trying to convince herself.

Ben glanced from Emma to Ree and back. "You're sure?" he said. "I could go instead ..."

Emma braced her shoulders and nodded. "No, I'm sure."

"Okay, then. Ree, whenever you're ready. Can you tell us exactly how it'll work?" said Ben.

"Actually—" Emma jumped in. "Actually, can she tell you that later? Can we just do this and ... I mean, not to get it over with, because I'm excited. But ... let's just get it over with, shall we?" She shuddered involuntarily.

"Sure," said Ben. "We can talk about all that later. Remember, I adjusted your iPert so hopefully it will tell you the year, at least, when you arrive, if not the exact date. Check it when you get there ... when you get *here*, later ... or whatever. Check it to see if it works, and let me know, when you get back." He looked at Dr. Waldo, who grinned and nodded approval. "Okay, Ree, whenever you're ready," Ben said.

Ree shuffled her feet in place and looked up at the sky. The day was cool but not cold; overcast but not raining. Below the cliffs, they could hear the sound of an occasional wave crashing against the rocks. Seagulls cried overhead as they wheeled and soared in search of their next meal. The wind ruffled the leaves of a madrona tree near the trail that led to the beach below. A slight breeze lifted Emma's dark auburn hair from her neck. She shivered and her heart skipped a beat.

"Okay," said Ree, "Emma, hang on to me." She extended her hand, but Emma reached over and grabbed Ree in a full body hug. "Don't let go," she said, squeezing her eyes shut and tucking her head into Ree's shoulder.

"I think we're good," Ree laughed, hugging Emma back with one arm. "All right, hang on tight."

Travel via the various methods the group used—the elevator, the pigeon and Dark MATTER, and Emma's mind—always felt disorienting, but time travel felt different from any of the ways they traveled through space. Emma clung to Ree, and then, when she could no longer feel Ree, she clung to where she thought Ree might be. She felt as though her cells were being lengthened, one end remaining behind while the other rushed forward into the unknown. The sensation wasn't exactly painful; it was a feeling of intense pressure, like every particle was being stressed at once. Like her cells were rubber bands being stretched to their limit. Finally, suddenly, Emma felt as though her cells released from the original starting point, snapped and returned to their normal length. She felt Ree in her arms again, and her muscles ached from clinging so tightly. Her knees buckled, and, letting go of Ree, Emma fell to the ground.

"Oh my gosh," said Emma. "That felt weird."

"I think part of it was because you were holding me. It doesn't feel quite like that when I do it alone," said Ree. "But we're here!" She sat on the ground next to Emma while each of them caught her breath.

Emma looked around. Ben and Dr. Waldo were nowhere to be seen. The lighthouse was still there, exactly where it had been when they'd left. The madrona tree by the trail to the beach, however, looked like it had grown. Or had it? Was she just imagining it? Emma couldn't be sure. The lighthouse had been old before, but was well maintained. If it was any older now, Emma couldn't tell.

"Did we travel?" she said. "What does the iPert say?"

Ree reached into a pocket of the bag she'd packed and pulled out the small device. After tapping around a bit, she looked up with a smile. "Eleven years forward. Not bad for an amateur!"

"Well done, miss," said Emma. Feeling balanced again, she stood. "Can we look around a bit before we go back?" She stared at the lighthouse. "Looks like it's empty." Then she noticed something around the back, a few hundred yards away. "Wait, there's a new building there. A cabin? What is that?" She looked at Ree. "Have you seen this before? Did you know that was there?"

Ree blushed and smiled. "Yup," she said. "So, in the future … well, in my future, on my Earth …" She paused, then reached for Emma's hand. "Come with me."

They walked quickly toward the cabin. It was small, nothing fancy, but it looked well made and cozy. "Who built this?" Emma said as they drew near. "Is it on state land?"

"No, just on the other side of the property line," Ree said, her eyes bright. She stopped just outside the front door and peered in the window. "She's home." Ree knocked on the front door and waited.

"Who?" Emma whispered. "Who's home?"

The door opened. Standing there, several months pregnant, first with a look of surprise and then a look of delight, was another Emma, eleven years older.

Emma's jaw dropped. She took in the woman's dark auburn hair, a little wavier than her own, perhaps, and a little longer. The eyes looked somehow more relaxed and content. Her smile made Emma think that their appearance was less of a surprise to her than it was to Emma.

"You're …" Emma started, but she didn't know how to finish.

"Future me," Ree beamed. "My Earth. This is me. Eleven years from now."

"Future Ree," said Future Ree. "Hello again, Past Ree, and I'm assuming this is Emma From Another Earth?"

"… Yes," said Emma, still blown away. It made sense to her that she and Ree, two separate people from separate planets, could exist in the same time and space. But two versions of Ree? The same person? Dr. Waldo had explained it, the whole molecule B and molecule C thing, but Emma hadn't really believed it. And yet, here they all were, standing together, and no one or no thing seemed to have exploded. Yet.

"Come in, come in," said Future Ree, waving the two inside the small cabin. "Don't want to let the bugs in!"

"I hate bugs," said Emma.

"I know," said Future Ree. "We do too." She shared a smile with her past self.

The inside of the cabin was just as cozy as the outside suggested it would be. Future Ree led them into a small living room. "Sit. I'll get us some lemonade, shall I?"

"Yes, please!" Ree said. She sat in a charcoal gray overstuffed chair, kicked off her shoes, and tucked her feet underneath her.

Emma, however, remained standing, mouth open, eyes wide, gaping at the cabin and not quite believing what was happening. "This is your house?" she said to Ree after Future Ree walked into the next room to get drinks and refreshments. "Future you? Do you—does she—live here alone?" she said, a pointed reference to the very pregnant state of Ree's future self.

"No," said Ree. "They—we—so, I haven't told you. But in my present day, on my Earth, this Earth but eleven years ago—oh, this is confusing. So, I'm dating Ben. Not your Ben, not the one you know. The one from my Earth."

At this, Emma plopped herself onto a couch that matched the chair Ree was sitting in. "You're dating *Ben*?" she said. Her mind could hardly handle all the new information that was being stuffed into it today.

"Yeah," said Ree, blushing. "I met your Ben just briefly, and then you all went off to chase after Eve's mom, and … well, I was curious. So I found a way to meet my Ben. I didn't know what would happen. I was just curious. We hit it off, though, and … we started dating. Nothing serious yet."

Emma looked around the room, and her eyes fell on a wedding picture. In it were a Ree somewhere between this Ree and Future Ree, and a man who most definitely was Ben. "Yet," she said.

"Yeah," Ree confirmed. "I guess I was curious, so I came forward in time just to see … you know, where things would go."

Emma looked through the doorway to the kitchen. "I guess things went well," she said.

Ree laughed. "I guess so."

Future Ree came in carrying a tray with a pitcher of lemonade along with cheese and crackers. She set it on the small coffee table, and joined Emma on the couch. "Am I getting you all caught up on everything?" she said. "I know, it's confusing, but you should be used to that by now."

Emma found she wasn't hungry. Needing to burn energy, she popped up from the couch and started walking slowly around the room. "Surely …" she started.

"Surely what?" said Future Ree, pouring the lemonade into three glasses. "Let me guess. Surely there are rules?"

Emma stared at Future Ree. That was exactly what she was going to say. But this was Future Ree, not Future Emma. It wasn't the same. It was a lot the same, but it wasn't the same. How did Future Ree know her so well? "Surely there are rules," she said. "The universes must have rules. Surely we can't be allowed to all be together like this."

"The universes do have rules," Future Ree said, "but we don't know them. Or we don't know most of them. We're just starting to figure it all out."

Emma noticed the use of the plural pronoun. "We," she said. "You and Ben?"

"All of us," Future Ree said. "We're all working on it."

Emma walked to the fireplace, to the assortment of pictures on the mantle. There were pictures of Ree and Ben, pictures of their families. Then she saw it: the picture they'd taken just a few days before in the Hub, the one Dr. Waldo had had so much trouble with. There they all were. Emma, Ree, Eve, Ben, Charlie and Chuck.

Charlie and Chuck.

Something her subconscious had noticed, but which her conscious self hadn't yet noticed, started to nag at her brain. What was it? What was she not noticing? Emma scanned the rest of the photos, a panic growing in her. There were more pictures of Emma and Ree together, older than she was now but younger than Future Ree. Pictures of Ree or Emma with Ben, and some with Eve and Dr. Waldo.

"Ree," she said. She felt her throat tighten. She went to the hallway, where more pictures were hung on the walls. She found what she was looking for: a photo of the entire wedding party. There again were Ree and Ben, and their families. And there was Emma. But …

"Where's Chuck?" Emma said. "Ree, where's Chuck? Where's Charlie? Why are there no pictures of Charlie after this one of all of us that we took the other day? Where is Charlie?" A chill ran up her spine and she felt cold from her core.

Future Ree met Emma's eyes with a look of intense pain and sadness. "Oh, Emma," she said, her own eyes filling with tears. "When did you say you're from?"

Ree had quickly caught on to what Emma was saying. She pointed to the picture they'd taken in the Hub. "That was this week," she said. "And Chuck and Charlie were fine. Just a few days ago. They were fine. Why? Where are they now? What are you saying?"

Emma started shaking, fearing what Future Ree would say next. Future Ree put her lemonade down and looked at her hands, then up at the picture, then back at the girls. "I'm so sorry. Ree, I thought you knew. You didn't say anything when you were here before. I thought you knew. Chuck and Charlie are gone."

chapter eight

On the simple, wooden table, Akala laid out an assortment of foods, all of which were unfamiliar to Chuck and Charlie. To their eyes it looked like an assortment of nuts, some root vegetables, a sort of salami or meat, something that resembled cheese and crackers, and berries or fruit.

"Juice?" said Akala, pulling a small container out of the basket. Without waiting for them to reply, she went to the cupboards and got three glasses and plates, poured the juice, and sat down. "Please, eat," she said.

Chuck dived in first, trying the cheese and crackers. After the first bite, he looked at Charlie, eyebrows raised, and shrugged in a gesture that said, "Sure, it's edible."

The wind outside was starting to pick up, and a flash of lightning brightened the cloudy sky. Charlie piled a plate with cheese and crackers, as well as some nuts and the mysterious meat. He hadn't realized how hungry he was, and the strange food tasted delicious. "Thank you, Akala," he said. "This is amazing."

Akala nodded in response, a small smile turning up the corner of her mouth. "Chuck and Charlie," she said, looking at them for affirmation that she'd remembered their names correctly. "Chuck and Charlie, tell me about your island? I have not been anywhere but here." She seemed shy and timid, as though talking to them took a great deal of courage but she was determined not to let the opportunity pass. Her large eyes were wide and bright.

"Oh," said Charlie, stalling for time. "It's … well, it's like anyplace, I suppose. Houses, people, jobs, schools. Just a normal place." He looked at Chuck for help.

"Yeah," said Chuck. "That pretty much defines it. We … well, we both have sisters, and we still live with our parents, but we've got this business idea and maybe will move out soon. I've been thinking, Charlie, we should get an apartment."

"Totally," said Charlie. "I've been thinking the same thing…" Noticing that Akala's wide eyes had grown even wider, he stopped. "Are you okay?"

"You live with your parents?" she said incredulously. "Both of you?"

"Well, yes," said Charlie, unsure why this was causing such surprise. "I mean, we're seventeen. It's not like we're thirty-five and still living at home."

But this comment only seemed to shock Akala even more. "Thirty-five! But only caretakers …" She stopped. For a while it seemed she was having a conversation inside her head, and finally she made the decision to speak. "We are *all* sixteen here," she said, and she paused, looking at them to see if they understood.

"You're sixteen?" said Chuck, puzzled. The wind was howling now, and lightning was coming in regular bursts. Through the window, they could see these were not simple bursts but rather webs of light, many-fingered bolts entangling the sky. But there seemed to be no rain.

"We are all sixteen," said Akala. "The others are all Memories now. Even our Memory Keepers have become Memories. Last year."

Chuck and Charlie exchanged a glance to see if either of them had a clue what she was talking about, but both were bamboozled.

"Sorry," said Charlie. "What? Memories? Memory Keepers? You're going to have to start at the beginning."

Akala took a deep breath. She seemed to struggle with whether she should say anything. Shaking her head, she spoke again. "We are all sixteen," she said. "The Memory Keepers moved on last year, when we were fifteen. This is the way it has been for generations." Seeing that Chuck and Charlie were still confused, she continued. "You live with your parents?" she said again. "They are alive?"

"Of course," said Charlie. "I mean, not *of course*, some people's parents are gone or split or whatever, but ours are alive. Is that so strange?"

Akala blinked rapidly. "We do not have parents," she said. "We are created in a laboratory. This is the way it has been for generations."

"Created in a laboratory?" Charlie had been about to eat another cracker with the soft cheese, but he put the cracker back on his plate. "You were created in a laboratory?"

"You were not?" Akala whispered. She again glanced furtively out the window to see if anyone was listening in the shadows, despite the wind and the lightning that was almost constant now. "Tell me more about your island," she said, a new edge of desperation inside her voice.

"I think … well, why don't you tell us about life here first? You are created in laboratories? All of you? And you are all sixteen? Start at the beginning," Chuck said.

Akala looked toward the windows again, then went and pulled the curtains shut before sitting. She bit her lips and started her tale. "We are all created in laboratories. This is not the same for you?

When a generation reaches thirty years old, they together work to create a new generation, in the laboratory. A group of the older generation are selected, by their genes, to become Memory Keepers and to raise the new generation to the age of fifteen. The rest of the generation of thirty-year-olds, the Elders, become Memories. They go to the Tower, and their Memories are saved forever. Each year on the first day of the year, the Memory Keepers install new Memories into our minds. When we turn fifteen, the Memory Keepers become Memories themselves, and they move on." She said all of this as though it was obvious, but her words left Chuck and Charlie's mouths hanging open in shock.

"The Tower? They become Memories?" said Charlie. "What do you mean?"

Akala frowned. "Their minds. Their thoughts and histories are extracted and stored in the Tower. They become Memories."

"But what happens to them after … after their brains are extracted?" asked Chuck.

"Not their brains. Their history. Their knowledge and wisdom. Their thoughts become a part of the collective Memories, which the Memory Keepers curate and pass on to us for the first fifteen years of life. After that, we have the wisdom we need and the Memory Keepers can move on."

Charlie shook his head. He had so many questions he didn't know where to begin. "Where do you keep the Memories?" he asked.

"As I said, in the Tower," Akala said. Her eyes drifted to the front door and a bit to the left; Charlie assumed she was looking in the direction of the Tower.

"For generations?" Chuck said. "It's been this way for generations?"

"We are the sixth generation," said Akala.

"So six generations ago, someone … they decided to … I'm sorry, but when you say 'move on,' do you mean the Elders are killed?" asked Charlie.

"No," said Akala defensively. "They are still with us. They are Memories. I told you."

"But their bodies?" asked Chuck.

"A body is merely a vase for a flower," said Akala. "The Elders never die."

"But flowers die," said Charlie.

Akala had no answer. She frowned.

"Why?" asked Chuck. "Do you know why they decided to live this way, six generations ago?"

Akala pursed her lips. "Because death is too painful. To have parents, grandparents, and to have them die, it was too painful for those left behind. When one person was gone and another had to live without them. They decided it would be a kindness to create a world where no one had to endure the agony of watching someone else move on unexpectedly. Too many broken hearts. Too many people wanted to die themselves, after watching someone else die. To live with parents and grandparents, and to watch them die, that is a cruelty. We do not suffer this way. We have evolved."

The words spilled from her lips as if she was reading them from a book, or remembering a speech someone else had given; it sounded rehearsed and stale.

"But that's …" Charlie wanted to say barbaric, but caught himself before speaking. It wouldn't be wise to draw too much attention to the fact that they were not familiar with the local ways. "That's interesting," he finished.

Akala's eyes grew wide again, and she stared at them intently. It was clear there was something on her mind that she wanted to tell them. Chuck and Charlie waited patiently for her to speak.

"Great cheese," Chuck said, as he finished it off. He licked his lips.

"All of it," Charlie said. "It was all good." He watched Akala to see if she would give voice to the words that were churning in her mind.

Finally, the intensity of her thoughts was too much. "I'm different," Akala said, the words themselves an exhale, a release.

Chuck tossed Charlie a look of caution. "Different how?" he asked.

"I'm different from the others," she said. "It happens. They are careful in the laboratories, usually, but sometimes mutants are born. I am one." She paused. "No one knows."

"Mutant?" said Charlie. He realized he didn't know what "normal" looked like here, so he could not well judge "mutant."

"I am different. My mind. I think differently," she said. "I ask questions. Not out loud; not anymore. But I think thoughts the others don't have. The others are content. I …" she glanced toward the windows again and lowered her voice. "I want to leave."

As soon as she spoke, Akala started packing the leftover food into the basket. "The storm is almost over," she said, sniffing the air. "I must go." She picked up the basket and left.

"What was that about?" said Charlie. He went to the door and looked left and right, but Akala had disappeared. "Do we smell bad?"

Chuck shrugged. "I don't know, but it does seem the storm's almost over," he said, opening the curtains at the window again. "Want to go look around?"

"Definitely," Charlie smiled, and the two headed out into the enclosure. The air felt clean and crisp, like the storm had cleared out all impurities, and the clouds were swiftly blowing away, leaving a bright blue sky behind. A few people started to emerge from their homes, peering out of doorways and looking up at the sky.

"All sixteen," said Chuck, looking at the beings who were, in turn, eyeing him warily with their wide dark eyes. "And for sure, they look like short-nosed meerkat heads with human bodies."

"I wish we could see what we look like to them," said Charlie in a low voice. "I'd love to see you with a meerkat head."

Chuck let out a guffaw. "Or Dr. Waldo! Can you imagine Dr. Waldo with a meerkat head?"

Charlie laughed too, and soon they both had tears streaming down their faces. The tension of the day had left them on edge, and it was a relief to be safe and outside. The homes they passed all had a worn look to them, as if they hadn't seen much care for years. The small gardens outside the houses were tidy and uniform, each with the same layout of plants: a small bush on either side of the door, a large patch of dirt with evenly spaced plants that may have been root vegetables or other produce, two old chairs sitting out front, and a row of flowers lining a low fence that delineated each home's space.

Two of the beings were watching them especially closely from the chairs of a home a few doors down from where the boys had been housed. Wiping his eyes, Chuck nudged Charlie in the side. "Don't look now, but is that Leidar and Corala? To your left," he said under his breath.

Charlie faked a sneeze and turned to look. "It's so hard to tell. But yes, I think that's the clothes they had on. Why are they staring at us like that?"

"I wonder if they saw Akala come out of our house? She seemed really nervous. Maybe they don't get along. Maybe they're meerkat spies," Chuck said. At this, the two burst out laughing again. They continued walking, pretending they didn't know they were being watched. After a bit, they saw a large tower in the distance, rising out from the top of a hill.

"Do you think that's the Tower Akala was talking about?" Charlie said, looking up at it in wonder. "Where the Memories are?"

"Yeah, what was that about?" said Chuck. "They take people's memories, and then put them back in other people? That's crazy talk."

"How do you suppose they do it?" said Charlie. It occurred to him that the Tower would make an excellent lightning rod. It seemed to be almost crackling even now; every now and then, he swore he could see a flash of electricity in the air surrounding it.

"No idea," Chuck said. "And I suspect I don't want to find out." He turned. "Come on. I can hardly keep my eyes open. I'm going for a nap."

Charlie shrugged. "Yeah, me too," he said. They headed back to their borrowed home, noticing that Leidar and Corala were still watching their every move. "I don't know why," he said, "but those two give me the creeps."

"Same," said Chuck. "Very much same."

They both fell asleep as soon as their heads hit the slim pillows on the narrow beds.

When he woke a while later, Charlie sat up abruptly. "Where am I?" he said groggily to himself. He looked around the room, not recognizing it. "What the heck?" he said, louder. "Where am I?"

The sound of Charlie's voice woke Chuck. Chuck sat up in his own bed and rubbed his eyes. Charlie saw him and gasped.

"Who are you?" said Charlie. "You look just like me. Who are you? Where are we?"

Chuck blinked hard and stared back at Charlie. "I'm Charlie," he said. "Who are you?"

chapter nine

"Gone?" said Emma. "What do you mean 'gone'? Gone for how long? Gone from where?" She felt nauseated, and frantically scanned Future Ree's walls again for more recent pictures of Charlie or Chuck, for anything that would prove this future version of her parallel self wrong.

"They disappeared from that planet," said Future Ree. She tilted her head toward the photo Dr. Waldo had snapped on Emma's phone. "Right after that picture was taken, they went out scouting possible planets for the travel company they wanted to start. Right?"

"Yes," said Ree. "We went with them. They were fine when we left them." She cast a glance at Emma. *This is impossible*, the look said.

"They were fine when we left them, too," said Future Ree. "But then they disappeared, and we never heard from them again."

Emma's heart dropped to the ground and she felt like all the air had been sucked from her lungs. "Never? But didn't you go back to look for them? Didn't you search? Why didn't you look for them?" she accused. Tears filled her eyes as she sorted through everything Dr. Waldo had told them about time. Time could be changed. This future didn't have to be her future … did it?

"Of course we looked," said Future Ree angrily. "Of *course* we looked."

"So what happened?" said Emma, an accusation in her tone: *Why didn't you bring them home?*

Future Ree sighed forcefully. "We went back. Their tent had been destroyed. We wandered around for five days, but we never found another sign of them."

"Where did you go?" asked Emma, pulling her ever-present pen and paper from her bag. "Draw me a map. Show me where you looked. We'll look somewhere else. We'll change the future. Our future, anyway. Maybe not yours." She desperately wanted to talk to her future self, not this Future Ree. Without a doubt, Future Emma would be more helpful. She could not believe Future Emma would have left Charlie behind. Logically, she knew that was the case; that if Ree had left Chuck and Charlie behind, Emma had as well. But she didn't believe it.

Future Ree rubbed her pregnant belly in a calming, meditative way. Whether she was trying to soothe herself or the baby within wasn't clear. "Okay," she said. "Well, we tracked their iPerts to a sort of encampment, a colony, out a trail that ran along the ocean and then inland a bit." She pulled out a piece of paper and stared at it a while, recreating the scene in her mind before beginning to draw. She labeled different parts of the drawing: tent, ocean, colony. Then she drew an outline over a large area. "This is where we searched. It's just a rough sketch, obviously. No one at the encampment knew who they were. They said they'd been out, had seen the tent that was destroyed, and had picked up the iPerts, but they hadn't met the people they belonged to and hadn't seen anyone. We kept looking for days, but eventually …" she stopped. She stared out the window, her mind filling with memories.

"You left them behind?" said Emma coolly. She would never have left. She knew she wouldn't have. With Ben and Dr. Waldo and all the scientists, surely someone would have been able to find them. She took the map from Future Ree and studied it, trying to recall the landscape they'd seen only briefly. "Did you go talk to another Future Ree first? Did this happen to another Future Ree and another Future Emma and another Future Charlie and Chuck? You had this same conversation?"

Future Ree poured herself more lemonade and drank a few sips. "More or less," she said.

"But not the exact same conversation?" said Emma.

"Not exactly," said Future Ree.

"What was different?" asked Emma.

Future Ree paused. "I don't think we asked the future me where they had gone to look for Chuck and Charlie."

Emma looked at Ree. "Let's go. It's up to us."

Ree stood, ready. "Up to us how?"

Emma's eyes fell on the picture of all of the gang in the Hub. "Remember the river of time? The rocks in the river? It's all about choices. We change our choices and we change the future. This Ree and Emma," she said, pointing at Future Ree, "they may have lost their brothers, but we're not going to lose ours. That Ree is molecule C. Her lost Chuck and Charlie are molecule C. But you and I and our Chuck and Charlie are in the present. We are molecule B. We haven't lost them yet, and we are not going to give up on them."

Emma grabbed Ree by the hand and headed to the door. "Nice to meet you," she called over her shoulder as she pulled Ree along, out of the house and down the trail back to the front of the lighthouse, where they'd first arrived. "Take us back," she said to Ree, and she pulled Ree into a bear hug and held on for dear life.

Ree slowed her breathing and concentrated hard. Their cells stretched again, like a rubber band, all the way to the end point, before snapping back. With a *whoosh*, the world around them reassembled. Ben and Dr. Waldo were still standing there, watching with looks of anticipation and worry in their eyes.

"You left just seconds ago!" said Dr. Waldo, his look of worry quickly changing to a look of delight.

"I've been practicing," Ree said with a self-satisfied smile.

Emma shook her arms and stamped her legs to get herself fully back in her body. Once again she felt like a small part of her had switched with some small part of the universes, but she dismissed the thought. There were much bigger concerns to deal with right now. "Chuck and Charlie," she said, out of breath. "Chuck and Charlie are in danger. We went and talked to a future version of Ree, and she said Chuck and Charlie disappeared from the planet they're on now, and never made it back. We are going to get them back." Her statement left no question. They had a mission, and they would succeed.

Emma and Ree quickly filled Ben and Dr. Waldo in on everything they'd learned as they raced into the Hub. "You need to land us exactly where Chuck and Charlie landed us last time," Ree said as Ben calibrated a Dark MATTER sphere for them to use.

"There's no room for error," said Emma, bouncing on the balls of her feet in her impatience.

Ben nodded calmly and made final adjustments to the sphere. "Should I come with you?" he said, concern furrowing his forehead as he looked at Emma. "I've been studying that planet. It has enormous electrical forces. In its storms, eighty percent of its lightning strikes are positively charged, unlike on Earth where it's only about five percent. Positively charged lightning can do a ton of damage. Maybe I should come with you," he said. "Just, you know, for another person to watch out for danger."

Emma suddenly remembered that Ree and the other Ben were

dating, on Ree's Earth. She liked Ben, but there was no time to think about that now. "No, you stay here. We need you here in case something happens."

Ben nodded again, disappointed but understanding. "Okay," he said. "Okay." He handed each of the girls a small bag. "Lots of pigeons and extra Dark MATTER spheres, all calibrated to bring you right back here. And Emma," he looked at her, his eyes filled with anxiety. "I know you don't like to do it, but you can get you guys home if you need to. I believe in you."

"Yes," said Emma. "We will be back, one way or another." Impulsively, she leaned in and gave him a quick kiss on the cheek. Immediately she blushed and she held out her hand for the Dark MATTER sphere to hide her embarrassment.

A swipe later, Emma and Ree tumbled through nothingness and came out the other side, their molecules quickly reassembling as they landed on the planet they'd been on just a few days before with Chuck and Charlie.

"I sure hope we're in the right time," said Emma.

Ree looked offended. "If we're not, it wasn't me. I didn't do anything." She brushed dust off her jeans as she rose from the ground.

"No, no," said Emma. "I know that. It's just, I never know how all this works. If we got here just shortly after we left, I'm amazed. It all seems so bizarre."

Ree seemed mollified. "Yeah, you're right. Ben is good, but as far as we know, it could have been weeks ago when we were last here." She looked at the iPert Ben had calibrated to tell time for their travels on her Earth. "This is no help. Ben will have to work on it some more. It only shows Earth time. And only *my* Earth, at that. And besides, I don't have a reference point from when we were last here." She tucked the device into her pocket.

The sun was hanging low in the sky, and the air felt sweltering, lingering hot and muggy. Emma took off her jacket and stuffed it into her pack. "Does any of this look familiar? Are we near where we were last time?" Had she known she'd be coming back on a rescue mission, she would have paid more attention. "I thought Ben was going to land us in the same place?" She shielded her eyes from the sun with her hand and scanned the horizon for anything she recognized.

"There!" said Ree, pointing to a clearing on her left. "Is that something?" She raced to the clearing, Emma hot on her heels. When they arrived they could see that this was indeed the right place, but nothing was as they'd left it. Charlie and Chuck's tent had been scorched and torn into shreds, and was strewn all over the area. The cooler Charlie had gone back for must have been lifted by a strong gust of wind; the lid was gone, and the rest was caught halfway up a bush. Some animals or other creatures had absconded with or ripped into all the food; only beaten, empty containers remained. One sleeping bag had been snagged by another bush; the other was gone. They searched carefully for any sign of the boys, anything that could lead them to their brothers, anything that could give a clue as to where they'd gone, but found nothing.

Emma could feel the blood rush from her face. Had the boys been here when this had happened? Had they, like the food from the cooler, been victim of scavengers? She knew Charlie well enough to know he might not have paid attention to the possibility of dangerous animals on this planet. In fact, if there were, it could have been a draw for him.

"I hope they weren't eaten by dinosaurs," Ree said softly, echoing the thoughts in Emma's mind.

"Me too," said Emma. "At least … I mean, at least there aren't bones." No sign of the boys at all at least meant there was hope.

Off toward the water, the seabirds called and rolled in the sky. A small splash in the nearby lake alerted the girls that something else might be even nearer.

"Okay," said Emma, collecting herself. "Okay. We have Ree's map of where they explored. When they came here—when we came here in the past—whatever it was—we tracked the boys. How do we track them?"

"Their iPerts," Ree said. "The other Ree said they tracked their iPerts."

Emma felt as though she was in shock, like she was acting through a fog and going through motions without those motions being fully attached to her brain. "Yes, iPerts," she said. She pulled out her own iPert and fumbled, staring at it blankly, trying to think what she needed to do.

"Here," said Ree, seeing Emma's confusion. "I've got it." She tapped and swiped on her own iPert for a few moments, then looked up toward the ocean. "That way," she said. "Along the coastline a ways, then inland a bit. Like Ree said."

Emma looked at the rough map Future Ree had drawn for her, which Dr. Waldo had helped her scan into her iPert and calibrate to a quickly approximated map of the planet. She turned it until she felt she had it oriented correctly to the land. "Yes. That makes sense," she said. "Here, it looks like the encampment they found would be that way. So," she said, turning and pointing in the other direction, "we go this way." She tapped an area on the map that Ree had indicated they had not already searched.

"Are you sure we shouldn't check the encampment first?" said Ree. "What if this Charlie and Chuck are there? What if we don't check and they're actually there?"

The parallel teens—Chuck and Charlie, Emma and Ree—had discussed their parallel Earths and parallel lives many times. They'd compared notes from their childhoods: "Did you get braces when you were twelve?" "Yes." "Did you skin your knee on a garden fence when you were eight?" "Yes." "Did you travel to Yellowstone Park when you were fourteen?" "Yes." "Are all your grandparents still alive?" "No." Not everything was exactly the same, and it seemed that ever since they'd met, their paths had started to diverge even more quickly, as though meeting had knocked them off the parallel course. When they'd first met, Emma had been more timid; more like Ree still was. Time and necessity had changed her, given her courage, toughened her up. Ree, who hadn't traveled with them, seemed more like Emma had been not so long ago, but they were, nonetheless, far more alike yet than they were different. It was strange, Emma thought, having a version of herself outside of herself; sort of like an out-of-body experience. And odd, too, how easy it was to love Ree, when she didn't always love herself. Everything that she hated in herself, she found she could like, or at least tolerate, in Ree. Like the way Ree was shy and reserved most of the time. Emma knew she was like that, too, a lot of the time. In herself the shyness seemed like a fatal flaw; an example of cowardice and a precursor to a life forever alone. But in Ree, the shyness and the reservedness seemed thoughtful, introspective, compassionate, and endearing. It was as though Ree was considering others, listening to them, not being full of herself like so many other people were. Maybe, Emma thought, she could start to see those qualities in herself the same way. Maybe she could start to appreciate in herself what she loved about Ree. Because she didn't love Ree *despite* those characteristics she hated in herself; she loved Ree *including* all those characteristics. She loved the whole of Ree. It was an overwhelming concept. She loved an exact replica of herself more than she loved herself. She vowed that she would start to look on herself with the same forgiving heart.

Right now, she could sense Ree's timidity, her fear of doing the wrong thing, her fear of risk, of going off in a new direction—literally. She'd been inside those fears so many times herself. "I know why you feel that way," Emma said. "It's tempting. It seems like a sure thing. But I think we need to make a different choice this time. I'm just thinking again about what Dr. Waldo said. It's our choices that can change the future. If we want Chuck and Charlie in our future, I think we have to do something different." A heavy weight suddenly fell on her heart. What if it didn't work? What if looking in a different spot wasn't the key? What if … what if they were already gone?

Emma felt Ree's arms surround her in a warm and comforting hug. "We are going to find them," said Ree. "We are the strongest Ree and Emma that have ever existed in all of time. If anyone is going to find them, it'll be us."

Emma let herself cry for just a moment, then squeezed Ree tight and let her go. "We are. We will." She looked at the map again. "Let's go," she said. "This way." The pair of Emmas started walking away from the water, into the unknown.

One of Dr. Waldo's more important inventions was a device that collected molecules from the air, separated the H and O molecules from the rest, and combined them to make water. They had the devices strapped to the top of their backpacks, so as the girls walked, the attached bags filled with clean water. After about an hour, Emma called a halt so they could eat and drink.

"I'm so thirsty," Ree said. She rubbed the bracelet on her wrist. "I wonder if the air here is breathable without the bracelets?"

"Let's not test it," Emma said. "But I'm curious, too." She took a protein bar that Ree handed to her and unwrapped it. "Totally craving a huge salad right now," she said.

"Me too," said Ree, munching on the nourishing but somewhat

dry protein bar. She gazed around the landscape. "Sun's getting lower," she said. "We'll have to find a place to camp sooner than later."

"Yes," said Emma. She unzipped an inner pocket on her jacket, where she was keeping some of the many pigeons Dr. Waldo and Ben had insisted they take. Their presence was a comfort, but her heart felt heavy. Where was she without Charlie? Who was she without Charlie? They had to find the boys. They just had to. *Charlie*, she called out in her mind. *Where are you?* There was no response.

Another hour later, the girls were feeling disheartened and tired. They had found a fairly large river and were following its banks, but they nonetheless felt directionless. "I guess I can see why the future Ree and Emma gave up," Emma admitted. "A week of this would be … I don't know. I don't know how long we can go. It feels hopeless."

"It's not hopeless," said Ree softly, reaching for Emma's hand. "We've just begun. We're strong. We can go on for a long time. And then, if we need to, we can go home, and come back." She stopped and sat on a rock, pulling out the bag of water for another drink. Her eyes looked tired.

A large splash upstream caused both girls to look up abruptly. "What was that?" said Emma. Thoughts of giant fish, alien monsters of unknown origin, and modern-day dinosaurs raced through her head as her heart pounded.

Ree stood and slowly crept toward the river for a better look, trying to stay out of sight of whatever might be looking back. Emma got up and followed her. They crouched behind bushes and rocks, peering around, waiting for another sound.

Then, another splash came, but this time there was another noise with it: something that sounded like laughter.

Eyes wide, Emma looked at Ree. “People,” she mouthed. Ree nodded.

They edged closer and closer to the river, craning their necks to see where the now frequent splashes and sounds were coming from. Finally, they saw them: three beings in the distance. Two were smaller and seemed younger; the third had a swath of gray fur or hair on its head.

“They look sort of like meerkats,” said Emma, staring at the creatures. “Meerkats without the snouts.” The taller one watched as the two smaller ones splashed in the river, arms and hands flying as they pushed water at one another, their enormous eyes full of delight. The one on the riverbank stood with hands on hips, smiling.

Something must have caught the eyes of the one on the bank, as suddenly it turned, sniffed the air, and looked straight at Emma and Ree.

The girls ducked behind a bush, but they knew they’d been seen. They could hear the shuffle of feet in the dirt as the being walked over to them.

“Hello?” the creature said, peeking over the bush they were hiding behind. The being then laughed. “Are we playing a game?” it said. “You do not need to hide. We won’t hurt you. My grandchildren,” the being said, pointing back at the river, “they are rambunctious but harmless. I promise.” The creature held out a hand to Emma, gesturing that it would help her up from her crouched position. Emma took its hand and stood, barely breathing.

“Are you lost?” the creature said, looking at Emma intently. It then sniffed the air again.

Emma willed her heart to calm down. “We … no. We’re not lost,” she said. “But our brothers are. Have you seen anyone …” she was about to say “who looks like us” but remembered that the bracelets would have concealed their true appearance. “Have you seen anyone you don't know? Anyone new?"

"Oh my," said the being. The younger creatures had discovered that their grandparent's attention was no longer on them, and had come out of the river to see what was going on. "They are missing? Where did you last see them?"

"Back there," said Ree, pointing in the direction they'd come. "We've been wandering for a couple of hours. We last saw them not too far from the ocean."

The being raised its eyes, which had clouded over with a look of concern. "Back by the ocean? Near where the Gleymara live?"

"The Gleymara?" repeated Emma. "Who are the Gleymara?"

The being looked deep into her eyes. "Oh my," it said, and then paused. "You'd better come with us."

chapter ten

Chuck and Charlie stared at each other, uncomprehending. They sized each other up, seeing each other as if witnessing a ghost. Each had the same wavy light auburn hair. They had the same green eyes, now filled with confusion and maybe a touch of fear. They were the same height. They had a similar casual sense of clothing. They booth stood with mouths agape.

Charlie looked around the room for a mirror. Had he somehow switched bodies with someone else, he wondered, and he was now actually looking at himself? That had to be the explanation, he thought. Otherwise, this made no sense. He raced from room to room until finally he found a reflective surface on a wall that would serve his purpose. He was staring at his own image when Chuck came into the room.

"Who are you?" said Charlie to Chuck, while still scrutinizing his own reflection.

"Charles Rainier Nelson," said Chuck. The two looked in the mirror, eyes shifting back and forth from one to the other.

"But *I'm* Charles Rainier Nelson," said Charlie. "Who are *you*?" He turned from the mirror to look Chuck up and down.

"I'm Charles Rainier Nelson," said Chuck insistently. He shook his head. "This is crazy. Did someone clone me?" He poked Charlie's shoulder. "Not a hologram," he said quietly, on finding that Charlie was, indeed, solid.

"Of course I'm not a hologram," said Charlie, rubbing the spot on his shoulder where Chuck had poked a little too hard. He poked Chuck back, and looked in the mirror again. At last he realized he not only didn't understand how there was another Charlie in the room, but also, he did not recognize this building. "Where are we?" he said. "Is this your house?"

Chuck shook his head. "No idea," he said. The two Charlies wandered slowly through the house. The furnishings were worn and sparse, but clean. "No," said Chuck, "this definitely is not *my* home. But I have no idea what *your* home looks like." He walked to a window and pulled open the curtains, then jumped back in terror. "What the . . . !" he whispered loudly, his eyes wide.

"What?" said Charlie. He walked to the window and peered out cautiously. There seemed to be more houses, similar to this one, each with a small yard. The area looked tired but clean. A larger building in the distance had the feel of a gathering space. There were no roads he could see; only pedestrian paths, maybe bicycle paths, all made of dirt. Everything was unfamiliar, but he saw nothing that shocked him. "What did you see?"

"Are they gone?" Chuck said. He pulled a corner of the curtain back slowly and looked out again, but the object of his fright had moved on. "People," he said, "but people that look nothing like people. Giant heads. Huge eyes. I swear it. I swear I saw people who weren't human."

Charlie scoffed. "Don't be an idiot," he said. "They must have been wearing masks or something." He followed Chuck's lead and pulled back another edge of the curtain, waiting for someone to walk by. The sky was clear; the air was fresh but scented with a metallic edge. "Ugh," Charlie said, putting his hand to his forehead. "I have the worst headache." He rubbed his temple gently.

Chuck looked at Charlie. "Come to think of it, I do, too," he said, touching his own head.

A movement outside the window caught Charlie's eye. Two people were walking along a path a few houses away. "What!" Charlie yelped. He slapped a hand over his mouth, quickly shut the curtains, and dropped to the floor. He looked up at Chuck, then stood and cautiously pulled the curtain back just far enough to allow him to see the people again. "What are they?" He looked carefully, trying to see if he could spot the edge of a mask. "Their heads," he whispered. "They're huge."

Chuck was peeking out the curtain on the other side of the window. "And their eyes," he said. "They look …"

"Like meerkats," Charlie finished. Suddenly, he noticed another person, this one walking alone. Walking toward them. "I think that one's coming our way," he said, his voice trembling.

A moment later, there was a knock on the door. Charlie and Chuck stared at each other, frozen, panic in each pair of bright green eyes. "What do we do? Do we hide?" Chuck mouthed. Charlie shrugged helplessly, his brain on full alarm, his body ready to go into fight or flight mode. If they couldn't flee, he would have to be ready to fight.

"Hello?" a voice called from the other side of the door. "Charlie and Chuck? Are you awake?"

"Charlie and Chuck?" Charlie mouthed, his eyes growing wider. Did this creature know them? And what's more—how could this creature speak English?

The door opened and a person walked in. "Hello? I brought you breakfast." On seeing Charlie and Chuck staring at her with abject terror in their eyes, the person spoke. "Chuck, Charlie. It's me, Akala." She studied them carefully. "Yesterday. We sat here talking for hours." Chuck and Charlie showed no signs of recognition. "Do you not remember?" Akala said. In her arms, she carried a basket filled with food. She placed it on the small table where they'd eaten the night before, then turned to the boys, hands on her hips. "Do you not remember me?" she said again.

Chuck and Charlie exchanged a glance. "Of course we do, Akala," said Charlie. He felt his heart in his throat, beating like a hummingbird's wings. How did this creature know his name? And what was she? Because very clearly, she was not human.

Akala sat down heavily in one of the chairs. "You don't remember," she said. Her large, dark eyes flew to the front door and a thought passed over her face, but Charlie had no clue what that thought might be.

"Did you sleep?" Akala said, looking at the boys warily.

"Like a log," Chuck said. He sat down on another of the chairs at the table, and lifted the basket lid to see what was inside. "In fact ..." he said, then stopped.

"In fact what?" said Charlie, but he didn't pursue the train of thought when Chuck didn't reply. He was afraid he didn't want to know.

Akala noticed Chuck peeking into the basket, so she got up and got plates and glasses for them all again, then unpacked the food she'd brought. This time there was a different assortment than the previous night, but the boys didn't know the difference. Akala brought out some unfamiliar fruits, a few soft biscuits, and a kind of cheese. She reached for a piece of fruit and took a bite. "If you don't remember me," she started.

"But we do," Charlie interrupted. "Of course we do."

Akala wasn't fooled. "If you don't remember me, then what is the last thing you do remember?"

Charlie looked at Chuck. Whoever this other Charlie was, Charlie felt like he could trust him. But he wasn't sure about this Akala. Who were these people, just roaming the Earth, looking like meerkats, eating strange food? And where was this place? Then, a bizarre and impossible thought crossed his mind: was this even Earth?

"Say, funny question," Charlie said, trying to sound light and breezy. "Can you tell me … what you call this … what you call our planet?" A tingle of fear shot up his spine.

Chuck turned to him abruptly, his eyes full of the sudden realization of what Charlie was implying.

Akala looked from one to the other. "Maluket," she said. "What do you call it?"

"Yeah, Maluket," said Charlie. "Same." He very consciously did not look at Chuck and could feel Chuck very consciously not looking back at him, and the energy between them was on the border of telepathy. *Where are we?*

Akala got up abruptly. "I need to go talk to someone," she said. "I'll be back, don't worry. The food … the food is safe," she said, then she dashed out the door without another word.

Charlie and Chuck stared at each other for a moment, speechless, then the words started pouring out.

"She knew us. Charlie and Chuck. One of us told her our name is Chuck," said Charlie. "Why would we tell her we are Charlie and Chuck instead of Charlie and Charlie?"

"We must already know each other," Chuck said, "but from where? And how?"

"Maluket," Charlie said. "That's not Earth. But how is that not Earth? Are we in another country? This looks a little like Spain, I think? I mean, from pictures I've seen? Maybe Maluket is the Spanish word for Earth?"

Chuck shook his head. "The Spanish word for Earth is Tierra. It means dirt, just like Earth means dirt in English. And that's another thing. She's speaking English, not Spanish."

Charlie started pacing the room, his legs trying to keep up with the racing in his mind. "She speaks English. But she doesn't look human. And she says the planet is called Maluket." He couldn't believe his own words. Picking up a piece of fruit, he turned it in his hands. "And what is this? Have you seen this fruit before?" He smelled it, and reached out his tongue to lick the smooth surface, but he stopped short of eating it.

"No," said Chuck, "but I'm not a fruit expert. I am, however, very hungry." He looked longingly at the food on the table. "Do you think it's safe?"

"She ate some," Charlie said, but that didn't answer the question. He stopped pacing. "She said it's safe. Why would she reassure us that the food is safe? Why would she think we would think the food isn't safe? Okay," he said. "You were saying you slept like a log. You were going to say that, in fact, you don't remember going to bed." Chuck nodded. Charlie continued. "What is the last thing you *do* remember?"

"We just got to the island," Chuck said. "An island called Dogwinkle Island. We're staying there for summer vacation." He picked up a piece of fruit and stared at it. His stomach grumbled.

Charlie blinked. What Chuck was describing was his own life. "You said 'we.' Who is 'we'?" His breathing was shallow, and he felt like he couldn't get enough air.

"Me, my twin sister Emma, and our parents," Chuck said.

"I have a twin sister Emma," said Charlie.

Chuck stared at him for a long minute. "What is the last thing *you* remember?" he said, finally.

"We just got to Dogwinkle Island for our summer vacation," Charlie said. "Emma and I were planning to borrow a truck and go stargazing."

"Borrowing a truck from Ed," Chuck said.

Charlie blinked. "Yes, from Ed," he said. He shivered, but he wasn't cold.

"Emma hates bugs," Chuck said.

"Emma hates bugs," Charlie confirmed.

The two sat staring at each other. Outside, they heard murmurs of voices. A bird of some kind squawked in protest or in song. Sunlight shined through a gap in the curtains.

"Charlie," said Charlie to Chuck. "*Where are we?*" Subconsciously, he'd been rubbing the bracelet on his wrist, and now the jewelry made its way to the surface of his mind. "What is this?" he said, now studying the bracelet more carefully and rubbing his fingers over the various stones. He looked at Chuck's wrist. "You have one too. What is this?"

Chuck looked down at his wrist at the bracelet he hadn't noticed before. "I have no idea. I've never seen it before." He took his bracelet off and put it on the table, rubbing his wrist where the bracelet had been.

Charlie left his bracelet on but continued to rub the stones. "I just don't have a good feeling about any of this," he said. "I think we need to leave."

"And go where?" said Chuck. "How can we go somewhere when we don't have a clue where we are? We have to figure out where we are first."

"That Akala," Charlie said. "Do you think we can trust her?"

"I don't know if we can trust her. But it sounds like we talked to her last night," said Chuck.

"Maybe she's the reason we can't remember," Charlie said. He looked at the food on the table. "She said she gave us food last night. Maybe something in the food made us forget." Now his stomach was grumbling, too, but suddenly eating any of this food seemed like a very bad idea.

The front door opened, and Akala walked back in. "I'm sorry," she said, then she stopped in her tracks, her dark wide eyes growing impossibly big. She stared at Chuck and her hand flew to her mouth as she stifled a scream. "What is that!" she cried, pointing at Chuck as he sat in the chair at the table. "What is that?! Where is Chuck? What is that creature? What has happened to Chuck?" She trembled visibly as she backed up to the door.

Chuck and Charlie stared at her in shock. "He's right there," Charlie said. He glanced at Chuck. As far as he could tell, nothing had changed. Chuck looked exactly the same.

"What did she say?" said Chuck. He knew Akala had spoken but her words had made no sense to him. "Why is she so scared?" He looked at Charlie, puzzled.

"What do you mean?" said Charlie. "She asked where you are. She asked what happened to Chuck." Charlie turned to Akala. "Akala, he's right there. That's Chuck. He's the same as he was when you left."

"That's not him," said Akala. Tears were welling up in her eyes. "This is some alien creature!" She walked backward, her hand reaching for the door.

"Wait!" said Charlie, his eyes falling to the bracelet on the table, then to the identical bracelet on his own arm. An idea struck him. "Chuck, put that bracelet back on," he said.

Chuck raised one eyebrow. "Put the bracelet on? Why?"

"That's the only thing that's different from when Akala was here a few minutes ago. Put the bracelet back on."

Akala stood, shivering, but now curious. "What is that one saying?" she asked Charlie, pointing at Chuck again.

"You can't understand him?" Charlie said.

Akala shook her head vigorously. "No, he is making no words. Just sounds."

"But you can understand me?"

Akala nodded, not taking her eyes off Chuck.

"Chuck, put the bracelet back on," Charlie said. "Try it."

Chuck shrugged, then complied.

Instantly, Akala's jaw dropped, and then her legs gave out and she dropped to the floor. She clapped her hands over her mouth to keep from screaming. Finally, she spoke. "What is this? What have you done? What kind of beings are you?" she whispered, shuddering.

"Chuck, talk," said Charlie.

"What do you want me to say?" said Chuck.

"Akala, can you understand him now?" Charlie asked.

Akala nodded. She closed her enormous eyes for several seconds, then opened them again, shaking her head.

"The bracelet," said Charlie. "It does something. I don't know how, but it does something. Don't take it off again."

Akala stood, her dark eyes flaring. "What are you talking about? What do you mean, this bracelet does something?" she said, pointing to the bracelet that was now securely positioned back on Chuck's arm. She put her hand to her chest. "Who are you? Are you magicians?" She cautiously peered behind Chuck. "How did you create this illusion?" She rubbed her shoulders as though she was cold, though the room was getting quite warm.

Charlie sat in a chair at the table and pulled another chair out, indicating that Akala should sit, too. "I don't know. We don't know. We don't remember how we got here and we don't remember meeting each other and we don't know where these bracelets came from, but there is something very wrong and we have to figure it out. We don't belong here. We need to get home." He sighed and looked longingly at the food as his stomach grumbled again. "Akala, can we trust you?" he asked.

Akala sat. "You can trust me," she said.

"How do we know?" Chuck protested. "'You can trust me' is exactly the kind of thing someone who couldn't be trusted would say." He rubbed his head. "We wake up in this strange place, both of us with headaches, not knowing who we are or how we got here, and you're the only person we've met, and you think we can trust you right away?" His stomach joined Charlie's in a chorus of grumbles, and he reached for the basket of food.

"You can trust me," Akala said, quickly reaching for the basket, "but I am not so sure you can trust everyone here." She took the cheese out of the basket and slipped it into a pocket. "This cheese, and the cheese you ate last night, others gave it to me to give to you." She cast her eyes downward. "Maybe you should not have eaten it."

"What?" said Charlie. "What do you mean? Who gave it to you? What could be wrong with cheese?"

Akala glanced at the windows. The curtains were wide open. "Corala and Leidar," she said. "They … I have suspected for a while they are … dangerous. Now I am more certain. I think they may have drugged the cheese so you would sleep."

"So we would sleep?" said Chuck. "Why would they want us to sleep?"

"So they could take your memories," said Akala. "They wanted your memories."

chapter eleven

The walk along the river to the home of the beings Emma and Ree had met was short, but the older companion was slow. To Emma's eyes, the landscape could have been a prairie in Minnesota. The tall grasses, vast fields, even the flying insects. She slapped her arm as one of the bugs landed on her, and wondered what sort of diseases these insects might carry. Alien malaria? The alien plague? Surely, she thought, there must be a stone they could add to their bracelets that would act as an insect repellent. If a stone in the universe could enable a person to understand a foreign language, create oxygen in an atmosphere with otherwise unbreathable air, or completely transform a person's appearance, then surely, surely there must be a stone that would repel bugs. Emma hated bugs.

As they strolled, the grandparent introduced himself.

"I am Nolor," he said, keeping his eyes on the rambunctious youngsters who were running back and forth. "My grandson, there, is Tygor, and my granddaughter is Sarya. They are the children of our daughter Maraya." His face darkened briefly, and then he pushed the darkness aside and continued. "You'll meet my wife, Daya, when we get to our home. Children! Careful!" he called out as Tygor and Sarya ran into the river to cool off.

"I'm Emma," said Emma.

"I'm Ree," said Ree.

"You aren't from here, I take it?" said Nolor. "If you don't know the Gleymara then you are not from here." He scratched at his nose with a long finger. Emma noticed that each of the fingers on his hands, thumbs included, had four knuckles. She wondered if the extra joint was a help or a hindrance to manual dexterity. His eyes were enormous—maybe twice the size of human eyes—and his head was bigger in proportion to his short body than on humans. His legs were also short and his gait was slow, but that could have been age. Emma found herself looking from Ree to Nolor to compare their appearances, and she wondered, as she always did with aliens, what she must look like as the Emma version of this creature.

"No," Ree was saying. "We're not from here." She didn't say anything more, however. The group had previously discussed that it was probably best on occasions such as this to offer as little information as was necessary.

"I see," said Nolor. With his left hand, he pointed to a building that was just coming into view. "That is my home, there," he said, and as he said it, his grandchildren ran ahead, with a wave behind them to their grandfather.

"Who are the Gleymara?" asked Emma. She warned herself to tread cautiously on the subject. It was difficult to navigate a conversation where she wasn't sure how much a native would know, but she couldn't know more than she did.

A soft breeze ruffled Nolor's short gray hair. He ignored her question. "We had a storm here recently," he said. "A bad one. I hope your brothers were inside when it went through." He looked at the girls for a response, but they had none. "How long have they been lost?" he asked.

How long, indeed, wondered Emma. Hours? Days? Weeks? "Long enough that we're worried," she said. "We saw their tent," she continued. "That must be what happened to it. It was a mess."

Nolor nodded. "Yes, a tent would not stand up to one of the Electrics."

"Electrics?" asked Ree.

Nolor lifted his eyes to hers, assessing, curious, but he left his question unsaid. "The electric storms," he clarified. "Enormous storms of electricity, mostly. Sometimes rain. Lots of wind. Mostly electricity. We just call them the Electrics. You have to be inside, protected. You would die outside."

"*Could* die?" asked Emma, swallowing hard. "Or *would*?"

Nolor shrugged one tired shoulder. "Could, I suppose," he said, unconvincingly. He thought, then nodded to himself. "Could."

Emma almost asked how an electric storm would kill a person, but then decided she didn't want to know.

By this time, they had reached the home. Another being was outside, waving at them as the grandchildren raced around her. "Daya, my wife," said Nolor. He returned the wave with a smile that spread to his wide, dark eyes. "Still beautiful," he said softly. "Still beautiful."

"Nolor!" Daya called out. Her eyes, wrinkled at the corners, were slightly bigger than Nolor's, and more of a warm charcoal gray. "The children say you have brought company!" She looked at Emma and Ree with a wide, kind smile. "Welcome, welcome," Daya said, waving them up to the front door. She was taller than the children, but shorter than Nolor, and all of them were shorter than Emma and Ree. Emma suddenly felt like a giant, and wondered if the bracelet she wore disguised her height as well as her general appearance. When they returned to the Hub, she thought, one of these days she'd see if Dr. Waldo could devise a way for them to see themselves as the aliens saw them.

Nolor rubbed his left cheek against Daya's left cheek, then repeated the action on her right cheek before touching foreheads with his wife. "I hope we gave you a rest," he said. "The children are very active today."

The look Daya gave Nolor was pure affection, which Emma could see even though they weren't human. "I had a small rest, yes. Thank you, Nolor. I am ready for the evening. And I will sleep well in the long night." She rested her slender hand gently on his shoulder while stepping aside for her guests to enter the home.

The house was made of large blocks of stone in varying shades of gray and beige, seamed together with a crisp white mortar, thickly spread. It looked solid, like it could easily withstand whatever storms might come through. The front door also seemed to be made of some kind of stone, but when Emma pushed it to open it further, it was surprisingly light. Inside, the floors were covered in more stone, with area rugs in shades of green and turquoise blue adding warmth underfoot.

Daya led them into a sort of living room. Although everything seemed slightly lower than the furniture back on Earth, the furnishings were surprisingly human-like, and Emma decided that any creatures with a generally human-like body would probably end up with similar furniture to support the body. A low, soft gray couch was draped with a cream-colored blanket knit from thick strands of some sort of yarn. Around the couch were spread three low chairs, in a color quite near the charcoal gray of Daya's eyes. Daya sat in one of these chairs, and Nolor in another. The girls sat together on the couch. Instantly, Daya popped up again. "Would anyone like something to drink?"

Nolor grinned. "Wae, please," he said.

Daya looked at the girls.

"Uh … yes, the same?" Ree said. Emma nodded her agreement.

Daya padded away quickly, humming a cheerful tune.

"You and your wife are kind," said Emma. "Thank you."

Giggling screams wafted through the air from another room. "No trouble at all," said Nolor. "We are happy to help strangers. This is one of our beliefs, always help strangers."

"Yes, about that," said Ree. "We don't want to be rude, but we're anxious to find our brothers. You said we needed to know something about the Gray … the Glay …? About some people?"

Nolor scratched his nose thoughtfully again. "Yes, the Gleymara." He shifted his eyes to look at the girls. "I'm surprised you don't know about them?" he said pointedly.

The girls said nothing.

"Well, then," said Nolor. "The Gleymara. They are a people of … a peculiar belief system, shall we say. Some might call them a cult."

A warm breeze drifted through an open window, carrying with it a sweet smell, perhaps of nearby flowers. The trill of a bird's chirp followed from afar. "Would *you* call them a cult?" Emma asked.

"I might," said Nolor, his dark eyes taking on a far-away look. "I might."

Daya returned, carrying a tray of mugs, which she set on a table between the chairs. She handed Ree and Emma each a mug, then gave one to her husband before taking the last for herself.

Emma sniffed at the liquid for any clues as to origin. The slightly fruity smell was enticing, so she took a small sip. What she tasted, she decided, was something between a juice and a tea. Regardless, it was pleasant enough, and she was thirsty.

"What more can you tell us about the Gleymara?" asked Ree, who was drinking the wae enthusiastically. "Why are they dangerous?"

Daya lifted her head, sniffing. "The children aren't near," she said to Nolor. "Go on." She pressed her lips together and sat back in her chair.

"The Gleymara," said Nolor. "The Gleymara are … well, I suppose I need to back up a bit. Who they are today is not who they set out to be. At least, I don't believe so. Back many generations ago, five or six or maybe more, there was a man, Stenar. Stenar was a strong young man, healthy, who married a smart and skilled woman, Jasla. They were together many years, and had three strong and healthy children. But one day, Jasla fell ill with Fermar Disease." He looked at them to see if they knew the term, but their eyes showed no recognition. "It is a serious disease, one that kills quickly. It invades the organs, devouring them like a monster, spreading like the Electrics, striking quickly and leaving little behind. After only a few months, Jasla died. She was still young, somewhere around thirty years, I think." He turned to Daya, who nodded agreement. "Stenar was devastated," Nolor said. He reached out a hand to Daya's knee and caressed it gently. "Jasla had been the love of his life, his reason for living. He was lost without her for months, maybe longer. Then one day he had this idea, an idea he thought was brilliant. He thought, if everyone is the same age, born at the same time, dies at the same time, then no one would have to suffer an unexpected loss ever again."

"But what about—" Ree started, but Nolor raised a hand in protest.

"Of course, of course, there is not absolute logic there. People die at all ages, not just thirty years. People can die young, not just old. Disease strikes like the Electrics; it doesn't care where. But in Stenar's mind, this was the solution. A community where everyone is born at the same time, and dies at the same time.

"Now," Nolor continued, "I forgot to mention. Stenar was a scientist, and an extraordinary one, at that. He worked in the study of the brain, of memories. He was interested in the ways memory is stored in the brain, and he was convinced that the electrical nature of Maluket could be a key to memory transfer."

"The electrical nature of Maluket," Emma repeated, trying not to sound like she had no idea what "Maluket" was.

"Yes," said Nolor. "As we all know, the planet has a tremendous electrical force, and Stenar believed memories were both chemical and electrical. He had already been working on the idea of transferring one person's memories to another, but with his new grand idea of a new community, he went at it with increased vigor." Nolor paused, seeming to flit through details in his mind, deem them irrelevant, and discarding them unmentioned. "At any rate, eventually he figured it out."

"He figured out how to transfer memories from one person to another?" asked Ree, sipping the last of her wae. Daya quickly refilled her cup.

"Yes," Nolor confirmed. "Which gave him what he needed to create the colony. So then he went to find others who understood his pain—others who had lost someone too early and who had never gotten over their grief. Together, they created the Gleymara. Gleymara—it is both the name of the people and the name of the place. A community where babies are made in a lab, memories are transferred to them every year, and then when they are fifteen, the Memory Keepers, the ones who have been raising them, are killed. They call it 'becoming Memories,' but the process of taking all their memories leaves them as shells. They die. When the new generation turns thirty, they mix up some new babies in the lab, and then they die, with only a handful living on as Memory Keepers. Those Memory Keepers live until the new generation is fifteen, and on the cycle goes."

"No one has stopped them?" said Emma. "That can't … I mean, it can't be legal, can it?"

Nolor sighed heavily. "The people are free to come and go," he said. "At least, that's what we are told. They are there of their own free will. But I believe," he shifted his eyes to a photo of his grandchildren on a shelf on the wall, "I believe they are not given the memories that tell them there are other ways. I believe they are, in essence, brainwashed. They are free, technically, but they do not have the knowledge or power of self to change."

"A cult, then," said Ree.

"Yes," said Nolor, "a cult."

Emma inhaled deeply, feeling grateful for her own freedom. But it occurred to her: how would a person know what they didn't know? How would they even know there was more to learn, if there was no one there to teach them? She could imagine that over time, so much knowledge would be lost. That people would lose their identities, and perhaps lose their reason to exist.

"Nolor," she said, "that all sounds awful. But why are they dangerous? How could they hurt our brothers?" Ever since they'd left Future Ree, her sense of anxiety had been growing. And she couldn't shake the feeling of regret and shame over having left Charlie on a fighting note. What had they even been fighting about? Oh yes, about her being the Chosen One. About how she wouldn't help him. She'd give anything to help him now, if only she could figure out how. One thing she clung to: he was still alive. She was sure of it. If he weren't, she would know. She was certain.

Daya had gotten up and returned with a plate of what looked like small biscuits or cookies. Nolor reached for one with a special smile for his wife. "My favorite. Thank you, dear," he said, and patted her knee again after she sat. He turned again to the girls. "You see, experiments such as this rarely go as expected. They may succeed for a while, but after not too long, things start to veer from the course, from the plan or the dream." He paused to munch on his cookie. "The Gleymara," he said, wiping his mouth with the back of his narrow hand, "they are bred to be all alike, all perfect. But that is not how nature works. Occasionally there are mutations. That is how we all evolved, after all. We are all mutations." He ate another of the small cookies. "Sometimes the mutations are good. Other times, not so much. But the effect is that what was meant to be uniform, has differences." Nolor shook his head. "No, that's not it. I don't know that that's it. Maybe it's just boredom. Maybe the lab in which they grew the babies couldn't account for personalities. Whatever it was, there are those within the Gleymara who … well, they rebel. They rebel in their way. Because everything they have is the same, anything different is like a drug. Some leave; they escape and never return. Others, well, there are those in the community who capitalize on the colony's weaknesses. They are the danger. They leave their colony during the day, during the night, and they come seeking memories. They find people on the outside who are living full, interesting lives, and they take their memories, and then they sell those memories within the colony. They sell memories like drugs. They steal the memories and they sell them like drugs."

"You mean…" Ree said, a look of horror growing on her face.

"Your brothers are in danger," Nolor said, "because the Gleymara might have taken their minds."

chapter twelve

"Wait," said Charlie. "They wanted our *memories*?" Ordinarily he would have laughed outright at this suggestion, but the fact that his mind was a blank since who knew how long ago gave the ridiculous notion some credibility. Neither he nor this other Charlie could remember anything, and the fact that there even *was* this other Charlie was something that had gotten lost in all the chaos. Somehow, he had been cloned and brought to either another planet or at least another country, and he very much wanted some answers. Having his memories stolen seemed pretty far-fetched, but he didn't have any better explanation at the moment.

"How would they take our memories?" Chuck asked. "How is that even possible?"

"It has to do with the Electrics, I think," Akala said. She shrugged. "I don't know. I wasn't one of those trained to pass on memories. My genes have flaws, they say."

"Your genes have flaws? Who says?" said Charlie.

"The Memory Keepers, the ones who created us for birth. After we were born they did tests to see which genes should be continued in the next generation." She started to reach for the cheese, then stopped herself. "They took your memories," she said, changing the subject away from herself. "Did they take anything else?"

Charlie laughed. "Well, you see, part of having your memory swiped is, apparently, memory loss. I don't even know how I got here, or how *he* got here. I don't even know where 'here' is. So I can hardly tell you whether I still have everything I brought along with me."

Outside, a motor of some sort started up. Charlie imagined someone somewhere mowing a lawn, and he wished he were doing anything that normal right then.

"Fair enough," said Akala. "Let's start with this. Where are you from?"

"Let's start with this," said Chuck. "Where are we *now*?"

"Maluket," said Akala. "Gleymara."

"And that's, what, near … Italy?" said Charlie. "Spain? Montana?" He glanced out the window again. The bushes, the flat plains, the sunshine, they could have been anywhere on Earth, he thought. Well, not Antarctica, probably. But just about anywhere. He had no point of reference to start from, and he felt lost. "Wait, where's my phone?" he said. GPS, of course. His phone's GPS would tell him where they were. He walked into the bedroom and searched in the bag he assumed was his, then in the bag he assumed was Chuck's, but found nothing. He flipped over the blankets on the beds, thinking maybe the phone had gotten caught in the sheets. Emma always yelled at him not to look at his phone at night—"You'll get a brain tumor from having that thing by your head all the time!" she whined—but he was still guilty of the habit. Nonetheless, his phone wasn't lost in the sheets or under the pillow, either. He then moved through the house, turning over items here and there, but it was sparsely furnished and there wasn't much to search.

"Nothing?" said Chuck.

"Nothing," said Charlie. "You don't happen to have a phone?"

Chuck felt at his pockets. "No," he said. "Weird. I never go anywhere without it."

They both looked accusingly at Akala. "Where are our phones?" Charlie asked.

"I don't know what a 'phone' is," Akala said, "and either way, I have not taken anything of yours. I am trying to help you. I could get in trouble, you know."

Charlie frowned. "They must have taken our phones, then, along with our memories."

"Same thing," Chuck joked. "I hadn't backed mine up for a while."

"Well, then, no GPS for now," Charlie said. "Maluket, you said? What's that near?"

Akala raised her eyebrows. "What is Maluket near?" she asked. "It is … well, it is the second planet. It is near Arumet, which is closer to the day star, and Sumet, which is the third planet. Is this a test? How much of your memory they must have taken!" she shook her head.

"Second planet … from the day star?" said Chuck, looking warily at Charlie. "You mean Maluket is the name of the planet? We're not … we're not on Earth?"

"You told me before that Earth is an island," Akala said, nodding her head in the direction of the ocean. "How did you get here?"

Chuck and Charlie looked at each other: apparently this was a story they'd told her before their minds went blank. It would be best not to contradict themselves now. "Again," said Chuck. "Again, part of having your memory stolen: no memory. Seriously. No, this is not happening. This is a reality show. Where are the cameras?" He waved at the walls. "Where are you? Come out! You got us!"

Charlie fell into the nearest chair and shut his eyes. He agreed with Chuck. None of this was really happening, he told himself. It couldn't be. This was all some bizarre dream. But when he opened his eyes, nothing had changed, and everything still made no sense. "Okay," he said, resigned. "Maluket. Not Earth. This … I don't even know. But whatever happened, we need to start by getting our memories back. Then, once we do, maybe you and I will know how there are two of us," he said, looking at Chuck.

"What do you mean?" said Akala. "You do not know each other?"

Chuck shook his head. "Not exactly," he said. "So where do we start? Where are our memories?"

Akala took a deep breath. "Well," she said hesitantly, "they might be stored at the Tower."

The tone of voice Akala used did not convince Charlie. "*Might* be?" he said. "Where else might they be?"

She sighed. "Corala and Leidar may have them. The day we met you, I had gone out with Corala and Leidar to see what they do when they leave the colony. They leave all the time, and I do not trust them. I think they knew I was trying to spy, and they did nothing unusual while I was with them; just walked around the land. But I believe that they are memory thieves. I believe they steal memories from others and then sell them to people in the colony. It is an excitement. It gives a thrill, for people to have other people's memories. Life here is, well, it's boring. There is nothing here. It is possible Corala and Leidar kept your memories for themselves. That they installed your memories into their own minds."

"Into their own minds?" Chuck said, flabbergasted. "What kind of planet is this?" he said under his breath.

Charlie stood again and started pacing. "What we need," he said, "is to get somewhere safe. We're not safe here." He looked at Chuck, who shook his head in agreement. "Okay. So we need to go somewhere else. We need to get away from here. But where? Akala—" he started.

"I will go with you," Akala said.

"I wasn't … I mean, I don't know," Charlie said.

"You can trust me," said Akala. "I'm here now, am I not? I have told you all this. I told you not to eat the cheese." She looked at Chuck and Charlie, who were exchanging meaningful glances. "If you don't have me, you will be more lost than you are. I do not fit in here. I want to help you. I am coming with you."

"But where are we going?" asked Chuck.

"I don't know," said Akala. She stood and put her hands on her hips for a few moments, thinking, then turned to the door. "Wait here. I will go pack. Do not let anyone in. Do not eat anything. It is nearing evening. We need to leave before it gets too dark. I will be back soon and we will go."

After she was gone, Charlie looked at Chuck. "What's going on here, dude?" he said. He didn't want to admit it, but a chill had gone up his spine. "And where's Emma? I mean, no offense, you're great, but where is Emma?"

Chuck shook his head. "No idea. But we'd better be ready when Akala gets back." He went off to pack what little he had. Charlie followed. They then went through the house to see if there was anything that might be useful, anything they might want or need. Chuck found a folding knife, and tucked it into a pocket of his bag. Charlie wrapped up as much of the food as he could, leaving the cheese behind. Then the two sat and waited for Akala to reappear. Sounds of people outside drifted in, chattering and people calling out to each other. From far off they heard a rhythmic thudding sound, a hammering of some sort. They continued to wait.

After several minutes, Chuck stood to look out the window. "Do you think we can trust her?" he said without turning. "What if she went to Corala and Leidar? What if they caught her and made her tell them what she knows? What if … I mean, what if they *do* have our memories? Even we don't know what's in them. But somehow, we got from Earth to here, and those memories must be in there. What if they decide they want more of our memories? What if whatever was in our brains was so juicy that they're on their way here now ... Here she comes," Chuck said. "She's walking fast. She looks worried. Grab your things."

By the time Akala got to their door, Chuck and Charlie were standing outside, backpacks on. "Are you ready?" Akala said, catching her breath.

"We're ready," said Charlie. He glanced back into the house, but he knew there couldn't be anything in there that they needed. They had taken everything that was of any use at all.

"Corala and Leidar have been talking," Akala said. "They have your memories. They have installed them into their own minds. I overheard someone else talking about it. You are not safe here. We need to go immediately." She raced off to the front gate of the colony without checking to see if the boys were with her, but she need not have worried; they stayed close behind. Soon, they passed through the gate they didn't remember entering through the day before. Akala looked left and right, making a decision. "This way," she said, turning right. "Let's run," she said.

They ran.

It didn't take long for the threesome to slow their run to a jog, then to a brisk walk, then a stroll.

"I swear I'm out of breath faster here than on Earth," Chuck said as they walked along the cliff over the beach. The dirt trail was narrow, a footpath at most, a scar along the edge of the land. It was used, but not often and not by many.

"You don't remember this place?" Akala said, stopping to gaze out at the ocean. "This is the same path we brought you in on, when we first found you."

"Not at all," said Charlie. He was troubled, unsettled. It was a bizarre feeling, having lost his memories. If not for the fact that he was, clearly, somewhere very unusual, where he clearly had never been before, he might not entirely believe that time had passed that he couldn't remember. If he were at home and no one told him that a day or a month or a year had passed—*how long had it even been?*—then he would have just gone on as if nothing had happened. As if the memories he'd lost had never been a part of him; as if he'd never had the experiences, the friendships, the love, the fear, the joy, the accomplishments, the failures, the adventures, the ups and downs of life. What had he even lost? Or who? He had no way of knowing. Everything he'd experienced in the past day, or month, or year, was gone. Completely and utterly gone. It was disconcerting to know that a part of his mind, his past, his self, could be taken from him, and he might never have been aware.

"Look!" Akala said, jarring Charlie out of his thoughts. "It is the time of Emergence!" Overcome with excitement, she pointed a finger at the ocean, where dozens if not hundreds of creatures had just begun bursting out of the waves like winged rockets heading up into the atmosphere. When they broke the surface of the water, they were nothing more than long, thick lines in the air. After surging out of the water and high into the sky, each one suddenly unfolded enormous wings of black and gold and turquoise blue, and began flapping, awkwardly at first, and then with a regal confidence. They then turned and flew off into the distance, a giant mass of birds erupting from the ocean and filling the sky like so many dragons.

"What are they?" asked Chuck, his mouth open in awe. The parade of birds seemed endless, dozens of the creatures emerging from the ocean every minute, to fly off to parts unknown. The flapping of hundreds or thousands of wings created a rhythmic hum in the sky, and a rippling breeze that reached the trio of onlookers and ruffled their hair.

"They are wunpada," Akala said with wonder. "They begin life at the bottom of the ocean, as creatures of the sea. Then they undergo a change. They build a sort of shell around themselves, and for months they are just lying on the ocean floor in their shells. While they are in their shells, they change into these birds. Then the day comes when all at once they begin to break free of their shells, and when they do, they can no longer breathe underwater, so they burst up and out of the sea to get to the air where they can breathe again. It is called the Emergence. It happens only once every three years, and no one knows exactly when it will be." She paused, her eyes bright with reverence. "And we witnessed it. We are here, witnessing it now." While she spoke, she never tore her eyes from the incredible sight of the massive birds rising from sea and taking flight, but a sudden thought made her look away.

Charlie swore she was blushing. "What?" he said. "What is it?"

"I have not been truthful with you," Akala said, watching the wunpada again. "Or rather, I have not told you everything."

A chill ran up Charlie's spine. "What?" he said, cautiously.

"The wunpada are not something we learn about in the colony," she said. "We do, but … we just learn that they are birds that come out of the ocean. The part about their being sea creatures first, that they change themselves from one thing into another, we don't learn that."

Chuck stared at her. "Then how do you know?" he asked.

"I have bought others' memories," she said in a shameful whisper, looking down and away again. "One time Corala told me she had memories from a scientist, and …" She stopped. "I am ashamed but yet I do not regret it. The memories of a scientist are … they are priceless. They are treasures. This scientist studied the wunpada. I learned what I know because Corala and Leidar stole her mind."

The wunpada in flight had now begun calling out, a long, keening cry that sounded so much to Charlie's ears like a discovery, like someone exclaiming *Ahhhhhhhhh! Ahhhhhhhaaaaaahhhhhhh! Ahhhhhhh!* "They're amazing," he said. He thought, though, about the scientist whose memories had been taken. For all he knew, he could be a scientist, too. He understood Akala's joy in the knowledge, in the learning, but to have taken that away from someone else seemed … well, in a way, unforgivable.

They sat on the ground for a while, watching the Emergence until it had dwindled to just a few birds per minute. "Is it over?" asked Chuck.

"Almost," said Akala. Her eyes were filled with tears.

Chuck looked back the way they had come. "We should probably move on, then," he said. "Will they come after us, do you think?"

Akala sighed heavily and got up. "Normally, I would not think so," she said. "But you are unusual. A rarity. I suppose it depends on what else is in your heads, and how much they want it. How valuable they think your memories might be." She took one last, longing look at the ocean, where a straggling wunpada had just breached the surface of the water and was flying to join the others, trying out its wings and growing stronger with each stroke. "We had better get moving again."

chapter thirteen

They find people on the outside who are living full, interesting lives, and they take their memories, and then they sell those memories within the colony … They steal the memories and they sell them like drugs. The words kept repeating themselves in Emma's mind, over and over, her terror rising every time. It was one thing for the boys to be lost … it was another thing entirely for the boys to be lost without their memories.

"How far back would they steal the memories?" Emma asked Nolor. A day of memories might not be too dangerous. But a month, or a year … all the memories of traveling through space and time … of the Hub, and Lero, of Dr. Waldo and Eve … what would someone do with that knowledge? What would a person who had no morals—who was so lacking in ethics that they would take someone else's memories—do with such information? Not only would Charlie and Chuck be in danger, but also Emma, Ree, Eve, Ben, Dr. Waldo, everyone in the Hub … maybe even all the universes. Emma shuddered.

Nolor shook his head. "It depends on how long they had. Extracting memories can take some time, you see, depending on their method. If they just had a short time, maybe a year or two. If they had access to the boys for longer, well, they could have taken everything."

Emma's heart deflated. "Everything," she repeated. The horror of it, the reality of it, instantly struck her. "And you say if all of a person's memories are taken ..."

"They die," Ree finished.

Nolor pressed his lips together. "So you see the danger. So we will find your brothers, then." He turned to Daya, who nodded the slightest nod. She understood what was at stake. "Where do we begin to look?"

The girls' conversation with Future Ree whirled in Emma's head. No previous Emmas and Rees had found Charlie and Chuck. Surely they'd all cared just as much as she and Ree did, but none of them had managed to find their brothers. In every future that they knew about, Charlie and Chuck were gone.

"That's not going to happen this time," she said out loud.

"What?" said Nolor. "What did you say?" He was perched on the edge of his seat, awaiting orders. Emma imagined he must have seen something like this before. He must have known someone who had suffered the fate she feared most for her brother.

She squinted her eyes. *Think, Emma, think!* She had been able to transport herself before, using the power of her mind, to other places, but she always knew in her mind where she wanted to go. And even then, she hadn't always gotten it right. *Think, Emma, think!* The idea of a future without Charlie started to haunt her, and the fear grew in her like a tornado. Charlie was more than a brother. Charlie was everything. Charlie was ...

"Ree!" Emma said, popping up out of her chair. "I know how to find them. I know how to get to them." She turned to Nolor and Daya. "I'm so sorry, we have to go. You've been beyond kind. Thank you."

"But—" Nolor started to speak, but the girls were already out the front door.

"Goodbye!" Ree waved as she chased after Emma.

Emma walked briskly away from the house, looking around the landscape. "We just need a bush …" she said under her breath.

"A bush? Emma, tell me what you're thinking!" Ree said, skipping to keep up with Emma.

"We have to get back to the Hub, but I don't want to just disappear while they can still see us," Emma said. She turned back, and, sure enough, Nolor and Daya were standing just inside the front door, watching the girls race away.

"Right," said Ree. She joined in the search for a suitable spot from which to disappear. "There," she said, pointing. "There's a hill and some bushes. That should do."

They raced to the spot Ree had found, crested the hill, walked behind the bushes, and turned back. "Can they see us?" Emma said, craning her neck.

Ree stood on her tiptoes and looked toward the house. "No, I think we're clear," she said.

Emma pulled a Dark MATTER from her bag. "Hook arms," she said, but Ree had already grabbed hold of her parallel twin. "Back to the Hub, Dark MATTER," Emma said, tapping in coordinates. "*Now.*"

The tumble though space felt almost normal by this time, and next thing they knew, Emma and Ree were back in the Hub, standing by their cottage inside the infinite space. They sat for a few moments, reorienting themselves as their cells merged back into place.

"Emma! Ree!" exclaimed Ben, out of breath from running. He had been working away at his workstation, but ran over when he saw the girls return. "Did you find them?" He looked around them for any sign of Chuck and Charlie. His brow furrowed when he saw they were alone.

"No," said Ree, "but Emma thinks she knows how." Ree turned to Emma, who had still not explained her idea.

"I need a pigeon," Emma said to Ben, urgently. "One that hasn't yet been calibrated. One that hasn't been set to anything. Your best pigeon," she said breathlessly.

"My best pigeon?" said Ben. Obediently he trotted toward where they kept the uncalibrated pigeons and the spare Dark MATTER spheres, a small locked cupboard near Dr. Waldo's desk. The girls followed. "They're all the same. You know that, right?" He looked at Emma, to make sure some of her cells hadn't shifted unexpectedly in the process of returning home.

"Yes, I know," said Emma impatiently. "I mean your most recent. Not an old buggy one. A new one."

Ben tapped a code into the short black cupboard, and the door sprang open. Inside were three bins: one filled with pigeons, one with Dark MATTER spheres, and a third, with devices Emma and Ree had never seen before. He grabbed two pigeons and gave them to Emma.

"But what are those other ones?" Ree said, as Ben closed and locked the cupboard.

He looked at Ree with an apology in his eyes. "Sorry," he said. "Can't say yet. There are two fresh, bug-free pigeons for you. One plus a spare. Where do you want to calibrate them to?" The pigeons always started out without any settings, and were then calibrated individually to a "home" setting; wherever a person was in any of the universes, with just a swipe, they would return to that place.

"Nowhere," said Emma. Ree and Ben looked at her, puzzled just as Dr. Waldo, who had seen the commotion, arrived.

"Nowhere?" said Dr. Waldo. He, too, had a confused look in his eyes, but behind his confusion his brain ticked and clicked, working to solve the puzzle. "No home calibration?" he said, still decoding Emma's plan.

"Nowhere," said Emma. "I need it to take me home." She watched Dr. Waldo, knowing her idea would come to him any moment.

And it did. A light bulb went off in the older man's head and his eyes brightened. "Of course. I approve." He tapped the pigeon affectionately. "That just may work, my dear, that just may work."

"But where?" said Ben. "I'm still confused. How will it take you anywhere without my calibrating it first?"

Ree, however, had caught on as well. "It's going to take us *home*. To Chuck and Charlie. Chuck and Charlie are home." She smiled, and a tear welled up in her left eye.

"Exactly," said Emma. She and Ree locked arms. "Think of Chuck with all your might, Ree," she said. "And I'll think of Charlie. Hopefully they're still together, wherever they are." She held the pigeon so tightly that she thought she might crush it, but she was not going to let go. "Pigeon," she said, "take us home. Take us to Charlie and Chuck. Take us home."

chapter fourteen

Not long after they started walking again, Charlie, Chuck, and Akala reached the point where the boys had first set up their tents. The former shelters were burned and in tatters, and little else remained of what they'd brought with them.

"This doesn't look familiar," said Chuck, trying to piece the tent back together. "Was it yours?" he asked Charlie.

"I don't recognize it, either," said Charlie. He rummaged through everything he could find, but still nothing sparked any memories. He turned to Akala. "You're sure this was ours? This is where you found us?"

"No, you were not here when we found you," she said. "But yes, I am sure this was yours."

Once again Charlie felt the sense of loss. How could he not remember? How could a whole period of time simply be wiped from his brain?

They forged onward. Akala stopped for a while, sniffing the air, trying to decide which way to go. Eventually she settled on a path and led the boys on through the flat, grassy landscape. The road they walked on was again little more than a dirt path, but it was enough that she felt it must lead somewhere.

"I think this is the way we went when I came out with Corala and Leidar," she said, and then she said no more. They passed by rolling hills and flat plains, short bushes and vast fields of tall grass, and an occasional small lake, but they saw nothing in the way of civilization. Charlie wondered if there really was anyone else out there, or if Akala was leading them to their deaths. But he couldn't see an alternative. Without her, they were lost for sure.

Eventually, the Charlies grew hungry. "Can we stop to eat?" Chuck said, already scoping out a nearby boulder as a nice place to sit.

"Yes, that is a good idea," said Akala. She sat on a large rock near Chuck, and Charlie found a flat spot on the ground. Akala pulled out from her bag some sandwiches she'd made before they left. She handed one each to Charlie and Chuck, then bit into one herself.

The air was still, and the shadows were long with a sun that had almost set. A few insects buzzed about their heads, alighting occasionally on flowers or blades of grass. One bug landed on Charlie's shoe. With its bright red shell and four red and yellow wings, it resembled something like a cross between a ladybug and a butterfly. Charlie sat as still as he could so it wouldn't fly away.

"Will this sting me?" he asked. He ate the last bite of his sandwich and slowly brushed crumbs from his lips.

The tiny movement startled the bug, and it flew away. "Now it won't," Akala said with a smile.

Suddenly there was a shift in the atmosphere, and Akala instantly turned her nose up to sniff the air.

"What is it?" said Chuck. "Another storm?"

"I can't say … it is different," Akala said, still sniffing.

Charlie tilted his head. "I think I'm getting acclimated to this place," he said. "I felt something, too. Maybe I can smell the storms when they come!"

Chuck laughed, but then put a hand to his forehead. "Whatever it is, I think I'm getting a headache. I feel a little woozy."

"You dorks," said Emma. "It's us. We just pigeoned in." One of the tricks of the pigeons and Dark MATTER spheres was that they created disturbances in the air, which disoriented the people in the landing area and helped disguise the fact that people had just arrived out of nowhere. Usually Emma and the others used this feature to help them get away if anyone noticed their arrival, but this time, she and Ree were so giddy that they'd managed to find Charlie and Chuck that they could hardly contain themselves. Each had a smile from ear to ear.

"Ahhhh!" Charlie screamed. Charlie and Chuck both popped up from their seats upon seeing their sisters. "Emma!" Charlie said. Then, his voice filled with confusion, he said, "And Emma? Which of you is Emma?" Charlie and Chuck both stared at the girls.

"Why are there two of you guys, too?" Chuck asked. "Are you real?"

After only a moment's hesitation to figure out which Charlie belonged to which sister, Emma flew to Charlie's side to give him an enormous bear hug, and Ree raced to Chuck to do the same.

Charlie about fell over with the force of Emma's hug. He laughed and returned the embrace, but then pushed her away to look her in the eyes. "Emma," he said.

"Charlie!" Emma said, gleefully. "We found you!"

"Emma," Charlie said again. "We are as glad as you are that you found us. But maybe you can give us some answers. Do you know why there are two of us? And why there are two of you?" He looked at Ree. "And where the heck are we?"

Emma's heart fell. "You don't remember?" she said, looking from Charlie to Chuck. "Or you, Chuck? You don't either?"

Chuck shook his head. "Everything's gone," he said. "Everything back to when we first got to Dogwinkle Island. However long ago that is. We have no idea."

"But that's …" Ree looked at Emma, counting in her head. "Well, that's months ago. Last year. You don't remember a thing?"

"Nothing," said Charlie. "And believe me, there's a lot of strange stuff going on, and it's about all I've been able to do to keep it all together, so if you, Emma, and you, other Emma, could explain some things to us, I think we'd both be mighty grateful."

Emma sighed. How in the universes to explain the past several months? She looked at Akala, sitting there watching, eyes wide, ears perked and absorbing everything. She had a look of terror on her face, but also she looked like she was not going to miss this for all the world. "Who's this?" she said. "Can we trust her?"

Charlie shrugged. "That's Akala. And we don't know if we can trust her, but she's all we have right now."

"You can trust me," Akala said. "I am glad to meet you, Emma, and Emma."

"They call me Ree," said Ree. "Middle name. Makes things easier since there are two of us."

Akala nodded. "Ree," she said.

"Yes," Ree confirmed. "That's Charlie and Emma, and we're Chuck and Ree. I'm still not quite sure how they got to use their first names and we got Chuck and Ree, but I guess maybe it's because they found the lighthouse first. But Ree's a good name. There are millions of Emmas. I've never met another Ree."

"We found the lighthouse?" said Charlie, tilting his head. "What lighthouse?" He scanned the plains but still, there was nothing but nature.

And so, as clearly as they could, Emma and Ree explained about the Balky Point lighthouse, and how it was a portal to all the other universes, or at least many of them. They described how Emma and Charlie had first visited an Earth that was parallel to their own and had met Chuck and Ree. And finally, they told them how Charlie and Chuck had decided to open a multiverse travel guide business, and how it was the act of scoping out planets to bring clients to that landed them here.

"Smart and entrepreneurial," Chuck said, nodding to Charlie his admiration for the two of them. "That makes sense."

"Sounds like us," Charlie agreed. "Spectacular idea, guiding tours through the universe. Who wouldn't want to go? I say we continue with the enterprise, what ho young man?"

"What ho indeed," Chuck said, mimicking Charlie's British accent. "Brilliant!"

Charlie turned back to Emma. "That's all great, and that explains why we're all here. And we know a bit about where our memories went, and who took them. But it doesn't help us figure out what to do next." He punched Emma in the arm, playfully. "But I'm really glad you're here, dork."

She punched him back. "Dork," she said, her smile growing ever wider. They hadn't told the Charlies that Emma and Charlie had been mad at each other when they last saw each other. She decided he didn't need to know.

Emma turned to Akala. "Do you know how to get their memories back?" she said.

Akala was sitting with her mouth open, absorbing everything she had just heard. She blinked, shook her head, and asked no questions. All of it was perhaps too much to comprehend, or perhaps too crazy to be true. "Getting their memories back is complicated," Akala said, finally. "I believe two others have put Chuck and Charlie's memories into their own brains. So we would first need to get the memories out of them, and then figure out whose memories go to which of your brothers, and then put the memories back in." She hung her head. "I do not know how to do all of that, no."

Ree sat on the boulder that Chuck had been sitting on earlier. "We need help, then," she said. She looked at Emma. "Maybe Nolor and Daya will know? They knew about the history of the Gleymara, and they knew something, at least, about how memories are stolen and stored."

"The Gleymara?" said Chuck. "What's the Gleymara?"

"That's the people you were with. At least, we think so. The cult. Where the memory thieves come from," Ree said.

Chuck and Charlie exchanged a look. "It's a strange day when you lose your memories on an alien planet and your duplicated sisters show up knowing more about where you are than you do," Chuck said.

"Certainly ranks up there in my top five strangest days," Charlie said.

Akala looked agitated. "I know there are other people on Maluket. There must be. I have not seen them but I know they exist. Corala and Leidar come out and take their memories. But inside the colony, we are told that there is no one but us and a few mutants who escaped. We are told that if they don't want to be a part of our colony, if they don't want to be like us, they leave and then they die out here. We are told there is no one else."

"But the scientist," said Charlie. "You got memories from a scientist. So you must know there are others out here."

"Yes," she said. "That is why I came out with Corala and Leidar the other day. I wanted to see more people. They must have known my plan, though. They walked around but we saw no one else. I don't think they wanted me to know what they really do, or where, or how."

Emma was absorbing this conversation, trying to make sense of it all. "Corala and Leidar, they're memory thieves?" she said.

Akala nodded.

"And they're the ones you think have Charlie and Chuck's memories?" Emma asked.

"That's them," Charlie confirmed.

"Nolor and Daya are a couple we met when we came looking for you before," Emma said. She surveyed the landscape. "They live near here—we need to find the river and then follow it to their house. They were nice, and smart. They may be able to help. What's more, we need shelter before it gets too late, and I'd feel safest inside a home." She didn't say it, but with people running around stealing memories, a night in the open plains seemed like a very bad idea.

"I think you're right," said Ree. She pulled out her iPert to see if it could help them find the river.

"New phone?" said Chuck, looking over her shoulder.

"No, it's the iPert. Don't you have yours?" Ree asked.

Chuck shook his head. "If I ever had one, I don't have it anymore. What's an iPert?"

"An iPert," said Emma, pulling out her own device, "is like a phone but it works everywhere. We can call to anywhere from anywhere with it. Anywhere in the universes. Well," she said, "almost anywhere. I don't think it works everywhere. But a lot more places than your regular phone. Dr. Waldo created them for us, so he could get in touch with us anytime. And so we could call each other."

"Across universes?" asked Charlie doubtfully.

"Across universes," confirmed Emma.

"Across time?" asked Chuck excitedly.

Ree shook her head. "Not across time, it seems." She blushed. She hadn't yet told anyone other than the Ben from her own planet that she'd tried making phone calls across time.

"How do you know it doesn't work across time?" Chuck asked Ree.

She stared into her brother's eyes for a few seconds. "We have a lot to catch up on," she said, then started tapping at her iPert without saying anything more. After a few moments, she looked up. "That way," she pointed, and she started walking in the direction of the river. The others followed.

They walked a while, the sun slowly dipping beyond the distant horizon. Akala sniffed at the sky a few times as they walked.

"What are you sniffing for?" Emma asked her. "What can you smell?"

"The Electrics," Akala said. "You can't smell it? I think there may be a storm coming tonight, but it's hard to tell just yet."

"You don't have weather forecasters?" asked Ree.

Akala looked away. "Maybe out here," she said. "But in the Gleymara, no. We don't."

She looked sad, so Ree and Emma didn't press any more. But the thought that there might be another storm that night made Emma all the more determined that they needed to get to Nolor and Daya's house quickly. She picked up her pace, and the others followed suit.

Soon, the roof of the house they'd been at just hours before came into view. "There," Emma said, pointing. She was sure she could hear the squeals and giggles of the grandchildren in the distance, and the thought of their happy faces put a smile on her own. Beyond ready for a rest, a place to put her feet up, and some wae, she walked even faster.

The children saw them coming from afar. They waved wildly at their new friends, then ran inside the house giggling and screaming at Nolor and Daya to come see who had come back. The older couple appeared in the doorway, smiling and waving at the traveling group with welcoming arms. Nolor turned his nose to the sky and sniffed, just as Akala had done, then motioned for them all to hurry up.

"You found them!" Daya exclaimed once everyone was in hearing distance. "Are these your brothers?" she asked, delight showing in every part of her face.

"We did!" said Emma. "Thank you so much!"

"You're welcome," said Nolor, "but we didn't do a thing! You found them yourselves!"

"Well, that may be true," said Ree, "but we have a favor to ask now. We need a place to stay for the night. A floor is fine. Do you ...?"

"Say no more," said Daya. "Plenty of room here. There is a storm coming soon and you must be inside, of course. Come in, come in!"

Introductions were made all around, everyone was invited to sit and settle, and Daya brought in a fresh pot of wae and a plate of savory biscuits. Emma was just about to launch into an explanation of what had happened and what they needed, when Daya put a finger to her lips, and with her other hand pointed at Chuck and Charlie. The two had seated themselves on the very cushiony and comfortable couch, and, exhausted, both had immediately fallen asleep.

"I think it's time for bed," Daya said softly. "You can tell us everything in the morning."

chapter fifteen

As humans from Earth who evolved on a planet with twenty-four hour days rather than thirty-hour days, a fifteen-hour night seemed extravagant at the outset. None of the teens would have imagined they could sleep so soundly for so long. However, they were sleep-deprived and exhausted, and they slept straight through the night. Each had awakened a couple of times with the powerful lightning strikes and thunder the Electrics brought, but they rapidly fell back asleep after every interruption. When the sun started to stream through a crack in the curtains of the bedroom Emma, Ree, and Akala had been given, Emma felt more refreshed than she had in years.

She padded out of the bedroom to find Daya, Nolor, and the grandchildren already up. The children were outside playing, Nolor was reading a book, and Daya was cleaning up after their breakfast.

"Would you like some wae?" Daya asked quietly, so as not to wake any of the others.

"That would be lovely, thank you," said Emma.

Daya poured her a cup and handed her the mug. "There's a swing out back that I find is a nice way to greet the morning," she said, and pointed to a door that led out from the kitchen.

Emma smiled her response and headed outside.

The morning smelled like dirt after a rainstorm; everything felt fresh and new, like possibilities and hope. Emma knew they were going to have to deal with some big challenges today, but she pushed the thoughts to the edge of her mind. *Not yet*, she told herself. *Not now.* She wanted to take this moment to appreciate where she was, to relish the impossibility of being on another planet, with kind aliens who had just let her and her friends sleep in their home, and who then had given her a morning drink to enjoy outside on a swing.

Emma found the swing easily. It was basically a rustic old bench, worn smooth with years of use, hanging freely on thick ropes from a sturdy branch of an old tree. Since she was taller than her hosts, Emma's legs swept the ground with every swing, so she pushed herself back and forth as she watched the sun rise over a mountain in the distance. Dust motes floated through the sunbeams, and birds chirped to welcome the new day. Emma sipped her wae, and thought this might be one version of perfection.

After half an hour or so, Emma decided it was time to think about the issues at hand. She pulled out her iPert to check for whatever information it might offer on this planet.

She heard the door to the house open, and looked up. There, hair tousled and skin crumpled from sleep, stood her Charlie. She shifted in the swing to make room for him, and he came and sat, carrying his own cup of wae.

"Morning, sunshine," Emma said, her heart so happy to have her Charlie back. *We saved him*, she thought. *None of the other Emmas did, but we saved him.*

"Morning, indeed," said Charlie. "What's that?" he pointed at the device in her hand.

"That's the iPert. Remember, we were asking if you still had yours?" she said.

Charlie took the iPert from her. "It's just a phone?"

"I mean, it's a lot more than just a phone," Emma said. "It's everything. It's amazing. Do you suppose the people who took your brain also took your phone?"

"One, they didn't take my brain; they took a few months of memories. And two, yes, I'd say that's a logical assumption," Charlie said. "Why is it called an iPert?"

"Well, that's Dr. Waldo's play on words. It's like an iPhone, but an expert level, so iPert. And also, it's named after Rupert. Rupert is … there's that phrase 'the elephant in the room,' and Dr. Waldo liked that phrase, so he created an elephant for the Hub. But Rupert is a two-dimensional elephant."

"Two dimensional," Charlie said, disbelieving.

"No, really, he is. Two dimensional. And we made a companion for him, too. Hermione. She's also two dimensional. I hope they're getting along," Emma mused.

"You hope the two-dimensional elephants are getting along," Charlie said, looking at Emma with sarcasm. He shook his head. "I really think I need to get those memories back. Seems like I'm missing out on a few things."

A small animal came bounding around the corner, startling the twins. "Oh my gosh!" Emma said, tucking her legs up under her. "What is that?" The creature looked something like a cross between a donkey and a small dog.

Within seconds, the screaming grandchildren followed, chasing after the donkey dog, which didn't seem to mind at all.

"Must be a pet," Charlie said.

"You just never know anymore what's a pet and what's a sentient being. Not after we met the oo'broo, or Klyvnini, depending on who you ask."

"The oo'broo or Klyvnini?" Charlie said. "What are the oo'broo or Klyvnini?"

Emma turned to him. She'd forgotten. Those memories were all gone for him. "Other aliens. On another planet we went to. They look like octopuses."

Charlie studied his wae for a while. "Emma," he said.

"I know," Emma said.

"We have to get my memories back," Charlie said.

"Have you tried?" Emma said. "I can't believe they could literally take your memories. It has to be like a computer file, and they took a copy but not the original. Somewhere in your brain are the original files. They have to be."

"To be honest, I haven't had time to try just yet. We've … I mean until you guys came along, I thought I was half delusional in believing there was another Charlie here. I didn't know what to make of that. Imagine waking up and there's another you, and you didn't know anything yet about parallel Earths, and there's no one to explain it, and what's more, you're surrounded by meerkat people."

Emma laughed. She loved her brother so much, his wit, his kindness, his way of making everything okay. "I know," Emma said. "We have to get them back, Charlie. I don't want you not to remember everything we've shared since we discovered the lighthouse. It's all been amazing, and it's great to have Ree around but she wasn't there for a lot of it, and Chuck doesn't remember and that's not the same anyway. I need you to remember our memories, too." She put her legs down again and kicked at the ground to make the swing sway. The sun was fully out from behind the mountain now, and the sky was clear of all clouds. The air did seem to sparkle more here, Emma thought. Maybe that was the electric charge Ben had been telling them about. She realized then that Charlie didn't know about Ree and the other Ben, or even the first Ben, or about Ree and Emma's travel forward in time, or so many new things, much less all the old things. It felt empty, in a way, having memories but having them without Charlie. "Charlie," she said, then she paused.

"What?" said Charlie. "You can't stop now. I know that tone. That's the 'I have something to say and I'm not sure how to say it' tone. Usually that tone is for someone else, not for me." He watched another of the ladybug butterflies float by, the somewhat lethargic beating of its wings nonetheless keeping it afloat in the air. "It's weird, getting older."

"Yeah," said Emma. "Well, so, when you get your memories back—and we will, I promise—but when you do, you'll find that you were mad at me last time we saw each other."

"I was mad at you? What did you do?" Charlie asked.

"I didn't do *anything*!" Emma said. "That's the thing! I didn't do anything, and you're mad at me." The hurt swelled up in her heart again, just thinking about it.

"Then why am I mad at you?" Charlie asked. "There had to be a reason. I'm very logical, you know."

Emma laughed and punched his arm. "Dork," she said. "You didn't tell me. You told Chuck who told Ree who told me." She couldn't quite keep the accusatory edge of hurt out of her voice. "You told them you're annoyed because I'm the Chosen One. Your words, not mine."

"I said you're the Chosen One?" Charlie said. He stared at his sister, trying to figure out what might make her so special that he would call her that. "In what way, exactly, are you the Chosen One?"

Emma sighed. Part of her would have been perfectly happy to just leave this memory behind and pretend it never happened, but she knew that wouldn't be fair to Charlie. His memories were his, not hers to manipulate. "Try to remember. You were pretty emotional about it. That memory has to be in your head somewhere."

Charlie put his feet firmly on the ground to stop the movement of the swing. He closed his eyes and breathed, in and out, in and out, in and out, slowly. His eyes moved back and forth rapidly under his eyelids as he worked to dive into forgotten depths of his mind, to dredge up whatever cells or chemicals might remain in which his past was still present. After a minute or two, he shook his head vigorously. Without opening his eyes, he said, "I don't think it's working."

"Keep trying," said Emma. "Relax. Let it just come to you." She reached for his hand. He squeezed hers back in response.

Charlie breathed in again, deeply, and exhaled. This time his eyes were relaxed under his eyelids, and he let his shoulders fall. His breathing grew slower and slower until Emma thought he might have fallen asleep. He flinched, pursed his lips, then relaxed again, breathing slowly.

Finally, he spoke. "This can't be right," he said. He opened his eyes and looked at his sister in awe.

"What?" she said.

"You can travel through space just using your mind?" he said, disbelieving his own words. "That's ridiculous. I'll try again." He started to close his eyes.

"No," said Emma, "stop. You got it. That's right. I mean, I think probably everyone can," she said, echoing sentiments she had repeated time and again. "I think it's up to the universes, really, and to the situation at hand. I think, you know, most people probably have just never tried. Well, I know you've tried. But maybe the situation was just not—"

"Wait," said Charlie, stopping his sister's stream of consciousness. "You can travel through space with your mind? And I was mad about that?"

Emma deflected, shrugging. She didn't want to talk about that until Charlie had more memories back, more context. "I guess you felt like it made you not special or something. That's not important. How did you get the memories back?" she asked.

"Well, it's hard to describe. I sort of focused and didn't focus at the same time. Like when you're trying to see something but you can't see it if you look at it directly. I focused on the edges of the idea, on the words 'the Chosen One' and on you, and then eventually it sort of shifted into view. The memory came back briefly, but I got excited and lost it. So I had to start over but this time I knew how to just sort of let the memory come. And there you were. The Chosen One. Traveling through space with your mind."

"What did you see?" Emma asked.

A pained look crossed Charlie's face. "I saw me holding you on the stairs of a lighthouse. I thought you were dead." He winced. "I remembered it was because you'd transported everyone through space. And I wanted to save you, but I couldn't." He looked away, the now-clear memory filling him with agony.

That memory was Charlie's alone. Emma had indeed been near death, and did not remember the moment he spoke of.

The children came screaming around the corner once more, following their miniature donkey-like pet and giggling as though giggling were all they knew how to do. Emma wondered for a moment when she she'd stopped giggling like that. She and Charlie used to build forts and play at being detectives and chase each other around the yard from morning to night. Certainly they'd fought, but most days they'd ended the day collapsed into a pile, laughing. She didn't regret growing up, but she did miss how simple things used to be.

"We should go inside," Emma said. "We've got to get you your brains back." She stood and reached for her brother's hand, and pulled him up out of the swing.

“I do still have brains, you know,” Charlie said.

“Jury is still out on that one,” Emma said, winking. “Oh, hang on,” she said, stopping just outside the house. She reached into her pocket and pulled out a pigeon. “Calibrated to take you back to the Hub. You swipe here to make it work,” she said, moving her finger just above the small sphere. “Ben made us each take a ton of these with us, just to be safe. Keep it with you. Don’t lose it. Use it if you need to, okay? Even if you have to leave me behind. Get yourself safe.”

Charlie locked eyes with Emma. “Emmzaloo. I am not leaving you behind.” He took the pigeon from his sister and gave her a hug.

When they walked through the kitchen door, Akala, Chuck and Ree were sitting at the table, each devouring a plate of something flat and round and covered in a spread. Akala was absorbed in a book she had open at the table.

“It’s like pancakes!” said Chuck through a mouthful. “Have some!”

“This topping tastes like applesauce,” Ree said. “Delicious, thank you.” She smiled at Daya.

Akala looked up, beaming. “Have you seen how many books Nolor and Daya have?” she said. “We have nothing like this at home. Our books are all very old. They told me I could borrow this one.” She went back to her reading, carefully holding the book away from the food.

Emma and Charlie joined the others and ate their fill as well, but Emma was eager to move to the sitting room to talk with Nolor and Daya about their situation. She had absolutely no idea how they were going to get the memories back, and she hoped they might have some insights.

As she was helping Daya clear the dishes, a knock came at the kitchen door, and then the person on the other side opened the door without waiting. "I'm here!" called out the visitor.

"Podor!" exclaimed Daya, and her smile had never been brighter. She rushed to Podor and pulled him into a tight hug. After a few moments, still holding him, she turned to the others. "This is our son, Podor. We … we called and told him to come over. We think maybe you will need him." When she looked back at her son, her eyes had a tinge of pain in them, which she quickly masked with a smile.

On hearing his son's voice, Nolor had come into the kitchen. "Let's move into the other room," he said. "Leave the dishes; we'll get them later." He embraced Podor, then slapped his son affectionately on the back.

They all moved to the more comfortable seating in the living room and sat. "So, I guess we need to explain," said Emma.

Nolor looked from Emma to the Charlies. "Unfortunately, I think we already know. You told us your brothers were missing. When you came back with them, it was clear not everything was right. That's why we asked Podor to come. You see …" he looked out the window toward where the children were playing. "We have experience with this ourselves. Our daughter, the children's mother, was a talented and respected scientist. She was out at the coast a few years back, studying the wunpada Emergence. She and her colleagues were staying in huts, waiting for the birds to come. You never know exactly when they'll emerge, you see." Chuck and Charlie nodded, remembering their own recent experience. Nolor took a deep breath, and Daya looked away at the wall, her eyes glistening. "Anyway, one night when they were all asleep, the memory thieves came. They took our daughter's memories, and those of several others. The thieves must have come back several times, because when the scientists were found days later, walking toward town but with no idea who or where they were, years of their memories had been taken. Decades." He paused again. No one spoke, and the room was filled with the heavy silence of loss. "Too many memories, it turned out. Too much. Most of the scientists died shortly after, including our daughter. The rest, well, they require constant care now. They have nothing left."

Daya's hand flew to her eyes, and she stood and walked quickly out of the room. With a nod to Podor, Nolor rose and followed her.

"I'm so sorry," Emma said. "We had no idea. We didn't mean to bring this pain back."

"The pain has never left," said Podor. "It's not your fault. They called me because after Maraya's death, I started studying memory exchange. I wanted to know, as you do, if memories, once taken, can be returned."

Emma was flooded with relief. "And?" she asked. "Can they?"

Podor nodded slowly. "Yes," he said. "I think they can."

chapter sixteen

Akala had been quiet to this point, absorbing the conversation, the books, and the new surroundings outside of her colony. But now she spoke. "Podor," she said, "you have told us that your sister was a scientist studying the wunpada Emergence."

"Yes," said Podor quietly. "She was one of the best."

"And you say she lost—her memories were stolen when she was out on the coast. Near us, near the Gleymara," she continued.

"That's right," said Podor. "She was on the coast, quite near you."

Charlie caught Chuck's eye. He suspected what was coming. Chuck nodded.

"I … well, I am ashamed to say this," said Akala. "I once bought memories. I had heard about it before, about stolen memories, but I didn't know if it was true until someone told me they were offering memories of people who studied the Emergence. I have always been fascinated by the Emergence. I didn't know anything other than the fact that at some point every few years, birds grew out of the sea. I didn't know about their life under the water. I didn't know about their change. But I wanted to know more. And one of the … of the memory thieves, she offered to sell me the memories."

Podor was still, listening intently.

Akala shuddered involuntarily. "I bought the memories. I bought the memories of a scientist studying the wunpada Emergence, and they were installed into my own mind." She looked deeply into Podor's eyes. "I don't know if the memories I have are your sister's, but it is likely that if they are not hers, then they are memories of someone she was with. If you would like to practice memory extraction on me, if you would like to try to get those memories back, then I am willing." She closed her eyes and inhaled deeply with her shame.

Podor let out a giant puff of breath. Emotions stormed across his face: anger, excitement, confusion, sadness. "You might have my sister's memories?" he said. "You know the people who killed her?"

Akala gripped the side of the chair she was in, as if reaching for strength, and forced herself to look Podor in the eyes again. "I might. I do."

Podor stood abruptly, pacing rapidly in small circles, thinking. "If we can … if I can … if we can get those memories back, we need to give them to Mother," he said. "She needs to have those memories. Whether they are Maraya's memories or those of a colleague, either way, we need to get those memories." Thoughts flew across his face. "Are you sure?" he said, and then his lips moved without sound as he continued a conversation with himself alone.

Akala took a deep breath. "Whatever you need to do, I am willing," she said. Then, more quietly, she asked, "Do you think it will kill me?"

As if a switch had been flipped, Podor finally saw Akala before him again as a real being, not just the potential storage unit of his sister's thoughts. "It shouldn't," he said gently. "Very unlikely. I can't promise anything, but just extracting those memories won't hurt you."

"Can you get just those memories," asked Akala, "or will you need to take others?" She set her chin. "You should do what you need to do. The memories are not mine. I had no idea that taking memories killed people. I had no idea of the impact on families. You may do what you need to do."

Podor sat next to her and reached for her hand. "Thank you, Akala. I think I can get just the stolen memories. I'll need your help to find them, but I think I can."

"Then we should begin as soon as possible," she said, "so your family may have these memories, and so we can help Charlie and Chuck get back their own memories."

Emma went to sit on Akala's other side, and took her other hand. "You're brave, Akala," she said. "And kind. Thank you. This means so much." She looked at Charlie. "Now what we need to do is figure out how we're going to get the people who stole your memories to agree to give them back."

"How are we going to do that?" asked Chuck.

"I have no idea," said Emma. "But we'll figure it out."

Shortly afterward, Podor whisked Akala off to his lab in town where he'd been working and experimenting. Daya had been torn; she desperately wanted the memories but also could not stand to see Akala get hurt. Podor had promised he would be careful, and Akala had reassured her that whatever happened, it was all in fairness; she'd had no right to the memories in the first place. Many tears were shed, but Akala and Podor went away, leaving high hopes and tense emotions in the house behind them.

Emma, Ree, Charlie, and Chuck sat once more in Nolor and Daya's sitting room, trying to hatch a plan. On the table in the center of the room was a large plate with a variety of biscuits, and a tray with cups and a pitcher of wae. "All brainstorming sessions require biscuits and wae," explained Daya, but Emma suspected Daya just needed to keep herself busy.

"All right," said Emma, taking a bite from a savory biscuit. "We need a plan. Anyone?"

"We need to go back to the colony," said Charlie, shrugging. "No way around it. That's where our memories are. That's where Corala and Leidar are. We have to find them."

"Well," said Chuck, "technically, we could wait for them to come to us. It sounds like their memory-thieving excursions are a pretty regular occurrence. We could watch for them, and capture them, and just take them to Podor's lab whether they like it or not," he said.

"We could," said Charlie, "but I like to think we might not have to stoop to their level."

"They don't really seem like the type who can be reasoned with," said Emma. She poured herself a cup of wae, then refilled cups around the room. The wae Daya had made today was reminiscent of ginger and lemon, with just a bit of sweetness. Emma wondered if she might be able to replicate it at home. Or maybe she could just have the Hub do it. "Make wae," she could say, and wae would appear, the perfect wae in the place where everything was possible. "Should we ask Dr. Waldo?" she said. "Maybe he would have an idea?"

"This isn't a science thing," Charlie said. "This is a people-skills thing. No offense to Dr. Waldo, but I think we've got this maybe better than he would."

Emma nodded. "I agree with that. And I agree we should try talking with them rather than accosting them out in a field somewhere," she said, "at least to start with. If that doesn't work, then we can reassess."

"Would you like to take one of our wheelboxes?" said Nolor. "It would be faster than walking. And you could get away faster, too, if you needed to. We have two; it wouldn't be a problem." He nodded his head toward a building that was detached from the main house.

"Wheelbox?" said Chuck. "I don't know what a wheelbox is, but I like the sound of that."

Nolor tilted his head. "You don't know what a wheelbox is?" he said, and then he smiled. "I know there are many things you all are not telling us. That is fine. You may tell us in your own time. If you like. But I want you to know, to believe, you can trust us."

"We believe you," said Emma. "Thank you."

"What, exactly, is this wheelbox?" said Chuck, bringing the conversation back to what he thought was most important. He was out of his chair and ready to go.

Nolor smiled. "Let's go have a look," he said.

The group filed out of the house to the building next door. Nolor pressed a code into a keypad, and a large garage door curled itself into the roof of the building, revealing two vehicles. One, painted a bright blue, looked very much like a low dune buggy with a roof; the other, painted a sort of cranberry color, looked more like a short station wagon.

Chuck and Charlie's eyes lit up. "Those are your wheelboxes?" Charlie said.

"We would love to borrow a wheelbox!" said Chuck. "Are they easy to drive?"

"You haven't driven one before?" Nolor said, exchanging a look with Daya. She looked skeptical, but Nolor waved away her concerns. "It's not hard. A few minutes of lessons and you'll be on your way. Who would like to try first?"

Chuck, Charlie, and Ree all raised their hands swiftly, but Chuck's hand was up a millisecond faster than the others. "Looks like it's Chuck," he said, "but it's easy enough. You all can learn if you like." He led Chuck to the bright blue vehicle, around to the side where it was plugged into the wall.

"Oh, it's not gas?" said Chuck.

"Gas?" said Nolor. "What do you mean?"

"How it's powered," said Chuck, realizing he sounded very much like an alien.

Nolor laughed. "It's powered by electricity, of course. What else?" He unplugged the car, then directed Chuck to get into the driver's seat. Luckily for Chuck, the steering wheel was on the same side of the car he was used to, so that, at least, was familiar. Nolor got into the passenger seat, and started the lesson.

Charlie, Emma, and Ree watched as Chuck guided the car around the property, slowly at first, then off to a road behind the house. "That road leads into town," Daya explained as they watched Chuck speed away.

While they waited, Ree turned to Emma. "Emma," she whispered so no one else could hear. "I keep thinking...." She paused and bit her lip.

"You keep thinking what?" Emma encouraged, her own voice a whisper.

"The way to fix everything," said Ree. "What if ...?"

"What if ... what?" said Emma.

Ree bit her lip again, then turned as Chuck and Nolor brought the wheelbox back to where they were standing. "Nothing," she said. "Never mind."

Emma frowned. What could Ree have been thinking? Another way to fix everything? But she wasn't going to force Ree to tell her if she wasn't ready. Still, Emma couldn't help but wonder.

"It sure is quiet," Charlie said as Chuck parked the vehicle.

"Is this your first time driving?" Daya asked.

"No, we all have licenses. Got them two years ago," Ree said.

Daya raised her eyebrows but said nothing.

"Easy!" said Chuck, climbing out of the driver's seat. Ree jumped in after him quickly, before Charlie could get into the car. Nolor taught her how to drive, then Charlie, and finally Emma agreed to take her own turn.

"You never know when you're going to need to know how to do something," Charlie said, and Emma found she couldn't argue.

Once Nolor was satisfied that all the teens had a reasonable grasp of how to handle the wheelbox, he sat in the driver's seat and input some information into the dash console. "GMS," he said.

"GMS?" asked Emma.

"Guiding Map System?" said Nolor, looking at her like she should already know this. "I've set the coordinates for the colony."

"Are there … are there roads?" Chuck asked. "We didn't see any on the way here. Just lots of fields and a few trails."

"There are roads," Nolor smiled. "Sometimes we only see what we are looking for."

Charlie, Chuck, Emma, and Ree piled into the vehicle with Charlie in the driver's seat, all of them ready to go and face their challenge. Nolor leaned toward the car, like its aura was dragging him in. He looked at Daya. "Maybe I should go, too," he said.

"No," Daya said.

Nolor met his wife's eyes for many long seconds, then nodded. His grandchildren rounded the corner, screaming and giggling and chasing their pet once again. He put a hand on the roof of the car, and spoke into Charlie's window, looking at each of the teens in turn. "I don't know where you are from, but someone needs you to get home safely. Be careful," he said. He patted the roof of the car twice, and stepped back to stand beside his wife. Nolor put his arm around Daya as if he could protect her from more pain than she'd already endured in this life. The two waved as Charlie eased the wheelbox out of the driveway and on the route the GMS system prescribed.

Once they were on the road, Emma spoke up. "It feels weird to lie to them," she said. "They're so nice."

"We haven't technically lied," Ree pointed out. "They haven't asked if we're from other planets, and we haven't denied it."

"But who would ever think to ask such a thing?" Emma said. "It just seems weird. Why don't we tell them?"

"Just how do you envision that conversation going?" asked Chuck.

"'Hey, Nolor and Daya, just a quick FYI, we're from Earth,'" said Charlie.

"'Earth? Where is Earth?'" said Chuck, joining the mock conversation.

"'Oh, it's another planet,'" said Charlie. "'In another universe. Actually, we're from two different Earths. Parallel Earths in parallel universes. Neither of which is this universe.'"

"'Parallel Earths? You're aliens? Wait! Our son studies brains! Can we dissect yours? Here, have some cheese. We've drugged the cheese, so you'll fall asleep and you won't feel a thing. Don't worry,'" said Chuck.

Charlie shook his head. "Yeah, been there, done that. And if they know we're aliens they might not stop with just a few months of memories."

"But why do we always assume people would be hostile to aliens? I mean, we didn't kill you guys when you found us," said Ree.

"Maybe because Emma and I looked just like you and Chuck," said Charlie. "You wanted information first."

"Okay, but you guys didn't kill Eve and her dad when you met them," Ree insisted. "Maybe we're making the wrong assumptions. Maybe we think they'd kill us when in fact they'd welcome us. They might be just as friendly and curious as we are. Obviously we're not here to take over their world."

"Yeah, we can't even keep our own brains," said Chuck.

"That's what I'm saying," Emma said. "It seems like for future alien relations, relationships between Earth and other planets, maybe we could be positive ambassadors. The first time they encounter aliens, we're good people. Then maybe they wouldn't be afraid the next time."

"That's true," said Ree. "And if you guys are going to do travel excursions," she said to Chuck and Charlie, "it wouldn't hurt to have the locals on your side. You might need them one day."

"Case in point," Emma said, "what would we do without Nolor and Daya? We'd be lost without them. People need each other, even if we're from different planets. We'll always need each other. It seems like a good idea to get to know each other. To trust each other. To be friends."

"Together we triumph. Alone we die," said Ree dramatically.

"Hmm," said Charlie. "Yeah, I see your point. But for now, we've got some more hostile aliens to convince." He nodded down the road ahead of them. "That's it, up there."

"Hello, Gleymara," said Chuck. "We've come to get our brains back."

Charlie parked the car outside of a wall that surrounded the colony. The foursome shut the doors with as little noise as possible, and walked quietly around the wall to the front. The gate was open.

"It looks so run down," Ree said. "Especially in comparison to Nolor and Daya's beautiful home."

"Akala said no one knows how to fix anything," Charlie said, and then he looked surprised. "Didn't she?" he asked Chuck.

"Not that I remember," Chuck said. "Maybe I wasn't there?"

"No," Charlie said, "I think that's another of my memories that they took. Maybe all the memories are still in there," he said, knocking on his head. He exchanged a glance with Emma, who winked at him. If she had to, she would work with him as long as needed to get those memories back.

"Well," said Ree, eyeing the dreary-looking enclosure. "I guess we need to go in." Her tone was far from enthusiastic.

Grabbing Charlie's hand, Emma started through the gates. The others followed. A few people were wandering around, and looked them over with something between curiosity and hostility. "Will you know Corala and Leidar?" Emma whispered. "Did you see them after you lost your memories?"

"After our memories were taken, you mean," Charlie whispered back. "I think so. Maybe my brain cells will act as a radar and lead me to them."

But they had no luck for a good while. They wandered aimlessly for about half an hour, trying to look like they weren't wandering aimlessly, before finally sitting at a public picnic table to reassess.

"This is not working. We need a better plan than this," Chuck said. He lightly punched the table, holding back pent-up anger.

"Any ideas?" said Emma. She, too, was feeling frustrated and helpless. Surely there must be something they could do. While they'd been walking around the colony she'd noticed that Ree's hair was fluffier than it was at home, and she imagined her own hair was the same. Even the hair on her arms was raised. She thought it must be the electricity of the planet, something about positively charged ions or who knew what. Regardless, it seemed that somehow, all that electricity must connect everything. There must be an underlying current—literally—that would help Charlie and Chuck find the memories that had been taken from them. Mustn't there?

"You said you can travel through space with your mind?" said Charlie. Chuck looked up. This was news to him.

Emma blushed. She didn't really want to talk about this right now. "Yes," she said hesitantly.

"Well, maybe, if you can move people through space, maybe you can move memories through space, too?" Charlie suggested. "How different can it be? Try it. Just think really hard about our memories, and see if you can't magically make my memories pop out of Corala or Leidar's head and back to mine."

"And mine, too," said Chuck. "Then maybe I'll know what you're talking about. You can travel through space?"

"Just using the power of her mind," said Charlie, proudly.

Chuck looked at Ree. "Can you do that, too?" he asked.

Ree shifted on the bench. "No," she said, but she caught Emma's eyes and gave her a long look. Then Ree stood and looked around, and then closed her eyes.

Instantly Emma knew what Ree was about to do. *Another way to fix everything.* "Ree!" she said. She jumped to grab hold of Ree's arm. A split second later, she felt her body dissolve into the push and tug of traveling through time.

chapter seventeen

Thin wispy clouds floated across two shining moons whose light illuminated the night sky. The moon Emma had seen when they first arrived, a bit smaller than Earth's moon but mesmerizing in its brightness, was high overhead. The second moon, slightly smaller and dimmer, was hanging low, just above the trees. The third moon, if it was above the horizon, was in hiding somewhere. Everything was still, but nonetheless the feeling of electricity Emma had noticed before, of energy, of hairs standing on end, filled the air.

"Where are we?" Emma whispered to Ree, but instantly she recognized the picnic table they'd been sitting at moments before. "I mean, *when* are we?" She rubbed her arms to help the molecules return to normal.

Ree scratched her forehead and shook herself. "In theory," she whispered, "it's the night before we first got to this planet. Or rather, early the morning before."

Emma looked around the grounds of the colony. No lights were shining in windows; no people were wandering around. They had arrived deep in the middle of the night, when everyone and everything was asleep. A night bird let out a low call, and in the distance, another answered.

"This is dangerous," Emma said. "Someone could have been sitting here. One of them."

Ree frowned. "I'm pretty good at getting my timing right," she said. "I've practiced a lot. And you didn't have to come. This was my risk. You're the one who grabbed me at the last second."

"Of course I wasn't going to let you go alone. We're in this together," Emma whispered. "We need each other." A soft breeze lifted her hair by her cheek. "So what's the plan?" she asked.

"We need to walk to where Chuck and Charlie set up the tents," Ree said. She sighed heavily. "I do wish I could travel in space, too. It would have been so much nicer just to transport there instead of here. I don't suppose you'd want to…"

Emma shook her head. "Can't risk anything else right now. Let's get going." She pulled out her iPert to call up the coordinates from their first visit, reached for Ree's hand, and the two started out on the long walk.

The light from the moons was bright enough that they could see their path easily. Emma was grateful for ignorance; the less they knew about the dangerous things that might hurt them in the night, the better. Whatever monsters this planet might hide in its dark hours weren't lurking in her and Ree's imaginations, and they walked on, blissfully oblivious. The night was cool, but not cold. Emma thought she could hear music in the wind, but when she strained to make out the sound, she heard nothing.

When they reached the coast, they stopped for a moment to look out over the ocean. Reflections of the moons shimmered on the surface of the waters, and an occasional splash indicated life below. Farther out, some small islands were enticing, covered in low trees and filled with the unknown. "It's not such a bad idea," Emma said longingly. "Chuck and Charlie with their travel excursions. I'd want to visit here if I were … well, if I weren't us."

"And if it were safe," said Ree.

"And if it were safe," agreed Emma. She sighed.

"It's beautiful," said Ree. A cold wind picked up and she rubbed her shoulders. "I wish we could have seen the Emergence. I'm a little envious." She stood silently just long enough that Emma started to figure out what she was thinking.

"We can't go to that time just yet," said Emma. "We have to save Chuck and Charlie first."

"I know," said Ree, smiling. A moonbeam bounced off her eyes. "Let's go."

They continued on the path in the quiet of the night. "You have a pigeon with you, right?" Emma asked, her eyes constantly scanning the landscape for any signs of danger. "Keep one in your pocket in case we need it."

"I do," said Ree, "already in my pocket. Great minds, and all." She looked at Emma and winked. "I like having a parallel twin," she said. "Charlie—Chuck—is great, of course. But as I get older, it's nice to have a friend who's a girl who understands me."

"I get it," said Emma. She smiled and linked elbows with Ree. It was true. No one would ever replace Charlie, of course. But having Ree and Eve around was nice. "I feel bad that Eve couldn't come with us. Not because I wish she were in trouble with us, but just because I like her company. I like hearing about her planet. It's so much the same but also so different. We should bring her next time."

"We should," said Ree. "We definitely need to make sure she does more stuff with us."

Something about Ree's tone concerned Emma. "What are you saying?" Emma said. "You said that funny. Like … I don't know, like she doesn't have a lot of time to do stuff. Have you … have you gone to her future?"

Ree said nothing. Emma didn't push. She didn't want to know.

They kept walking, checking their iPerts on occasion to make sure they were still headed in the right direction. Emma rolled the pigeon around in her pocket. "I wonder," she said. "I have this pigeon set to take me to the Hub. I wonder, if I used it now would it take me to the Hub in our normal timeline, or in the time we're in now? That is, a few days ago? Or however long it's been?"

"I don't know," said Ree. "I haven't tried that. My guess is that it would take us back to our own proper timeline. I'm thinking about the whole thing Dr. Waldo said about the river and time, and molecule A and B and C. If we're molecule B, then we belong in the molecule B timeline. I feel like somehow the pigeons would know that. But," she smiled, "I also think we should give it a try and find out sometime."

"Sometime," said Emma, also smiling.

"Sometime," said Ree, "but not now. "We are on a mission." She checked her iPert. "Almost there."

"We're early," said Emma. "When we got here before, it was nearing sunset. We're hours ahead of time."

"I know," said Ree. "I thought it was safer to land us in the middle of the night in the colony. If we'd gotten there in the daytime then people would have seen us." She shrugged. "Once again, I'm thwarted by only being able to travel in time, not space."

"Thwarted again," said Emma. "Thwarted. Good word. Maybe together we could figure out how to get you to move in space, too. I really think you could do it if you wanted to."

"Don't say that, Emma," said Ree, suddenly frustrated.

"What?" said Emma, confused. "Why?"

"You say that all the time, that any of us could do what you can do, if we just tried. That implies that we're not trying hard enough. Charlie has probably about broken his brain, trying to travel through space like you can."

Emma stopped. "What do you mean? He hasn't told me that. He told you?"

"He told Chuck, who told me," Ree said, also stopping. "It's just, not everyone can do everything. Everyone has their own skills. If you keep saying that everyone can do what you can do … I don't know. It just feels like you're telling us we're not trying hard enough. That we're failures."

"But that's not what I meant at all," Emma said, her eyes stinging with tears she was trying to hold back.

"I know what you mean. But maybe you just have to accept us for who we are, not who you think we could be if we tried harder. I can move through time," said Ree. "Maybe that's enough."

Emma started walking again, silent but lost in thought. She'd never meant to imply that anyone else was a failure. She'd just meant to imply that she wasn't special. It hadn't occurred to her that maybe it was okay for everyone to be special in their own way. Including her. Maybe everyone didn't have to be the same, or to even want the same things.

She was still deep in thought a few minutes later when Ree stopped again. "This is it," Ree said.

The sun was just starting to come up and the girls were exhausted. They found a bush that would hide them from Charlie and Chuck—and themselves—when they arrived, got as comfortable as they could on some flat rocks, and fell asleep.

Later, the sounds of their brothers talking and laughing first seeped into Emma and Ree's dreams, then woke them completely.

"They're here," Emma whispered to Ree, rubbing her stiff neck and brushing dirt from her face. She peeked over the bush to the strange sight of Charlie, Chuck, Ree, and herself. Except somehow, having gotten used to being around Ree, seeing another Emma and another Ree was not nearly as strange as she thought it might be. "So many Emmas," she said.

Ree laughed. "So many Emmas." She crawled next to Emma and poked her own head over the bush. "That's before we went to see me in the future, right? Will we mess everything up if we stop you and me—that is them—from going to see her?"

Trying to sort it out made Emma's head hurt. "Maybe? But on the other hand, our whole point in being here is to change the choices they make."

"To change the choices the *Charlies* make," Ree said. "Not the Emmas. I woke up earlier and couldn't stop thinking about this. I think we should wait until you and I are gone."

Emma thought this through. "But if we do, the Charlies will come back and you and I might not go see you in the future."

"No," said Ree. "Remember? The reason we went back was because I'd told you I can travel through time, and you said we needed to get back and tell Dr. Waldo. That won't change."

The thought of spending several more hours on the very hard rocks was beyond unappealing, but she could see Ree's point. "Okay, but I need to eat something." She hadn't had time to get her backpack before grabbing Ree when she'd seen Ree about to jump through time. Luckily Ree had hers, and the water-gathering device Dr. Waldo had created had been collecting water all night long. Ree handed Emma a protein bar and filled a bottle with water for each of them, and they hunkered down once again.

They watched as the other versions of themselves repeated their own actions. Emma cringed when she saw herself yelling at Charlie, and wished she could go in and tell herself to stop. Eventually, everyone went into their tents for bed, taking all the artificial light with them, and Emma and Ree were left outside under the moonlight again, munching on the last protein bars. "Not very observant, are they?" Emma whispered after a while. "They didn't look around, didn't look in our direction at all. We'll need to talk with them about that." She put her hands under her cheek and rested.

Finally, they heard noise from the campsite again, and they knew this was the other version of Emma and Ree packing to go. Ignoring how hungry they were, they each drank more water, and waited until they saw that the other Emma and Ree were gone. Then they moved in.

Charlie, as before, was not yet awake, but Chuck was up.

"Back already?" Chuck said. He turned toward where their tent had been, and back to the spot they now stood. "How did you get over there?" He scratched his head and then the tip of his nose.

"We're the future you," said Ree. "That is, we are you, but a few days ahead of you. We traveled back in time because we need you to go home."

Chuck rubbed his eyes and looked at the girls, then back to where their tent had been, then back to the girls.

"Right," he said.

"No, really," said Ree. "We're serious. We're from the future, and this is important."

"Charlie needs to hear all this, too," said Emma, heading to get her brother. "Hang on."

Chuck shrugged his shoulders. "Okie dokie," he said.

A few moments later, Emma emerged from Chuck and Charlie's tent with Charlie in tow. Charlie looked very disheveled and groggy. "What is so important?" he said, grumbling, irritated. "I didn't sleep well. Can't a man have some peace on an uninhabited planet?"

"That's just it," said Emma. "It's not uninhabited."

"What?" said Charlie, starting to wake up. "How do you know?"

Emma took a deep breath and let it out. "Okay. Chuck: Ree and I just left, right?"

Chuck shook his head. "Um, yes?" he said. "But I'd also like to point out that you obviously did not leave because you're standing right here."

"And before we left," Ree said, ignoring her brother, "we told you that I have learned how to travel through time using just my mind, a lot like Emma can travel through space. Right?"

Charlie rolled his eyes. "Of course," he said under his breath. "*Of course* you can travel through time just by thinking about it."

"Listen, Charlie," Emma said. "I know you're upset, and I get it, and we can talk about that later. Because you're the most important person in the world to me and we're going to work it out. But you need to listen to us right now."

"Whatever you say, Chosen One," Charlie sneered.

Emma gave Ree a look that said, "You're in charge here."

Ree nodded. "So, where to begin," she said. Her eyes flitted left and right as she sorted through everything in her mind. "Okay. Well, first thing to know is that we're not the Ree and Emma that just left."

Chuck stared at them for several long moments. "Are you from other parallel Earths, then?" he asked.

"No, no," said Ree. "I mean, we *are* that Ree and Emma, but we're from another timeline. A timeline that's just a few days ahead of you. In our timeline, everything that happened has happened the same as it happened for you, up until now."

Chuck and Charlie exchanged doubtful glances.

"Go on," said Charlie, his eyebrows raised as high as they would go.

"When we left—just now—but in our timeline, we went back to talk to Dr. Waldo about my … my time-travel thing," said Ree. "He wanted me to give a simple demonstration, so I took me and Emma ahead in time, where we met up with a future version of me, many years from now."

"'Future Ree,'" said Emma. Seeing the looks on Chuck and Charlie's faces, she clamped her mouth shut.

"We got to talking to Future Ree," said Ree, "at her house. And suddenly Emma noticed something weird." She paused and looked at Emma.

"The photos on Future Ree's walls," Emma said. "You guys weren't in them. You were missing."

The looks on Chuck and Charlie's faces changed from irritation to confusion.

"Why?" said Charlie, his animosity gone. "Why weren't we in them?"

Emma reached for her brother's hand, suddenly feeling very emotional. "She told us that after you guys came to this planet, you were never seen or heard from again. When we left just now," Emma nodded to where the girls' tent had been, "that's the last time we ever saw you." Tears sprang to her eyes and a lump caught in her throat.

"Future Ree told us that in every timeline, that's the way it was. Emmas and Rees from other timelines came back every time to find you, and every time, they failed," Ree said.

"But we remembered something Dr. Waldo told us," Emma said. "He said that our choices can change our future. He told us about time being like a river. It's complicated, but, basically, every version of us, in every timeline, exists at the same time. So if we think of all the versions of us, Future Ree is farther down the river, and she's molecule C. She's Ree C. We're at our point in the timeline, and we're molecules B. Emma B and Ree B. You guys are behind us in your own timeline, and you're molecules A. You're Chuck A and Charlie A. So we are the same people, but we're sort of not. I don't know exactly how it works, but your Emma and Ree are still back at the Hub with Dr. Waldo in the A timeline, and we're in the B timeline, and Future Ree is in a different timeline."

Charlie let go of Emma's hand. "Time is a river, and there are infinite versions of us all along the timeline? You're B and we're A? Then how does one life move through the river? It doesn't make sense."

"I don't know," Emma said, waving her hands aimlessly. "It's complicated. But the point is, we decided that we weren't going to be like all the other Emmas and Rees that had failed to find you, so we came back to this planet and started searching. And we found you."

"Well!" said Chuck. "Good job! But what's the problem then?"

"The problem," said Ree, "is that by the time we found you, the memory thieves had already stolen part of your memories. Everything from the time each of you first came to Dogwinkle Island. Everything about the lighthouse, and the Hub, and Dr. Waldo, and even about each other, about parallel Earths and parallel selves. The memory thieves stole your memories, and we're having a hard time figuring out how to get them back. So I thought, well, I can travel through time, right, so why not come back and tell you just to go home? Don't wait around, don't go wandering like you did when you were discovered by Corala and Leidar and Akala."

"Corala and Leidar and Akala?" said Charlie.

"Aliens," said Emma, and then she shook her head. "Well, no, we're the aliens. They're from this planet. Corala and Leidar are the ones who took your memories."

"So you guys need to just pack up and go home," said Ree. "I know that's not what you want to hear, but …"

"But we can't lose you," Emma said, eyes locked on Charlie's. "We cannot lose you. You'll find another planet for your travel business. It's a great idea. It is. But not here. We need you to go home."

Even through his irritation, Charlie could feel the sincerity of Emma's plea. He knew she wouldn't ask such a thing if it weren't truly important. Charlie looked at Chuck and shrugged. "Sounds pretty convincing to me," he said. "I mean, it's pretty obvious, we're indispensable. They need us."

"We need you more than you know," said Emma. "I can't lose you."

Chuck stood and gave Ree a hug. "Okay," he said. "We'll go home."

The girls helped Charlie and Chuck pack quickly, then sent them on their way.

"I guess we need to walk back to the colony," said Emma. She looked around at the space where their camp had been; where, in their own timeline, the scorched tents had alerted them to so much trouble. Having Charlie and Chuck just leave to return to the Hub seemed somehow anticlimactic. But it was a relief. Everything was okay again. "Once we're at the colony, you can transport us back to the picnic table where—I mean *when*—we were, in our own timeline."

"Can't we just go home?" said Ree. "I mean, we've fixed it, right? Do we need to go back to that place? I hate it there." She shuddered.

Emma thought a moment. "Yeah, I guess you're right. No need to go back. We'll see them at the Hub." Everything was so confusing, but it seemed to her this solution would work.

"Okay, but first, there's one more thing we need to do," said Ree.

It didn't take them long to walk back to the cliffs that looked out over the ocean. "This should be a good spot," Ree said. "Now if I can just get the timing right." She grabbed for Emma's hand, and concentrated hard on what Chuck had told her.

With a familiar *whoosh*, Ree took them back just a few days. Her timing was impeccable: as they were regaining their composure and recombobulating, the Emergence began.

From the depths of the sea, the wunpada that had begun life as sea creatures started to burst forth into the sky, gaining familiarity and use of their wings as they flew up to the clouds. They spread their glorious, wide, black and gold and turquoise-blue wings, and Emma and Ree gasped with delight.

"They're enormous!" said Emma. "I had no idea they were so big! Do you think …"

"I think they'd be too small to ride on," Ree said, reading Emma's thoughts. "But it would be amazing, wouldn't it?" They watched in awe for many long minutes before Ree spoke again, in hushed tones. "If you could choose between flying or being able to travel through space like you can, which would you pick?"

Emma pondered this a while. "I don't know. That's too hard. It would be amazing to fly. To soar in the sky and feel all my fears and worries falling off behind me in the wind. Not to be weighed down by gravity and life. But on the other hand, all these universes," she said. "Traveling through them … I don't know. It's corny, but I feel like the universes are music, and I'm part of the song. Having experienced that, I don't know if I could give it up." She felt with tremendous certainty that all the atoms and molecules she'd lost by traveling through space had been replaced by something bigger, something unimaginably beautiful. The universes were a part of her now. "What about you?" she asked. "Flying or time travel?"

The Emergence was still ongoing, and Ree's eyes were glued to the scene before them. "Flying, for sure," she said. "Time travel is interesting, but everyone I love is in my own timeline. Right where I want them. Safe," she said. "Flying, though, flying would be amazing."

"Yeah," said Emma. "It would be."

They watched a while longer, and finally the Emergence dwindled down to just a few birds per minute, then fewer than that, then none. "Time to go home," said Ree.

As they stood, movement farther down the cliffs caught Emma's eyes. "Wait," she said. "What's that?"

Ree followed Emma's line of sight until she, too, saw what Emma was seeing. She gasped. "Is that … is that Chuck and Charlie? And Akala?"

Emma's heart filled with dread. "But why are they there? We told them not to stay," she said. "Why are they there?"

"Molecule B," Ree said in horror. "We're looking at molecules B."

"What?" said Emma. "I don't understand."

"We saved molecules A. But the Chuck and Charlie from our own timeline were already past that moment."

"Molecules B," said Emma.

"We need to go back to the colony," said Ree, trembling. "We may have saved Charlies from another timeline, but I'm not so sure about our own."

chapter eighteen

"… Well, maybe, if you can move people through space, maybe you can move memories through space, too?" Charlie was saying. "How different can it be? Try it. Just think really hard about our memories, and see if you can't magically make my memories pop out of Corala or Leidar's head and back to mine."

"And mine, too," Chuck said, smiling at Emma, who was standing by the picnic table. "Then maybe I'll know what you're talking about. You can travel through space?" It was moments before Ree was about to make her dash through time, about to attempt to fix everything by warning Chuck and Charlie about the future.

"Just using the power of her mind," said Charlie, proudly.

Chuck looked at Ree. "Can you do that, too?" he asked.

Ree shifted on the bench. "No," she said, but she caught Emma's eyes and gave her a long look. Ree stood and looked around, and then closed her eyes.

Charlie felt a tremendous *whoosh*. Not a gust of air, really, but a gust of … what? Energy? *A disturbance in the force*, he thought. He put out a hand to the table to try to steady himself. The sun was glaring in his eyes, disorienting. Were there two suns? No, just the one. The air was wavering. Were they going to have another storm? They hadn't learned enough about the Electrics, he realized. They weren't prepared. They needed to be better prepared. He looked over at Emma. Wait, where was Emma? She had just been standing there, but now she was gone, and so was Ree .... He closed his eyes, and felt another swirl of energy. *Definitely a storm on the way*, he thought. When he opened his eyes, Emma was there again, standing right next to Ree. *Maybe I need to eat something*, he thought.

"What was that?" Chuck said, looking around as though some unseen force had whacked him upside the head.

"Maybe an electric storm," Charlie said. He saw Emma and Ree exchange a long meaningful glance, and he remembered they'd just been talking about Emma's ability to travel through space using the power of her mind. Had she ...? He waited until his sister caught his eye, and raised his eyebrows. Emma responded with the tiniest shake of her head, which Charlie understood to mean, *we'll talk about this later*. He noticed that Chuck was having a similar exchange with Ree.

"Okay, then," said Charlie. "Back to the matter at hand." He shook his head fiercely to try to get rid of the muddled feeling in his brain. "How are we going to find Corala and Leidar?"

A sudden flurry of noises came from the bushes near the group.

Charlie felt a hard thump on the back of his head.

And then everything went black.

As Charlie opened his eyes, the room came into focus slowly at first; the light was diffused and objects were blurred at the edges. When he sat up, a sharp throbbing pain at the back of his head made him instantly regret the move. He lay down again, settling his head as gently as he could on the thin gray pillow on the bed.

He stared at the ceiling, trying to be as still as possible to let the pain subside. The ceiling was high and unfamiliar; its surface was rough, with flaking white paint. Charlie moved his eyes left and right, trying to see as much as he could without moving his head. Sun streaming through a tall curtainless window let him know it was daytime. Dust danced silently in the sunbeam, mesmerizing Charlie for a moment until he noticed the window was not only tall, but also it had thick metal bars running its full height. He sat up again quickly, feeling suddenly panicked. "Where am I?" he cried out. He noticed there were three other people in the room, each lying on a narrow bed just like his.

His words awakened the others. With relief, Charlie saw that Emma was there with him … wherever "there" was. If Emma was near, she could always get them out of anything. Plus, she probably knew why they were there in the first place.

But then, one of the two others sat up, and Charlie felt a depth of fear he'd never experienced before. This person looked exactly like him.

And the fourth person was a replica of Emma.

"Emma?" Charlie said weakly, looking from one Emma to the other. "Is … is one of you Emma?"

"Yes," said one Emma, her eyes flitting from one Charlie to the other, to the duplicate Emma, and back.

"I'm Emma," said the other Emma, a little defiantly. Watching her clone, she put her hands to her own face as if to check that it was, in fact, her face. She then looked around the room. "Is there a mirror?" she asked.

But there was not. Aside from the beds and the teens themselves, the room was empty.

Charlie stood and went to the door, fearing what he would find. Tentatively, he tried to turn the doorknob. His heart sank. "Locked," he said, then he tried again. "Still locked." He banged his head lightly against the faded wood of the door.

"Charlie," one of the Emmas said, but then she paused, looking from the Charlie at the door to the Charlie still sitting on one of the other beds. "Which of you is Charlie?" she said. Her dark auburn hair was sticking out at all angles and her eyes begged for someone to explain what was happening.

Charlie sat back down on his bed, keeping his eyes on the others at all times. He looked from one Emma to the other, his mind churning. "Emma," he said. "What's your middle name?"

The first Emma that had spoken, spoke again. "Ree," she said.

"That's my middle name, too," said the other Emma. She squinted her eyes at the first Emma.

"And what's my middle name?" asked Charlie.

"Probably Rainier," said the other Charlie. "Same as mine."

Charlie rubbed his eyes and was cognizant again of the pain at the back of his head. "Emma," he said. "Where were we born?"

"Minnesota," said the first Emma. Charlie nodded.

The second Emma looked from Charlie to the other Emma, her eyes wide. "Minnesota?" she said. "Where is that? That's not right."

The other Charlie looked at her. "Where were you born?" he asked.

"Minsota," the second Emma said. "South of Canada. East of Dakota. North of Iowa. West of Wisconsin."

The second Charlie nodded. "Yes, that's right. That's where I'm from."

The first Emma looked at them. "Minsota isn't a state," she said.

"Of course it is," said the second Emma. "Where did you say you're from?"

"Minnesota," said Charlie. "South of Canada. East of North and South Dakota. North of Iowa. West of Wisconsin."

The teens stared at each other. Something was off, but none could figure out what.

Charlie stood again and walked to the window to look out. "I don't remember how I got here," he said. "Do any of you?" He shook his foot, feeling a rock in his shoe by his big toe.

"Not at all," said the first Emma. "We were … well, we were heading to Dogwinkle Island. That's the last I can remember."

The second Emma stared at her. "What are you playing at? *We* were going to Dogwinkle Island, too." She stood and joined Charlie at the window. "Are we on the island?" she said.

Outside, the day was bright and the air had a shimmery quality to it. Whatever building they were in, they were quite high up, and they seemed to be on a hill. Craning his neck, Charlie could see the building was made of stone, though the bars were metal and seemed to hum when he touched them. A current coursing through them sent a soft shock up his arms, and he let go quickly.

"Wherever we are," Charlie said, shaking his arms, "I think we need to get out."

The other Charlie walked to the door and tried the lock. He, too, was unsuccessful.

"I tried that already," said the first Charlie.

"I know, but I don't know what else to do," said the second Charlie. He kicked at the door, hard. "Ow," he said.

The first Charlie walked over and tried kicking the door as well, winding his leg up first for as hard of a kick as he could possibly give. His foot met the door with a resounding thud. "OUCH!" he cried.

"Yeah, I tried that already," said the second Charlie.

"No, there's a giant rock in my shoe," said the first Charlie. He sat on the edge of his bed and pulled it off. Out tumbled a small sphere. Charlie looked inside the shoe again, and pulled out a crumpled note. "What the heck?" he said under his breath.

The first Emma caught the sphere as it rolled away, and came to sit next to Charlie. After examining the sphere, she handed it back to him. "What's it say?" she asked, nodding at the note.

"It's in my handwriting," Charlie said, looking confused. He started to read aloud.

> *Dear Charlie,*
>
> *You wrote this message to yourself. If you're reading this and you don't remember writing it, then your brain has probably been wiped (again). I can't possibly explain everything in a way that will make sense so you'll just have to find someone who can. That's probably Dr. Waldo.*

Charlie looked up. "Who's Dr. Waldo?" he asked.

Emma shrugged.

"Beats me," said the second Charlie. "Keep reading."

> *... That's probably Dr. Waldo. Hopefully, wherever you are, you're with Emma and Chuck and Ree. Chuck and Ree are another Charlie and Emma, but they're from a parallel Earth in a different universe. At least, that's what Emma and Ree told us, because you and Chuck have been through this already and don't remember that part. They're legit. Don't worry about them. They're safe.*

"A parallel Earth?" said the first Emma, looking at the duplicates of herself and her brother.

"A different *universe*?" said Chuck.

Charlie looked at the first Emma. "You must be my Emma," he

said. “If we’re both from Minnesota.” He turned to the others. “We must have decided to call you Chuck and Ree. You must be from the other Earth.”

Chuck raised an eyebrow. “You serious, bro?” he said. “You believe in a parallel Earth?” He moved closer to Ree.

Charlie shrugged. “I mean, none of this makes sense, but I left myself a note, and that’s all I have to go on. I trust myself.”

“It sounds like we need to find this Dr. Waldo,” said Emma, poking Charlie in the side. “Keep reading.” She craned her neck to try to read the note over his shoulder.

Charlie continued.

You wouldn’t believe me, even if I did explain everything, except for the fact that there’s another Charlie and Emma, because they’re hopefully right there with you, but even that might freak you out. Wherever you are, the best thing to do right now is to get back to Dr. Waldo.

Read this part carefully. You—all four of you, don’t leave Chuck and Ree behind—need to link arms and hold hands and DO NOT LET GO. Then, take the sphere I put in our shoe, and swipe that blue part. It’s going to transport you through space to a place where all the universes merge. We call it the Hub. It’ll feel weird so be prepared. Again, this is what Emma tells me. I can’t wait to get my memory back but at least I have more memory than you apparently have now. So, point being, get going, hang on to each other, swipe the blue part, and then when you get to the Hub, ask for Dr. Waldo. You’ll probably need people

on this planet, too, when you come back to get your brain. You can trust Nolor and Daya, and their son Podor, and Akala. Other than that, watch out. If there's a storm, go inside. Good luck, dude. Be safe.
Charlie

Charlie turned the paper over, but there was nothing written on the other side.

"On this planet?" said Ree. "This *planet*? Are we not on Earth?"

"Not even *your* Earth?" said Charlie. "I mean, if there are two Earths, why are we somewhere else? And why can't any of us remember? If I really did write this, I sure wish I'd put in some more details." He walked to the window and looked out over a landscape that seemed unfamiliar but not impossible. "I guess the thing to do is try it. What harm can there be in linking arms and … swiping a ball?" He wrinkled his nose. When he said it out loud, it seemed ridiculous. He looked up at the ceiling. Were there cameras? Was this all a prank? But if it was, then where did the prankster find people who looked exactly like him and Emma? And where were *their* memories?

A noise outside the door drew everyone's attention. "What's that?" Emma whispered.

"Sounds like footsteps on stairs, maybe?" said Ree, her ear turned toward the door. They all held their breaths to hear better. Sure enough, the slow, muffled sound of someone climbing up wooden stairs was approaching.

"Whatever this ball thing is, we need to try it now," Charlie said. "Everyone come over here." The others gathered around him, holding hands and linking elbows and hanging on to each other as tightly as they could, none of them knowing what was about to happen.

Satisfied that everyone was holding on as tight as they could, Charlie put his finger on the blue spot on the sphere, squeezed his eyes tight, and swiped.

The air crackled and sparked, as though all the excess electricity of the planet was suddenly focused inside that small room. Once again, Charlie felt a shock coursing through his body, but he did not let go of Emma or the others. Then, suddenly, he felt as if he were falling and floating at the same time, like he'd become completely untethered from time and place. He could no longer discern where his body began and ended; everything outside of him became a part of him and he became a part of everything outside of him. For the briefest moment, he even was a part of all the thoughts of the universe, all the memories of all time; he even had the tiniest glimpse into his own forgotten memories, for just a split second. Then, the memories were gone and his consciousness dispersed to become part of all consciousness to where he could no longer differentiate self from other, and he was no longer Charlie but finally he was one with the universes. And then, just as quickly, the process reversed, his body began to take form again, his thoughts collected back around his own experiences, his world narrowed and grew small, and once again, he was just Charlie.

But where was he? He looked around the vast space; they were definitely no longer in a tiny cold room at the top of a tower on a hill. No, this space felt almost infinite, somehow; unconfined and uncontainable.

"What the heck," said Emma, and Charlie realized he should check to see if the others were all there with him. There was Emma, and the other Emma, and the other Charlie. Wherever they were, they'd all gotten there together.

"You're back!" a voice cried out, and a young girl with translucent skin and pale blonde hair came running toward them. "We were so worried! Did you get your memories back?" She started giving hugs all around.

Emma returned the hug, but with an air of unfamiliarity that the girl caught right away. "Emma!" the girl said. "You know who I am, don't you?" She looks around at the others. "You all have all your memories, right? Right?" Her eyebrows furrowed in concern.

"Well," said Charlie, "if you know us, then you're ahead of us. I'm Charlie, and that's Emma, and this is another Charlie and another Emma, and based on a note I seem to have left for myself in my shoe it sounds like we call them Chuck and Ree. But I'm sorry, we have no idea where we were, or where we are now … or who you are."

The girl's face fell. "Oh no," she said. "Oh nooooo. We need to get Dr. Waldo." She started to run off, then turned back around. "I'm Eve," she said. She held up a hand. "Stay there. Don't move." She turned again, and raced to find Dr. Waldo.

"At least that part is right," said Emma, trying to sound hopeful. "We were supposed to find a Dr. Waldo, and it sounds like we're in the right place."

"But what *is* this place?" asked Chuck, looking around in awe. The space was informally divided into several sections. Where they had landed seemed to be a lounge of some sort, with overstuffed chairs and comfortable couches; just the kind of place they might like to gather with friends. But off in the direction the girl had run, several people were milling about in white lab coats, talking amongst themselves, gazing at computer screens, working at lab stations or desks. Far in the distance they could see a building that seemed to flicker in and out of existence, and beyond that were some cabins. Whether they were inside or outside wasn't clear.

"Is that an elephant over there?" Emma said, pointing toward the cabins. "*Two* elephants, I think!" she corrected herself.

Charlie followed her line of sight. "I think so," he said, but then added skeptically, "but they look like they're two dimensional? That can't be right." He frowned. It *couldn't* be right. But somehow, it seemed it was. When one of the pair turned toward them, it was clear: those elephants definitely did not have depth.

A few short minutes later, the girl came running back to them with an older man racing behind her. On his face was a look of glee tempered only slightly by a look of concern. "Children! Children!" he said breathlessly as he caught up to the girl. "You have returned! But Eve says you don't have your memories?" He looked from one to the other for answers.

"You're Dr. Waldo?" said Emma. "It sounds like you know us. We don't remember you," she said, indicating herself and the others. "Charlie found a note in his shoe that said to use that black ball thing to come here and ask for you. Can you tell us … anything? Last we remember, we were coming to an island for vacation."

And so they all sat on the comfortable couches and chairs, and Dr. Waldo and Eve patiently explained everything to Emma, Charlie, Ree, and Chuck, from the beginning, from the time when Emma and Charlie first met Eve, and then how they all started traveling the universes via the elevator inside the lighthouse, how they discovered new worlds and saved the multiverse, how they found Eve's mom, and then finally, how they'd headed off to that uncharted planet where Charlie and Chuck had planned to start their travel business, but where everything had gone so very wrong. At one point, Ben saw the gathering at the lounge and joined them, casting quick, concerned glances at Emma and Ree every now and then.

When Dr. Waldo and Eve were done, the twins from both Earths sat, stunned, absorbing all that they'd just heard.

Finally, Chuck turned to Charlie. "I still think it's a good idea," he said.

"The travel business?" said Charlie. "I agree. Even without our memories, we are stunningly entrepreneurial."

"I'm thinking we should call it 'Unparalleled Travel,'" said Chuck. "Get it? Parallel universes? Unparalleled Travel?" He nodded slowly at his own brilliance.

"I love it," said Charlie. "It's perfect." He leaned over and high-fived Chuck.

Eve rolled her eyes and let out a laugh that sounded like crystals chiming in the wind. "You may have lost your memories, but at least you haven't lost your personalities!" she said.

Charlie smiled at the girl. In their explanation, Dr. Waldo and Eve mentioned that they were from a planet called Lero, but they hadn't gone into much detail. The idea of visiting other planets was incredible—even though, apparently, they'd just been on one. But there wasn't time to worry much about that just yet. "It sounds like the memories we're missing are some pretty good ones," he said. "I don't know how we're going to get them back, but I, for one, would really like mine back." The others whose minds had been taken nodded in agreement.

"Dr. Waldo," said Ree, "this Hub here, do you have scientists who might be able to just restore our memories? I mean, if everything is possible here, then it seems like by default, that's possible, right?"

Dr. Waldo's eyes opened wide. "Well, now, yes, that's a very interesting question, yes, interesting indeed, hmmm hmmm hmm," he said. "I think you are probably right. But the question is, *how* do we do that?"

"You said you have run tests on us," said Emma. "At least on Ree and me. Maybe you have … I don't know, like, a backup of our memories? Like a computer backup?"

The elderly doctor tilted his head, his face an expression of doubt and intrigue. "Hmm, well, maybe, we certainly, yes, maybe …" He turned to Ben. "Ben, why don't you look into that?"

Ben looked like a deer caught in headlights. "Look into … restoring their memories from a backup? How would I do that?" he asked. "I'm not quite sure where I'd … I mean, with a computer, I'd have to plug in the backup drive. I don't know how I'd plug their memories into their brains?" He pressed his lips together, thinking hard, but apparently coming up with nothing. "I'll keep thinking," he said, shaking his head.

"I am worried that if we wait too long, the memories will be gone," said Charlie. "I want to go back to the planet and get our memories." He looked at Chuck, Emma, and Ree, eyebrows raised in a question. "What do you all think? Do you want to go back?"

Emma and Ree hesitated, but Chuck immediately answered. "Yes," he said. "If that's where our memories are, then that's where we need to go."

Charlie looked back at Emma and Ree. "What about you guys. All for one and one for all?"

Emma looked at Ree, and then back at her brother. "We're in," she said.

chapter nineteen

"Are you sure this is a good idea?" Ben said, as he crammed extra pigeons into all the pockets of the new travel backpacks he'd gathered for the four teens, all of them calibrated to bring them back to the Hub. "Here," he said, his hands full of more of the small spheres, "put them in your shoes, like Charlie did." He shook his head. "Charlie, that was maybe the smartest thing you've ever done. I can't imagine what would have happened if you hadn't done that and written yourself a note."

Charlie shrugged off the compliment. "No idea what I was thinking, since I can't remember anything, but probably it was Emma's idea." He winked at his sister. She punched him affectionately on the shoulder.

"I really think we should come with you," Eve said, her anxiety emanating from her like heat.

"No, you need to stay here in case something goes wrong … again," said Ree.

"But if we came with you," Ben protested, "maybe we could prevent something from going wrong again." His dark eyebrows were in a permanent frown of concern.

Eve nodded as she joined him in checking the travel backpacks. "Food, water generator, pigeons … the problem is, we want you to have a way to get back, but I worry about what happens if all this gets into the wrong hands," she said, as she put another iPert into the bag.

"But the wrong hands wouldn't know how to use that iPert anyway," said Chuck. Dr. Waldo had had to explain it all to them again—the pigeons, the iPert, the water generator, and more. Dr. Waldo had reluctantly declined to give them anything too powerful, including the Dark MATTER spheres, for the very reason Eve was citing. They had no idea, for example, who had the iPerts they had lost.

"For what it's worth," said Charlie, "may I point out, there's no reason to assume the worst in other people. I think we need to have a talk when we get back. It sounds like we've been operating on the assumption that any time we meet new people, a new species, we should just assume they're dangerous."

"That's how survival works," said Emma. "Assume there's danger until we know we're safe."

"Yeah, but that just seems like a self-fulfilling prophecy," Charlie argued. "If we think they're dangerous, our brains will be primed to see the dangerous stuff. We might miss the welcoming stuff and maybe miss the bigger picture."

"I agree," said Ree. "And besides, if it's aliens we're dealing with, I mean, we won't know how they communicate. We can't go in assuming they think like humans. The things they do might seem weird to us, but that doesn't mean they're being hostile. What's more, Charlie's note listed four aliens who we decided we could trust. That's a start."

Emma thought on this for a bit. Charlie had always been the more open of the two of them, the more welcoming and friendly. At times, she'd seen it as a flaw. He trusted people too soon, she thought, and the proof of it was in the fact that he'd had his memory wiped not once now, but twice. On the other hand, Ree had a point. The people they were about to face saw things differently. She couldn't know their intentions ahead of time, and maybe it was wrong to assume. Maybe the ones who had stolen their memories had some redeeming qualities. "Okay," she said. "Okay, fine. I'll go in with an open mind."

"Literally, haha!" Chuck said, elbowing Charlie and laughing at his own joke. Charlie snort-laughed heartily, and the two high-fived.

"Get it?" said Charlie to Emma. "*Literally* an open mind, because they took your brain? Get it?" He nodded vigorously, tremendously amused with himself and his parallel Earth twin.

Emma rolled her eyes. "Yes, Charlie. I got it. Thank you." *My brother,* she thought. *Can't live with him, can't live without him.*

Ree zipped up the last pocket on her new backpack. "Are we ready, then?" she said. "No time like the present." She smiled a little smile to herself. One of the things Dr. Waldo had told them, that none of them had remembered, was that Ree had learned how to travel through time. Emma knew without asking that Ree was eager to give that skill a try. She knew because once she learned she could travel through the universes using her mind, she'd been thinking about almost nothing else. She wanted her brains back so she would know again how to do that, because could there be anything more amazing than traveling through time and space like that? She caught Ree's eye, and exchanged a knowing wink.

"What, exactly, is the plan?" said Emma, slipping a pigeon into her shoe and checking her bracelet to make sure it was secure. "Do we have a plan?"

Charlie shrugged his backpack onto his back. "We have a plan," he said. "We're going to talk to the people who took our minds. But first we're going to find Nolor, Daya, Podor, and Akala. The people I mentioned in my note to myself. I hope I was correct that we can trust them." He looked at Ben. "You think you have the right coordinates on them, based on what we told you before we forgot everything?"

Ben nodded, his brow still wrinkled. "Yeah, I think so. Are you sure I shouldn't …"

"We're sure," Ree said, her eyes kind but firm.

"Okay, then," he said. He held out a Dark MATTER sphere that he'd calibrated to take the group to Nolor and Daya's home. "Whenever you guys are ready. Be alert, okay? Don't turn your backs to anyone, ever. Sleep in shifts. They've figured out by now that you're from another planet. Your brains are probably worth a lot to them. Just … just be careful." He handed the sphere to Emma. "Come back safe."

"And bring your memories with you!" Eve said. "You can do it. I know you can. You guys are resourceful and you're good problem solvers. You'll find a way. I believe in you." She pumped her hands in the air in support of her team.

A look crossed Charlie's face. "Wait," he said. "I just remembered … I think I just remembered meeting you, Eve." He blushed. "Were there hay bales? Why am I remembering hay bales?"

Eve laughed. "There were hay bales! All those memories, they're still in there. One way or another, we'll get you back." She looked at Ben, who nodded. They would not give up on their friends.

"But first, we'll give this a try," Emma said. "Everyone, gather," she continued, and the foursome huddled together, linking elbows and holding hands. "We'll be back soon!" Emma said, and she swiped the sphere.

"Whoa," said Chuck, blinking rapidly to readjust his eyes. "That is trippy. And we do that all the time?" Swaying a bit, he put his hands on his knees to steady himself.

"Apparently so," said Charlie. He looked up at the house before them. "So this is Nolor and Daya's house?"

"Hopefully," Emma said. She squinted at the sun, and wiggled her toe against the pigeon she'd put in her left shoe. Another pigeon was pushing against the toes in her right shoe, and she thought she could feel the edges of the notes Ben had written and placed in everyone's shoes as well. They had taken every precaution this time. She hoped it would be enough.

The front door to the house opened, and two creatures walked out. Emma almost squealed. Ben had tried to describe to them what these beings looked like, but all he had to go on was what she and Ree had told him before they last their memories, which wasn't much. None of them had any memories of any other aliens, except, of course, for Eve, Dr. Waldo, and the other Leroians working in the Hub. And as far as aliens went, Leroians were pretty similar to humans. But these creatures … were they actually intelligent? Emma wondered. They looked so very much like a combination of a meerkat head and a human body. Emma gulped and smiled.

"Hello," she said hesitantly.

"Emma! And Ree, Charlie, Chuck! You're all back!" One of the creatures rushed forward to give Emma a hug.

"I'm so sorry," Emma said, gently returning the hug, "but I have to tell you. We've all had our memories taken from us. We don't remember you. We just know that Charlie left a note in his shoe saying Nolor, Daya, Podor, and Akala are safe. Are you … well, are you one of them?" She blushed. Admitting that this person before her held no meaning to her was embarrassing.

The being held her at arm's length and looked deep in her eyes. "Oh dear. Not you, too?" After a deep sigh, the creature spoke again. "Well, then, we'll start at the beginning once more. I am Daya. This is my husband, Nolor," Daya said, indicating the short being beside her. "Yes, we have met before. You stayed with us." She looked at Nolor. "I was afraid, Nolor. I was afraid this would happen." Her eyes filled with tears.

Despite not knowing this being, Emma's heart surged with empathy. "It's okay, we're fine, don't worry," she said, softly rubbing Daya's shoulder. "It's okay."

Nolor looked up at the sun and sniffed the air. "There's an Electric coming soon," he said. "You'd better come inside."

Daya quickly had the group settled in on the various couches and chairs in the living room, with blankets on their laps, not because she thought they were cold but because she thought they seemed unsettled. "I'll get the wae," she said, and then trotted off to the kitchen, leaving the teens wondering what "wae" was but knowing they'd soon find out. Already, the air had shifted.

"Your hair is floating," Ree said to Emma. "Like, it's lifting away from your head," she giggled.

"Yours is too," said Emma, looking around for a mirror but realizing Ree was just as good as a mirror.

"That's the Electrics for you," said Nolor. "Truly hair-raising." He sniffed the air again. "This could be a big one. I'm glad we got you inside before it started." He glanced at the windows to make sure they were all closed. "Might even get some rain with this one," he said.

Daya returned with a tray of wae and biscuits, then headed quickly back to the kitchen, returning again shortly with another tray of mugs. "There's plenty more," she said. "Take all you like." She started pouring the hot liquid into the mugs, handing them around to the people in the room. Finally she poured the last mug for herself and settled into a seat next to her husband. Nolor put his arm around his wife and gave her a light squeeze.

"Well, then," he said. "So you have all had your memories taken?

Not just Chuck and Charlie this time?"

"Yeah," said Charlie. "We're the lucky ones who got it done twice, but we don't remember it," he said.

Nolor was quiet for a moment, looking at his wife. "You won't remember our story, then," he said softly.

The air in the room shifted again. Emma wondered if it was the Electric that was coming, or the way Nolor looked when he spoke his words.

"No," she said gently. "We're sorry. Would you tell us again?"

Daya looked down at the mug in her hands, then closed her eyes. Nolor squeezed her arm again, this time holding her longer. "We won't go into all the details. But our daughter died from having all her memories taken." He looked out the window, seeing far past whatever was outside.

"Oh, I'm so sorry," said Ree. She looked at Emma, who understood the meaning behind the intense gaze: *died*? From having memories taken?

"You were going to go back and get your memories, and we should have stopped you," said Nolor. It was clear from the way he was shaking his head that he blamed himself. "We should have stopped you," he repeated.

"Nolor," Emma said. "I don't remember what happened when we were here last, but I can assure you, I know how stubborn we all can be." She stopped for a moment and thought, *I don't actually know how stubborn Ree and Chuck can be. But I can guess.* "It's not your fault."

"I didn't think they'd go back for you a second time," Nolor went on, shaking his head sadly. "Didn't occur to me for a minute. You're young. They can't possibly make any money from your memories. No offense. But it's such a waste. Such a waste." Next to him, Daya started to sob.

Thick clouds had darkened the sky, but a sudden flash of lightning filled the room with light, followed moments later by a deafening boom. Emma thought she could feel residual crackling within her ears. She wished Ben could have come with them. Not that she wanted to endanger his life, as well, but she knew how much he would have enjoyed the spectacle of the storm. As she had the thought, she realized: *that was a memory*. The memories that had been taken from her pre-dated the day when she met Ben. How would she know Ben would love being there, witnessing the storm, meeting the people? Eve and Charlie were right. The memories were all still within them. They just had to figure out how to get them back.

Charlie raised his chin, which Emma knew was a sign he'd decided something. Before she could stop him, he spoke. "I think we should tell you something," he said.

Emma flashed him a warning look, but he willfully avoided her gaze.

"What?" said Nolor, now curious. Daya, too, looked up from her mug.

"We're not from here," Charlie said.

Nolor smiled and waved his hand. "Oh, we figured that out. You don't need to worry. We are not like the Gleymara. We are kind to strangers." He reached out for another biscuit and took a bite, wiping crumbs off his shirt with his other hand.

"No," Charlie said. "I mean, we're from another planet."

"Charlie!" Emma said in a loud whisper, as if by whispering she could take back her brother's words.

Nolor looked up, his eyes a mix of amusement and puzzlement. "You're from another planct?" He looked to the sky just as another flash of light filled the room. "Another planet around our sun? But that is impossible. Scientists know there is no other life on the other planets." He shook his head. "And further, I don't understand why you are saying this? Is this helpful?" His face fell into a look of disappointment.

"No," Charlie objected. "I'm serious. We're not from here. We're from a planet called Earth. I'm telling you because … I guess because I want to be honest with you, because we need your help. And if you're going to help us get our brains back in order, you might need to know that our brains are different from yours."

Oh, thought Emma. *Of course.*

"You're from a planet called Earth? Which planet is that?" Nolor asked. Daya gazed out skeptically from under her eyelids.

"It's in another solar system," Charlie said. "I don't know how far from here. Another universe. It's …" he paused. "It's complicated to begin with. How we got here, how it all works, all of that is in the memories we lost. They took all our memories from the time we learned how to travel through space."

"Space and time," Ree said quietly.

Nolor sighed heavily and leaned forward, elbows on his knees, cupping his forehead in his hands. "Another universe," he said. He turned to look at his wife. They looked at each other for a very long time.

"The bracelets," Emma said. She remembered that Ben had told them the bracelets allowed them to breathe, and she thought for a moment whether it would be smart to take it off. "I can only take this off for a second. I'm not sure we can breathe without these." As the words slipped from her mouth, she realized what dangerous information that was. If someone stole her bracelet on a planet where she could not otherwise breathe, she was as good as dead. But they had trusted these people before. She decided to trust them again now. "When I take this off, you'll see what I actually look like. Are you … are you ready?"

Nolor shrugged, his body language indicating that he didn't really believe her, but that she should go ahead.

Emma inhaled and exhaled deeply a few times, then took in a deep breath and held it. With a bit of tugging—they'd secured the bracelets extra tight to avoid their slipping off accidentally—she took the bracelet off and set it on the table.

Daya gasped. Was that just the tiniest bit of curiosity and delight that Emma saw in Daya's eyes, though? Emma couldn't be sure, and when she looked again, whatever Emma had seen was gone. Daya covered her mouth with her hand.

Nolor dropped his jaw. His eyes showed no curiosity at all; only terror.

Emma felt herself about to explode from not breathing so she quickly put the bracelet back on and let out a long exhale.

Nolor stood. "What is this?" he said, his voice louder than they'd heard before. "Who are you?" He stood, moving himself between the teens and his wife. "What *are* you?" he asked.

"We're human," said Emma, rubbing the bracelet. "We don't mean you any harm. I swear. We're not here to hurt anyone."

"You know us, Nolor," said Ree. "You met us before. We can't remember it, but you can. Did we seem dangerous to you when we were here before?"

"Bogs in the clothes of fells," said Nolor, waving his hand dismissively.

Emma frowned at the unfamiliar words. Charlie leaned over to her. "Probably something like 'wolves in sheep's clothing,'" he whispered, then shrugged.

"I know this is … well, distressing," said Emma, trying to figure out how to smooth everything over. "We can't remember anymore what it was like when we first met people from another planet, because those memories are gone. But I can just imagine it would be completely shocking. It was shocking enough when we went to the Hub and Dr. Waldo told us where we were."

"The Hub?" said Nolor. He was still standing protectively in front of Daya, but he now sat down, his body still shielding her from any possible danger.

Emma sighed. "Oh, it's all so complicated. And we barely know any of it ourselves. All those memories, from when we first started … traveling through space," she glanced at Nolor and Daya, hoping the words wouldn't cause them too much alarm, but their faces did not change. "All those memories are gone now. Taken by people on your planet." *If they're going to be alarmed at our being aliens*, she thought, *they should remember that all of this was the fault of their people. Not ours.*

But her words did not have the placating effect she thought they would. Instead, she seemed to have agitated Nolor further. "We did not tell you to come here," he said. "We did not ask you to come here. If, in fact, you are telling the truth at all." He reached for Daya's hand. A flash of lightning lit up the room again, followed almost instantly by a roar of thunder that shook the very foundation of the home. Nolor turned to his wife and gave her a meaningful look.

"We can't turn them out," Daya said to his unspoken question. "Not in this storm," she said.

Nolor looked out the window and watched as a spider's web of lightning wove its way across the sky, this one rumbling and threatening from farther away. He closed his eyes, and seemed to be having a conversation with himself in his head. After a while, he opened his eyes. "Will you all please go to the kitchen," he said evenly, "so Daya and I may talk in private."

Charlie scratched his head, then stood without saying anything and headed toward the kitchen. The others followed. Nolor stood and shut the door behind them.

"So," said Chuck, taking a seat at the table and tucking his feet behind the legs of the chair. "That didn't go as well as hoped."

Ree sat next to him. "No, but at least they didn't kick us out completely. That's a bad storm out there." As if in answer, another bolt of lightning struck, again quite close. The thunder reverberated through the walls, and Ree shuddered in response.

Emma pulled her iPert out of her pocket and studied it. How much had she once known about how to use it? There hadn't been time for Ben to brief them on the device beyond its basic uses: how to call him and Dr. Waldo and Eve in the Hub; how to bring up information on the planet they were on, or at least, however much data the device was able to gather. She tapped the screen, hoping to gain some insights on the planet's weather and other potential natural disasters. The last thing they needed now would be a hurricane or an earthquake. All the iPert told her, however, was "High probability of regular and irregular electric storms. Positive-charge lightning." *Thanks*, she thought, and she returned the iPert to her pocket.

Muted sounds of Nolor and Daya talking filtered through the door. At times, the discussion was clearly an argument, with Nolor's voice getting louder, and quieter pauses when Daya must have been trying to reason with him. At other times, the conversation was just a low hum, mumbles that no one could decipher. Charlie tried putting his ear to the door to hear better, but he could only make out an occasional word or phrase.

"What are they saying?" Emma asked. She was thirsty, and wondered if it would be rude to get something to drink in a home where she wasn't sure she was even welcome. She then remembered the water-generating device, and pulled it out of the backpack she'd brought with her into the kitchen. Following the quick instructions Ben had given them before they left, she set it up on the floor and left it to collect water from the air.

"Can't really tell," Charlie whispered, concentrating. "Something about someone else whose memories were stolen. Must be their daughter. But a lot of it doesn't make sense to me." He shrugged, and went to sit at the table. "Make some for me, too," he said to Emma, seeing the water-generating contraption on the floor.

After a while, the raging storm subsided, the lightning strikes hitting farther and farther away until they had stopped completely. Nolor and Daya were still talking, but the bursts of anger seemed fewer and further between.

"Think they'll kick us out now?" Ree said, noting the calm skies.

A crackling noise outside caught their attention: the sound of tires on the ground. Emma looked out the window and saw another being coming toward the kitchen door. Moments later, the door opened, and a being walked in.

"You guys are back!" the person said with a wide smile, which waned when the smile wasn't returned in quite the same fashion.

"So you've met us?" Charlie said, standing and putting his hand out for a handshake. "We don't remember anything. Seems we've had our memories taken … again. I'm Charlie."

The being reached out and clasped Charlie's hand. "We have met. I am Podor, Nolor and Daya's son. They've taken your memories again?" he said, his smile gone. He then heard another burst of volume from the other side of the door. "Why are you in the kitchen with the door closed?" he asked.

"It's a long story," said Charlie. "Maybe you should go talk to them."

Podor studied Charlie's face for several seconds, and then turned to look at the others. Then he silently opened the door to the living room, and went on through, closing the door behind him.

chapter twenty

After what seemed like ages, the door opened. Podor poked his head into the kitchen. "Come on back," he said, standing aside to let them pass.

Emma tried to read the look on his face. Curiosity, she thought; definitely some curiosity there. Maybe even guarded excitement. Certainly not the anger and hostility she'd felt from Nolor and Daya. A sign of hope, she thought. Or hoped.

Nolor and Daya were sitting side-by-side on the couch, watching the teens carefully as they re-entered the room. Everyone sat again and the room was silent, but the air was bursting with unasked questions. Finally, Podor spoke. He turned to Emma. "Can you show me …?" he said, nodding toward the bracelet on her arm.

Emma's heart leaped into her throat, though she couldn't say why. She felt as though the safety and maybe future of her group of friends somehow rested on this moment. *That's ridiculous,* she told herself. *Just show him*. She took a deep breath, held it, and removed the bracelet long enough for Podor to see her in her human form. She then put the bracelet back on and exhaled slowly, watching him closely the whole time. First, he gasped, but his eyes lit up with delight. *Maybe it's a generational thing*, she thought. *Maybe younger people can handle this sort of thing better than older people*. Then she remembered Daya's reaction, the curiosity she was sure she'd seen there. *Don't make assumptions*, she told herself.

"That … is astonishing," said Podor. He stood and walked to Emma, staring at the bracelet the whole time. Kneeling down in front of her, he held his hand over the bracelet, clearly wanting to touch it. "May I …?"

Emma held out her arm to him, and Podor ran his fingers gently over the bracelet, caressing the individual stones. Emma turned her wrist so he could get a better view of the other side. Podor's eyes were wide with wonder. Finally, he returned to his seat. "Amazing," he said. "Amazing."

The whole time, Nolor sat on the couch with his arms crossed. Daya sat beside him with legs crossed, but a more amenable look on her face. "You understand our concerns," was all she said now.

Emma nodded, eager to make amends with these people they needed, but who also she thought had become their friends; at least, they had been when they had their memories. "We absolutely do. We would be scared, too."

Daya nodded, looking kindly into Emma's eyes. "Our Podor is a scientist, you know," she said. She nodded at her son, indicating that he should continue the conversation from there. Nolor frowned, but nodded in a way that expressed great regard for his son.

Podor looked from his parents back to the teens. "I am, in fact, a scientist. Not a … well, not a planetary scientist, not one who studies aliens, but I run in circles with a lot of scientists, naturally," he said. "We've had conversations about aliens before. As one does. Dreaming, speculating, imagining, always; never actually thinking the speculating would become reality. Always hoping we'd one day find out about life on other planets, but never knowing or believing that could happen in our lifetimes." He shook his head. "And yet here you are. You say you're from another planet, another universe. I have no reason to believe you, but at the same time, no reason not to. Turns out I wasn't prepared for this. We always thought it was a certainty that there's life on other worlds, but I guess I never actually thought I'd be one of the ones to …" He looked at Emma, and then the others. "To meet you." Suddenly, he burst out laughing and shaking his head. "Aliens!" he said. "Amazing." He studied them carefully. "The bracelet does that?" he asked, incredulous. "The bracelet masks your actual form?"

Charlie looked at his own bracelet. "Yeah, we don't remember a lot, to be honest," he said. "All that is gone. Dr. Waldo and Ben and Eve didn't have time to explain everything to us before we came back."

"Maybe we should have given them time," Ree said under her breath.

"We don't have a lot of time," Chuck reminded her.

"We have *all* the time," Ree said.

Podor watched the exchange with joy. "Could you … could you all do me a favor? Could you all remove your bracelets at the same time? I want to see you. See how you're different, and how you're the same."

"Okay," said Charlie, "but if you say anything while we have them off, we won't understand you. One of the stones is a translator, too."

"A translator!" Podor said. He definitely had a scientist's joy at all this new information, Emma thought. He was someone who saw something unusual and unexpected, and couldn't wait to figure it out.

The teens looked at each other, and on cue they all inhaled, then removed their bracelets. For a split second, Emma worried that Nolor might jump in and grab the devices, potentially killing them all if the atmosphere wasn't fit for them to breathe. She rubbed her toe against the pigeon in her shoe, wondering how fast she could get to it, or if she could even swipe the blue part with her toe.

Podor spoke, but without their bracelets they couldn't understand him. Charlie replied. "We can't understand you, and probably now you can't understand us." Having used up the oxygen in his lungs, he put his bracelet back on, and the others did the same.

"Amazing," said Podor. "Amazing." His eyes were filled with the desire to tell others, to call his friends, to share. "This Dr. Waldo," he said. "Where is he, exactly?"

Chuck laughed. "That's sort of a complicated question," he said. "Dr. Waldo is in the Hub. The Hub is a place where all the universes converge. It's sort of everywhere and nowhere at the same time."

"But how did you find it?" Podor asked.

"It's inside the lighthouse," Emma said, repeating what Ben had told them. "To be honest, we don't remember a lot. We are going to have to get our memories back before we can tell you more."

Podor nodded rapidly, his mind whirling. "Could I meet this Dr. Waldo? Could you take me to him?" he asked.

Emma nodded. "We can," she said, "but you have to be willing to help us, too. We need those memories."

Podor beamed. "It's a deal," he said.

"Take Podor to this Hub first," said Nolor, his arms still crossed. "Then your memories. Prove it to him first."

It was clear this was not negotiable. Emma looked at Charlie, then nodded. "Okay," she said. "Let's go to the Hub."

Disbelief and utter excitement glowed on Podor's face. "Now?" he said "We're going now? You're taking me now? This is amazing. Incredible. I really can't even believe this is going to happen." He jumped lightly a few times, too excited to stand still, then crossed the room to hug his parents, whose faces showed more concern than joy.

"Is it safe?" Daya said, her son in her arms. "You must come back to us soon."

Nolor said nothing as he hugged his son, but he held on for a very long time.

His goodbyes done, Podor turned back to the teens. "What do we do?"

In the meantime, Charlie had fished a pigeon out of his backpack. "We use this," he said, holding up the small ball between his thumb and forefinger.

Podor scoffed. "*That* will take us to a place between the universes?" he said. The look on his face said that his doubts were growing.

Charlie shrugged. "It worked before. Like we told you, we don't remember much. Dr. Waldo will be able to tell you more."

A giant smile broke out across Podor's face. "This is incredible, just incredible," he said. He rubbed his hands together. "Let's go. Let's go now."

The teens all hooked arms and held hands, and drew Podor into their circle as well. "Hang on tight and don't let go no matter what," Emma said. "We don't want to lose you."

Daya gasped, but said nothing.

"Ready?" said Charlie, looking to each person in the group for confirmation. They all nodded. "Here we go!" He swiped the blue part of the sphere, and they dissipated into billions of molecules spread to the universes, their bodies reforming in the lounge at the Hub as though nothing had ever happened.

Eve had been at her desk, working on some calculations and twisting her mind through a scientific puzzle, when the disturbance in the air by the lounge caught her eye. She put down her pen and watched as her friends reappeared, and jumped up in delight to join them. "Ben!" she shouted as she raced by the lab station where he was working. "They're back!" She ran to the lounge and scooped Charlie and Ree, the people nearest her, into a bear hug. "You're back!" she said. "Did you get your brains back? Is everything okay?"

She then saw Podor. "Oh, a new friend! Who's this?" Eve untangled herself from the hug and held out her hand. "Hello, I'm Eve. From the planet Lero. Welcome to the Hub!"

Podor's eyes were filled with wonder as he tried to take in what had just happened and what he was seeing. He held up his arms in front of himself, staring at them as though he'd never seen them before, then patted his body to make sure it was all there. Finally he noticed Eve's outstretched hand, and he grasped her hand in both of his own. "Hello," he said. "I am Podor. From the planet Maluket. Nice to meet you." He stared at her eyes, her translucent skin, her long white-blonde hair. "Lero," he said. "You would definitely stand out on Maluket."

"Eve," said Emma, "I'm confused. How can we understand you, but you look like you're from Lero now? You have a bracelet on. I thought that would make anyone looking at you think you looked like their own species?" She looked at her bracelet and tried to compare it to Eve's.

"Oh, yes," said Eve. "That's new! The bracelets you all have do have that stone. But here in the Hub, it's no fun having everyone look like ourselves! So Ben and I just created new bracelets that don't have that stone. That way we get to see everyone looking like themselves. Having everyone look just like me is boring! We'll still use the original bracelets when we travel," she said, "but here in the Hub, there's no need. Anyone who comes here knows about aliens." She smiled broadly and Podor smiled back, caught in her joyful spell.

"Incredible," he said. He surveyed the area further. "This place," he said. "They tell me this place is in between universes. That can't be right?" Off in the distance he saw Rupert, the two-dimensional elephant, cavorting in a large field. Unseen birds were chirping in the air. Scientists conducted experiments, formed hypotheses, and fretted over calculations in another area. The Experimental Building flickered in and out of existence.

"Yes, that's right," said Eve, smiling broadly. "Everything is possible here."

"Oh!" said Podor. "Incredible. Amazing!" It seemed like he had no idea where to look; fascinating sights caught his attention from all sides. "Then you can get your friends' memories back here?"

Eve's smile fell. "You didn't get them back yet?" she said. "I hoped you had. We're trying to figure it out—Ben is working so hard—but we still have work to do."

This time Podor frowned. "I was working on this myself. I believe I can get the memories out of one person and put them into another; I have done so once. But that requires the cooperation of the person from whom the memories are being extracted. In this case, Corala and Leidar. I don't know if they'll go along with this."

As Podor was talking, Dr. Waldo and Ben joined the group. Ben stepped forward. "Hello, I'm Ben. This is Dr. Waldo," he said, stepping back to let the scientist greet the newcomer.

"Yes, yes, Dr. Waldo, that's me," said Dr. Waldo, shaking Podor's hand. He seemed more harried than usual, more worried. Wrinkles lined his forehead even as he smiled.

"Podor," said Podor, shaking Dr. Waldo and Ben's hands in turn. "I understand you're the one who can explain all this to me," he added, sweeping his arms wide to include the entire space. "Traveling from one planet to another, one universe to another … as a child I always dreamed of this. But we never imagined it possible. Your friends here can't remember how they first discovered this … this space travel. They said something about elevators, and a lighthouse, but they don't remember much. Can you tell me?"

"Ah yes," said Dr. Waldo. He motioned for everyone to take seats in the lounge, and then sat himself on the edge of a cozy chair.

"Well, simply put, every planet—at least, every planet we've managed to visit so far—has what we call 'thin spots.' At these thin spots, there are what we call 'elevators,' though some might call them 'portals.' It's just what we call them. You can travel to other universes by entering these elevators, if you have the key."

Eve held up her necklace, a small gray rock with a white stripe around it, attached to a long string. "A wishing rock. Not all wishing rocks open the elevators, but this one does. When I get near an elevator, if I'm wearing this necklace I'll start to sort of feel the energy of it. When I get closer, the door to the elevator will open."

Podor's jaw dropped in disbelief. "You're kidding." He paused, thinking, for a long moment. Then he said, "Do you think a person might be able to feel the energy of an elevator even without the key?"

Dr. Waldo nodded. "Yes, indeed, indeed I do, I think many have felt the energy of these places, but not many have figured out why." His eyes twinkled. "Are you thinking of such a spot on your own planet?" He rubbed his hands together in glee.

Slowly nodding his head, Podor said, "I do. Maybe. Our planet has a high electrical force, but more so in some places than in others." He turned to Charlie, Emma, and the others. "And I think it's just where we need to go. The Tower. Where memories are stored. Based on what you told us, I suspect that's where you were when you woke up without your own memories."

"If that's the case," Charlie said, "then I agree that's where we need to go." He stood. "Are we done here?"

Podor did not stand just yet. "But this place," he said, his eyes unable to stop drinking in all the wonders. "I would like to come back." He looked at Dr. Waldo and raised his eyebrows in question.

"If this Tower is indeed an elevator, then it may be as easy as that," said Dr. Waldo. "We will get you sorted, young man. But I can see our friends here are eager to get going, and I think this time the rest of us will go along."

His statement left no room for argument, and the teens didn't bother. Eve and Ben brightened at hearing they would be going along on the adventure. Ben quickly gathered up travel packs for everyone, and gave Dr. Waldo, Eve, and himself pigeons to stuff into their shoes. "You never know," he said. "It saved them once already." He then handed Eve and Dr. Waldo different bracelets to put on. "So we don't look like aliens," he said, changing the one on his own wrist.

"The Tower coordinates, you think that's where you came from last time?" said Eve, securing the bracelet on her wrist. "That's where we should go now?"

"Well, yes, but we don't want to end up locked into a room at the top of the Tower again," said Emma. Thinking about it made her feel claustrophobic all over again. "Can we put ourselves like fifty feet away? Outside?"

"But what if that's in the middle of a lake?" said Chuck.

"Well, we ended up underwater once and survived," laughed Eve, but the looks on the others' faces reminded her that they had no recollection of that adventure. She sighed. "Okay, then. How about we go to the room you came from, assess the surroundings, and then use another Dark MATTER sphere to jump outside? Sort of a small job for a Dark MATTER sphere, but it would be safest."

Everyone agreed, while Podor just shook his head. "Incredible," he said under his breath.

The group gathered around Eve, who had the first Dark MATTER sphere set to go. "Group hug!" she said, clearly delighted to be part of the adventure again. Everyone locked arms and held hands, and she swiped the sphere.

chapter twenty-one

The room high up in the Tower was cool when they landed back on Maluket, but one thing had changed: the door was no longer locked. It had been opened and left ajar. Whoever had abandoned them in the room before knew that they'd been gone.

"Is this the right place?" said Podor, scanning the bleak interior, furnished with nothing but six sparse, narrow beds. "You were locked in this room?" He walked to the window and grabbed the bars as he looked out. "Oh, wow," he said, quickly releasing the metal. "Lots of energy in those." He touched a bar again with his finger, tentatively, carefully. "That'll keep a person inside," he said.

"This is it," said Chuck. Aside from the open door, nothing had changed. He crossed to the window where Podor was standing and lightly touched the bars, jumping back at the shock. "Was this once a prison or something?" he asked. The walls were made of giant blocks of gray-brown stone, held together with a mortar of some sort.

Podor tilted his head. "In a sense, I suppose," he said. "This is where they bring the Gleymara who have turned thirty, to take all their memories. Of course they die after that," he said. He paused, lost in thought, listening, maybe, for the ghosts of those who had died there. "It's their choice, in a way, but it's not an informed choice. They've been brainwashed their whole lives to think they'll become a part of everything when their memories are taken. That they'll live on somehow. Some run away, but that doesn't even occur to most of them."

Emma trailed her fingers along the stones. She couldn't imagine the horror of being trapped in here any longer than they had been. "This is the place you think has an elevator?" she said.

Eve pulled out her necklace. "If it does, it's not in this room," she said. "I would have felt something by now." Nonetheless, she walked the perimeter of the room to see if there were any changes in the energy. "You're right, though," she said, gazing up at the high ceilings before looking out the window, carefully, without touching the bars. "There's a ton of electricity here."

"You should have seen the storm," Ree said. "It was insane."

"Last night?" Podor said, winking. "Just another day on Maluket." His gaze fell on Eve's necklace. "That rock," he said to her. "I have seen rocks like that around here, too. Down at the water's edge. Will they open elevators, too?"

"Some of them, probably," Eve said, "But not all of them."

"How might I know which ones will open the elevators?" Podor asked.

"We have ways to test the rocks back at the Hub," Eve said. "But to be honest, I start by trusting my gut. You have to sort of listen to the rocks. Pay attention. Just like people, they can tell when you're really paying attention. Everything has a story in it, if you're willing and able to listen. The ones that are keys to the universes, I feel like they sort of guide me to pick them up. I can't really explain it." She shrugged.

Podor laughed. "That's not exactly an answer. But I will give it a try. In the meantime, maybe we can walk around the Tower and see if your necklace tells us whether there's an elevator here?"

Ben spoke up. "Or," he said, "maybe that can wait? Not that it's not important, Podor, but ..." he looked at his friends. "We don't know the effects of prolonged ... I guess prolonged memory loss. I think the sooner we get these guys' brains back, the better."

Podor nodded. "You're right, of course."

"Any ideas on how we're going to do that?" Emma shivered. Hearing about how people died after their memories had all been taken away had not been at all comforting. More and more she was starting to think maybe she could learn to live without her memories, if it meant she could just go home.

"I think we start by getting out of here," said Charlie. He came over and wrapped an arm around his sister's shoulder. "Don't worry, Em. It's going to be okay."

"Getting out of here sounds like a good idea," said Chuck. He then noticed Dr. Waldo at the window, tapping the bars quickly with his fingers, his eyes lit up with joy. "Dr. Waldo? Something interesting?" he said.

Dr. Waldo's smile grew as he continued to study the bars, holding up a device he'd brought with him that was scanning the atmosphere, its readout flashing wildly as it filled with information. "Fascinating, simply fascinating," he said, mostly to himself. "This planet is amazing!" He turned to Podor. "To be honest, I don't get out of the Hub much myself anymore. I have been remiss in exploring. Your planet intrigues me greatly. Once we get these children's minds back, I would like to talk with you about your culture, how advanced your science is," he said. "Yes, yes, we will certainly have you back to the Hub, and we will talk."

At this, Podor beamed with delight. "That, sir, would be my greatest pleasure."

"In the *meantime*," Charlie said, heading to the door and not waiting to see if anyone was following him, "we need to get out of here before they come back and shut us in again." The others trailed behind him out the door. Immediately before them was a circular stone staircase, leading both up and down.

"Maybe we can come back and look around a bit, once we're all fixed," Ree said, looking up the staircase and craning her neck to see what she could see. Another floor up, a window next to the stairs filtered in some daylight from outside, but beyond that, all they could see was more stairs. Carefully steadying themselves against the wall, they started their descent.

After two more flights of stairs, Charlie stopped at a window. It was very narrow, but not covered in bars. "We're still pretty far up," he said. "Podor, how big is this building anyway?"

Podor joined him at the window and looked out at the landscape, but from his viewpoint was unable to see much more of the building. "Pretty big," he said. "I haven't been by for a while, but as kids we used to come here and dare each other to get close to it. The tower part of the Tower is five or six floors high itself, I think. Then there's the base. I think it's two floors high. It might have a floor or two below ground level, though. I don't know. It's pretty big."

"A floor or two below ground level?" said Chuck. "Like a dungeon?" He made his eyes big and spooky.

"I suppose it could be," said Podor matter-of-factly. He started down the staircase again.

Chuck looked at Ree. "I was kidding about the dungeon," he said.

"Apparently he wasn't," said Ree.

Eventually they came to a closed wooden door. Charlie stopped in front of it and put his ear against it, holding a finger to his mouth to indicate the others should be quiet. He listened intently for several seconds. "I think I hear voices," he whispered. "People talking." He listened for a while longer, while the others all held their breaths.

Emma crawled up next to her brother and quietly pressed her own ear to the door. "I hear them, too," she mouthed.

"How many?" whispered Podor.

Emma shrugged. The voices on the other side grew louder; perhaps an argument, Emma thought. Then, the voices stopped, and they could hear footsteps coming toward them.

Emma looked at the others, her eyes wide. "They're coming!" she whispered, and she flattened herself against the wall and closed her eyes, unsure what else to do.

The others were all still standing on the landing, wide-eyed and bewildered, when the door burst open. There stood two beings, looking at the group like an accusation. One then shifted the grimace on her face into a forced smile.

"Hello?" she said, sweetness dripping from her voice. "Can we help you?"

Podor stepped forward, holding one arm back as though protecting the others. "Are you, by any chance, Corala and Leidar?" he asked.

The beings looked at each other, and the one who had spoken nodded once. "Yes. I'm Corala. Can we help you?" she repeated.

"I think you have something that belongs to my friends," Podor said.

A small smirk turned up the corner of Corala's lip. "I can't imagine what you mean," she said. "Interesting friends you have," she tossed over her shoulder, as she turned and walked back into the room.

The others followed her through the door. The room was enormous. While the structure itself had the feel of an old English castle, the space was filled with unfamiliar technology. Vast shelving units held row upon row of tall, rectangular, metal plates, sealed inside transparent plastic covers, with cords traveling from each plate to the shelf it sat on. More cords connected all the shelves, and yet more cords connected the various shelving units. Green and yellow and red and blue lights blinked and cycled silently and computers hummed throughout the room. Beyond glass walls was another room with even more shelving units with even more metal plates, and some furniture that looked like an ominous dentist chair, with a helmet that would come down on the patient's head, straps for arms and legs, and cords, not currently attached, that ran from a table by the chair to a bank of computers behind it.

"Oh my," said Dr. Waldo, the lights of the computers reflecting in his glasses. "Oh my, indeed."

"Are these … are these the brains?" Emma asked in horror, looking at the metal plates. "Is this where our minds are?"

Leidar chuckled, a menacing sound. "No, no, your brains aren't there. We have them," he said. He pointed to his head. "In here. I'm glad you're back, though, because there's something that makes no sense. What's very strange," he continued, with a long look at Corala, "is that we can understand you now, and we recognize you as the people we met before. But in your memories …" He looked the group up and down. "In your memories there's no one who looks like you, or us, and you're all speaking a language we don't understand." He stopped, staring them all down for answers.

Ree gasped. "Ohhhhhh," she said. "Of course."

Emma felt a flood of relief wash over her. If they couldn't understand the language, there's no way they could know … well, at least they couldn't know *everything*. Although they were pretty smart. How much had they figured out?

Leidar had been watching the wheels turn in her expressions. "At first we couldn't figure it out. We've never taken memories like yours before. It was as if your memories were all just dreams of some strange alien planet." He paused, again watching their reactions. After a moment, he nodded. "But then, there *were* strange aliens and planets. Creatures we'd never seen before. An underwater world. Times when you were in one place one moment and another the next."

"We were wondering," Corala said, her tone saccharin-sweet, "if you'd care to explain? What, exactly, are we seeing here in your memories?"

The Earthlings and Leroians were quiet for a moment. Then Charlie spoke up. "If you don't understand our memories, then why keep them?" he said. "They're meaningless to you. Why not just give them back?"

"Well that's just the thing, isn't it?" Corala said. "Maybe you have more memories like this that you would like to share with us?" She leaned against a lab table and reached for a long, menacing-looking iron rod. She tapped it lightly against the palm of one hand.

"Wait," said Charlie, his eyes on the rod. "Stop. Here's a question for you. Why do you steal memories? Why do you do this in the first place?"

"Ugh," said Corala, putting the rod back on the counter and shaking her head. "Really? You want to get philosophical? It should be obvious. Because life in the colony is so *boring*. Nothing changes. It's all the same, all the time, all day long. *Boring*." She rolled her wide eyes.

"But do you realize that when you take all of someone's memories, they die?" Podor said quietly. He looked at the racks of metal plates and clenched his teeth. "My sister, for example. You took all of her memories. She is gone."

A moment of fear flashed across Corala's face before she composed herself again. "I'm sorry," she said. "It just happens."

"It doesn't *just happen*," Podor said, less quietly. "You made that choice. You make these choices. These kids didn't lose their memories by accident," he said, waving an arm to indicate the foursome from two different Earths. "That was your choice."

"Your choices have the power to both create and change your future," Ree said, half to herself. "I remember!" she whispered to Emma. "Do you remember that? Our choices have the power to create and change our future."

Emma shook her head lightly. She didn't remember that conversation. But the fact that Ree did gave her hope.

"What?" said Corala, looking on Ree with great disdain. "What did you say?"

Ree looked at Dr. Waldo and straightened her back, standing a little taller. "It's what Dr. Waldo told us. Our choices have the power to create or to change our futures."

Dr. Waldo smiled broadly.

Leidar shrugged, sneering. "What does that mean?"

Ree took a deep breath and let it out. "It's complicated. But time is like a river, and all of time is happening at once." She blinked. These were among the lost memories, coming back to her in sudden flickers. "I can't remember." She looked at Dr. Waldo for help.

"Ree is exactly correct," said Dr. Waldo, looking as stern as any of the teens had ever seen him. "And, and, may I point out, you have these memories, you have this … this knowledge, and it's worthless to you because you stole it without experiencing it. Someone else cannot learn your lessons for you, and you cannot understand the universes by taking someone else's memories. You are stealing memories, and all you are doing is harming others. Has taking what is not yours made you happy? Or has it just made you want more?" he stammered. "You must stop. You must stop now. Ree is correct. Time is all happening at once. Past, present, and future, they all exist right now. But you still have the power to make different choices. The future is not set. You may change the future by making different choices."

Charlie took a step forward, glancing around at all the equipment and storage units and other contraptions they did not understand. The lights on the computers blinked and the whole room hummed. "Look, why don't we go outside and talk out there. It's making me nervous being in this room," he said.

Corala grinned a non-reassuring grin. "Scared?" she laughed. "Of us?" Her eyes drifted to the dentist chair behind the glass wall. "Do you even remember what you have to be scared of?"

"We are definitely going outside," said Charlie, moving to leave.

"What if we don't follow you?" said Leidar. Clearly he was more curious than Corala, who seemed to be completely without interest.

"You'll never find out what I'm offering," Charlie said. He turned and walked out of the room, and his friends followed.

Leidar turned to Corala, who was watching the others go. He huffed, and walked after the group. With a casual, disinterested look around the room, as though no one was making her decisions for her but her, Corala loped along as well.

By the time everyone was outside, Charlie had already found a spot on the ground in the shade of the Tower and was sitting on a large boulder. The day was warm and a bit humid. Emma felt like even she could smell a storm coming.

"How often do you have the … the Electrics?" Emma asked Podor, finding a rock near him on which to sit.

Podor sniffed the air, then smiled. "Maybe you are more like us than you realized," he said.

"Is there another one coming soon, then?" Emma strained her neck to look up at the top of the Tower. Now that they were outside she could see its structure: made of large stones, with a wide base several stories high, and a narrow tower rising up from the middle. That must have been where they'd been trapped, she thought.

"Yes," said Podor, sniffing again. "Not immediately. But soon."

"Do you smell it?" Emma asked. She sniffed the air herself, searching within the scents for something that would indicate a storm. What would a storm smell like, she wondered. Hot? Would it sting her nose? Would it hurt?

"How do you know on your planet what the weather will be, if you can't smell it?" Podor asked eagerly. The excitement he felt at being able to talk to aliens was more palpable than any incoming storm.

"A weather app on my phone," Emma said. "Weather forecasters, I guess." She pulled out her iPert and scanned the icons, wondering if Dr. Waldo had put a weather app on this device. Of course, he had. She smiled, pointing to the icon of a sun, cloud, and rain. She tapped the icon, but the screen simply came up with the message: No Data. "Bummer," she said.

"But how do your weather forecasters know the weather?" Podor asked. "Do they sniff the air?"

Emma laughed. "No, not that I know of! They … well, I guess computers, probably. Satellites, maybe." She scrunched up her face. Exactly how *did* weather forecasters come up with their forecasts? She realized she didn't know.

"And they are always correct?" Podor said.

"Not exactly," Emma smiled. "But close enough, I guess."

Podor sighed with delight.

"You're excited," Emma said, her smile growing.

"I can't believe this," Podor said. "Finding out how aliens from another planet predict their weather. Sitting with an alien and talking about the weather. It's a dream come true." He laughed. "As ridiculous as that sounds, it is a dream come true. I hope that after you have your memories back, we will have a chance to continue talking. I would hate to have aliens drop onto my planet and then leave without my having a chance to ..." His smile fell.

"What?" said Emma. "What were you going to say?"

"I was going to say how much I want to know everything you know." He looked over at Corala and Leidar. "I suppose if I were them, if I didn't know another way to gain the knowledge, I might want to take your memories, too." He watched Corala and Leidar, who had not yet joined the group but were talking quietly to each other a short distance away. "It's important always to try to see things from the other perspective," he said.

"Hmph," Emma said. "That may be true, but that doesn't give them the right to take our brains."

A muffled, distant sound filtered through the thick air, and Podor looked around to find its source. Finally he saw it: a small figure running toward them, waving her hands in the air. The light of a remembered thought crossed his face. "Akala!" he said. "I think that's Akala!" Seeing the blank look on Emma's face, he continued. "I haven't had a chance to tell you about Akala. You don't remember her, I suppose. But ... well, she had some stolen memories. We were able to take them out of her and give them to someone else. That's progress, I guess."

"Akala," said Emma, searching her mind as she watched the figure approach, trying to prod it for memories, but none came. "I know that name was on the note Charlie wrote to himself, but I can't remember her. That's her?" she said, nodding toward the quickly approaching girl.

Podor nodded toward Akala. "We thought Akala might have had some of my sister's memories, but it turns out they were from another scientist my sister had worked with. We took them out and gave them to the man's mother. Akala has been with them. It was

… difficult. There was much anger mixed with the gratitude for the returned memories."

"You gave the memories back?" Emma's heart fluttered with hope. Even though she couldn't remember her memories, she missed them.

"Well, not 'back,' since the man was dead. But we returned them … we returned them home."

The girl was no longer running, but had slowed to a walk. "Do you know who has your sister's memories?" Emma asked.

"No," said Podor. He sniffed the air again. "Maybe they're inside," he said, "on one of those shelves."

Emma turned to look at the Tower. Was it possible? Could they somehow reunite all the memories with their rightful owners, or at least the families? Or would even their own memories be lost forever?

chapter twenty-two

Akala reached the group just as Corala and Leidar finished whatever discussion they were having.

"Akala?" said Corala, staring at the girl, puzzled. "What are you doing here?"

"Podor's parents told me they were here," she said, nodding at Podor and breathing heavily. "So I came."

Corala squinted. "Yes, you're in their memories," she said. "I thought that was strange. But helpful. The only time we could understand what anyone was saying was when they were talking to you, or Podor or his parents. They seem to have held back some information, though. You would be wise not to trust them, Akala." Corala dipped her head sweetly. "We will keep you safe. Don't worry," she said.

"Not trust them?" Akala said. She looked at Podor. "Why? And what do you mean, I'm in their memories?"

"They took more of Chuck and Charlie's memories, and took some of Ree and Emma's, too," Podor explained, his voice flat.

"Oh!" said Akala. A look of horror crossed her face. "But why? Why would you do that?"

"That's what we're saying," said Leidar, mimicking Corala's feigned concern. "You can't trust them. You have no idea who they are. They've been tricking you. They've been tricking all of us."

"Tricking us?" Confused, Akala turned to Podor for confirmation. "Tricking us how?"

Podor shook his head. "They may not have told us everything," he said, "but they had good reason. Now is not the time to explain, but ..."

Charlie stood up. "No, I think now *is* the time to explain. I've been sitting here trying to remember, and I've had some flashes of memories. I've been thinking," he said. "Thinking about how we got here—or at least, what they've told us, combined with those bits of memory that are coming back." He looked at his sister, and their parallel twins from another Earth. "We can't remember exactly, though, because you took our brains." He leveled a gaze at Corala and Leidar. "And *why* did you take our brains? Because you were *bored. Because you were bored.* Because you live in a colony that was built years ago out of cowardice and fear. Built because people didn't want to feel pain. Built because death is hard, and watching someone die is unbearable, and they didn't want to feel that anymore, so they decided to create a new and better world." He started pacing, his tone taking on that of a speech. Emma watched, wondering where this great orator had come from. She felt a twinge of pride in her heart.

"Now, I admit, I'm just guessing on some of this, but this is what I think happened. This world, your colony, was started with good intentions," Charlie continued. "People wanted to do good. Build a place where people would be safe and happy. But then things got a little weird. Because people in the colony wanted to only grow the best of the best people," he raised an eyebrow as he looked at Leidar, "they started to manipulate the genes of the babies they were raising. They started to create babies that were all alike, supposedly all perfect. But here's the thing." He repeated himself for emphasis: "*Here's the thing*. Who decides what is perfect? Problem is, one person's perfect is another person's nightmare. And what's more, when everyone is alike, when you all think alike, you start to lose what makes being alive special. You get rid of ideas that don't match your own, and guess what? You start to get bored. You get rid of ideas that don't match your own and you get rid of creativity, innovation, diversity, art ..." he paused, thinking, and then went on. "You lose the ability to think critically. First, the people in your colony just rejected new ideas. Then, they became *scared* of new ideas. But where did it all lead? Intelligent life craves creativity and ideas. Intelligent life is curious. But you took it all away and what happened? You got bored."

Charlie turned and saw Akala. He stared at her for several long moments, his eyes flashing and mind whirling. Finally, he turned back to address Corala and Leidar. "And also, you lose knowledge. Your colony is run down. People don't know how to fix things anymore. It is an unsustainable culture. Your ancestors created the colony so you wouldn't have to watch other people die, but now all of you are dying, together. Not in ten or whatever years when you all go to the Tower archives, but now, slowly, dying of a lack of richness. I don't mean money. I mean a lack of different people, different ideas. Having different people around, people who know different things, love different things, bring different skills to the group, that is what makes a culture rich."

Leidar had seated himself on a rock, and the discomfort on his face looked more than just physical. He avoided looking at anyone, even Corala.

Corala, however, was defiant. "Who are you to come here and tell us this? You're not even from this planet!"

Podor glanced at Akala, expecting this to be a surprise to her, but she was calm. "I knew," she said to him, quietly. "They talked about it in front of me. I didn't believe it, but ... I knew. It's impossible, but it is the only explanation. Don't worry. They have not been deceiving me. They are my friends."

Podor nodded and smiled. There was much to discuss, later.

Charlie watched this exchange and gave Akala a smile and a wink, then continued as though no one had spoken. "You lost everything when you created a colony where everything was the same, and so you got bored, and you craved new ideas and knowledge, but you didn't have any of your own, so you went out and stole them. But you didn't have to. You didn't have to steal, and you don't have to kill everyone when you turn thirty. None of it, none of it is destiny." He looked at Ree. "*We change the future by changing our choices*," he said, and he smiled and turned to Emma. "Emma, I'm remembering. All of it. It's still in there. I'm remembering," he said to her, softly.

"This is it," he went on to the group, his voice booming now. "This is the way forward. You are outsiders. You are rejected by the rest of your world because even though you are all the same to each other, you are different from everyone else. But it doesn't have to be that way. You can make a new choice. You can decide to become a part of the bigger world. And Akala," he turned to the first friend they'd made on the planet, "they're right. We were not up front with you at the beginning. We are from another planet, but we didn't tell you at first because we, too, were scared. We were scared you'd hurt us, or reject us, because we are different. Because we're not like you. No one wants to be rejected. But we're all different ... and yet, we're all the same." He took a deep breath and looked directly at Corala and Leidar. "This is what I propose. You give us our memories back. And we will work with Podor, and Nolor and Daya, and Akala, and all the people in your colony, to welcome you into the rest of the world. You don't have to steal memories.

You can create your own memories, just as amazing and exciting as anything you've ever seen in someone else's minds."

Corala's face showed a struggle of emotions. She looked toward Leidar, but he still was looking away. "The outside world does not want us. We have seen their memories. They hate us," she said.

Akala spoke softly. "They do, yes. But they hate us because of how we hurt them. I just spent hours talking with the family of the scientist whose … whose memory I bought from you." She ducked her head in shame, but then lifted her chin. "We took everything from them. That's why they hate us. But what if … what if we stopped doing that? I think what Charlie says is worth thinking about. He's right. Everything is falling apart back home. No one has … purpose, I guess. No one cares about anything. It's not a life worth living. I've talked with Podor, and his parents, and with others, and … well, I liked it. I liked being with people who know things I don't. Who have new thoughts to share with me. You should see the books they have! You could spend a lifetime in those books! It all makes me think, and I have not done much of that in my life." She turned to Charlie. "I think it is a good idea, Charlie. You are well spoken."

Corala turned toward Leidar. She stood and waved her hand indicating that he should follow her. He pulled himself out of his daze and they walked a fair distance away from the rest of the group.

Emma jumped up and ran to Charlie. Pulling him into a big hug, she whispered, "Charlie. Charles. That was amazing. You were amazing there. Who knew you could speak so well?"

Charlie hugged his sister back, then sat down on his rock again. She sat next to him. "I don't know, Em," he said. "It all just came out. And all my memories," he said, amazement in his eyes, "they're just coming back. I'm remembering things." He looked at her. "I'm remembering, for example, that last time, before you had lost your memory but after I'd lost mine, you told me to try. You believed in me. You believed I could do it." He punched her lightly on the arm.

"You are amazing, Charles Rainier Nelson," Emma said, tears in her eyes.

"Well, let's see if I made a difference before we jump to that conclusion," he said, but nonetheless he blushed, and smiled.

"You said you're getting your memories back?" Emma said. "How? Are they just coming back on their own?" She tapped her knuckles against the side of her head. "I wish mine would."

"I don't know, exactly," Charlie said. "Yeah, sort of they're coming back on their own, but it's like I'm willing them back. Maybe it'll work for you?"

"I've been trying, too," said Emma, "but nothing has worked yet. I'm holding out hope that we'll convince Corala and Leidar."

But it didn't seem Corala and Leidar had been convinced. They were talking in quiet tones, too low to be heard, but there was a lot of shaking of heads and hands on hips, and some pointing and waving as well. Finally, Corala walked away from Leidar and back to the group.

"The answer is no," she said. "We know better than to believe that anyone would accept us in the outside world. They would shun us and we would be worse off than before, and have nothing. We say no."

Akala stood suddenly. "No," she said. "You don't get to decide." Her voice wavered, but she stood firm.

Corala slowly turned her gaze to Akala. "What?" she said. She laughed maliciously. "Stop talking. You are nobody. Sit down."

Akala straightened her back, though her face showed how scared she was. "No," she said. "You don't get to decide for everyone. There's a whole group of people back there." She waved her hands in the general direction of the Gleymara colony. "Not as many of us as there used to be, but we are more than just you two. We will take this information to everyone and have … we'll have a vote. That's the way they do it on the outside world. Their decisions are not all made for them in advance by someone else or by tradition. People discuss, and they think about the positive sides as well as the consequences, and then they vote. And that's how we're going to do it."

Corala stared at Akala, stunned and flabbergasted at being challenged in such a way by such a person. She looked at Leidar. "Do you have nothing to say to this?" she sneered. When Leidar remained silent, she rolled her eyes. "You are worthless." She turned back to Akala. "You can do whatever you want, but you need us to get their memories back. You can't do it without our being present. So what are you going to do about that?" she huffed.

"Corala." All eyes turned to Leidar, who suddenly broke his silence. "Akala is right. Charlie is right. Life in the colony is awful. You said it yourself. You say it all the time. It's so boring. It's not a life. I … I want more." He stood and looked at Charlie. "Do you really believe the outsiders would welcome us?"

Charlie put his arms out, facing up. "I don't know, dude. But if life inside the colony is awful, isn't it worth trying? All we can do is try, man. If you don't try, you'll never know."

"You'll have us on your side," said Podor. "Akala, me, and many others I can talk to. I can help them understand. Life is about change. We do the best we can. Then when we learn more, we do better. That's how it is."

Leidar looked at the ground, watching his feet as he shuffled them in the dirt. Then, looking at Corala, he walked over to Charlie and reached out his hand. "Yes," he said. "I will try." He turned back to Corala. "We will go to the colony, and tell the others, and we will vote, as Akala said. You can come with us, or you can decide to be forever bored. As for me, I know an opportunity when I see it, and I am not going to miss out. Besides," he said, "I don't want to die when I'm thirty. I know from others' memories that watching people die naturally is painful, but I want to live."

Ree walked over and gave Leidar a hug. "It's all hard," she said. "Life outside, it's all hard. Well, not all of it. A lot of it. But it's also all worth it. And you have some great people who will be helping you."

Leidar smiled and blushed. "Thank you," he said.

"Well, Corala?" said Akala, her confidence growing stronger. "Are you with us? We still need to go to the colony and talk with everyone. Will you help us help them understand?"

Corala's face was red, tears threatening to fall down her cheeks. She looked at Leidar as though he'd betrayed her; as though she was completely alone now. Her eyes took in the Tower beside them, and she was quiet for a long time as everyone watched her, expectantly. She shook her head in the tiniest motion, and kicked the ground. "I will go with you, but I will not support your cause," she said.

A smile grew across Leidar's face. "But you'll go with us?" he said.

Corala said nothing, but she nodded.

"It's a start," Charlie said. "That's all we ask. That you start."

It turned out that the number of people in the colony was down to just over fifty. With Leidar's help, Akala gathered everyone into the main hall, where they started to explain about the outside world. It was quickly apparent that those who weren't tired of their sheltered, boring life were in the minority. Corala tried to argue her own side of the debate, but she soon realized she was outnumbered. Almost all of the people in the colony had, at one point or another, partaken in the wares the memory thieves offered, and had seen what they were missing out on in life. Most eagerly welcomed a change, though many were wary, as Corala and Leidar were, that they would be accepted. Podor had called some of his friends to come and talk with them as well. After a few hours, it was clear the people of the colony were ready to make a decision. Akala called for a vote, and everyone in the room voted to open up the colony and join the rest of the world. Almost everyone, that is. Corala still voted no.

"She's just being stubborn," Charlie said to Emma. "You'll see."

Afterward, people mingled about enjoying food and drink that one of Podor's friends had brought as a gesture of goodwill. The air was buzzing with a feeling of possibility. But Charlie, Chuck, Emma, and Ree were ready for the next part of the agreement.

Chuck waved Leidar over to where the Earthling teens were standing. The look on his face as he met them was light, excited.

"This is not what I expected," he said. "I'm actually looking forward to something for the first time in … ever. Podor's friends are nice. Interesting. Smart." He looked down. "I guess we owe you some apologies."

"Yeah, sure," Chuck said, "we can get to that later. But first, there's the small matter of our brains."

"Small matter indeed," Eve joked. Chuck leveled her a look of fake offense. "What?" she said. "Too soon?"

"Everyone's a comedian," Charlie said, smiling.

"Okay," said Leidar. "You're right. Akala seems to have everything under control here. Let's go now." He caught Corala's eye, and she came to join them. "We're heading back to the Tower," Leidar said. "Time to give back."

Corala, Leidar, the Charlies, the Emmas, Eve, Ben, Dr. Waldo, and Podor all made their way back to the Tower. As they approached, Podor turned to Emma. "Do you feel it?" He said. "I swear there's some sort of energy here that you don't find anywhere else. There's something about this place. If there's an elevator on Maluket, this is it."

Emma stopped walking and focused her attention. The air was both calm and electric; it felt expectant, like it was waiting for something to happen. If she listened carefully, it almost seemed like she could hear sounds that, as far as she could see, had no origin. There was the faintest smell of distant smoke and honey. "You're right," she said. "I wonder if that's why they built the Tower here, whoever built it. They could sense something." She started walking again. If there was something otherworldly about this place, it could wait until after they had taken their memories back. They had waited long enough.

Everyone gathered in the large room with the rows of shelves full of metal plates. "Back there," Corala said, indicating the room with the menacing chair. "So, I have Ree's and Charlie's memories. Leidar has Emma's and Chuck's. Who wants to start?"

Emma shot her hand up. "Please. Unless someone else wants to," she said. The others all nodded consent.

"Okay, so first we take your memories out of Leidar," Corala said.

"I've been working out how to do this," Podor said. "Do you mind if I watch?"

"Sure," said Corala. She, Podor, and Leidar went into the glass room, and Leidar lay down on the chair, leaving the rest to watch from the main room.

Dr. Waldo crept up to the glass separating the two rooms, eyes wide with interest. He nodded as Corala spread a gel on Leidar's temples and forehead, and then attached diodes over the gel. She then placed a helmet over his entire head.

"Do you think it hurts?" Ree whispered. As far as they had seen, Leidar hadn't taken any painkillers.

"I'm guessing there's a numbing agent in the gel," said Ben, who had come to stand by the window as well. "You'll be fine," he said. He put a reassuring hand on her shoulder.

Corala tapped something into the keyboard on the computer next to the chair, then flipped a switch. There was a flash, then a hum, then lights on the computer flashed rapidly. Leidar flinched slightly and blinked several times, but didn't seem to be in pain. Ree let out a deep sigh.

After a few minutes, the flashing on the computer slowed, then stopped. Corala toggled the switch off and removed the helmet and diodes. She handed Leidar a towel, and he wiped the gel from his forehead. Corala nodded at Emma that it was time.

The entrance to the glass room was down a hallway on the side. Emma's heart fluttered as she walked down the hallway to the door. Halfway down, she stopped. There was another hallway to the left. Where did it go? There was something about it … She shook off the foreboding feeling and continued into the glass room.

Podor tossed her a look of support. "You'll be fine," he said, seeing the fear on her face.

She lay down on the chair and felt the residual warmth from where Leidar had been. Facing the ceiling, she noticed how high the ceilings were, something she hadn't noticed before. She felt a chill as Corala spread the gel over her forehead, and then a slight pressure as the diodes were attached. Was there already an electric charge surging through them, or was she just imagining things? Suddenly Emma felt nauseated. As Corala placed the helmet over her head, Emma started to feel claustrophobic, like she wanted to jump out of the chair and run for the hills outside. She looked at Corala, but the look Corala returned was far from reassuring. Suppressing the urge to flee, Emma forced herself to take deep breaths. Podor reached out and held her hand. Leidar stood by Corala, watching her closely.

"I don't know what will happen if you're holding her hand while the process is going," Corala said to Podor. "It's probably fine, but I don't guarantee anything."

Podor gave Emma's had a squeeze, then released it. "Sorry," he said. "I don't want anything to go wrong."

"It's okay," Emma said with a smile of gratitude. "Thanks." She squeezed her eyes shut. "I'm ready," she said.

Emma heard Corala tapping away at the keyboard again. She took deep breaths, counting to four as she inhaled and exhaled.

"Corala!" Leidar called out suddenly. "What are you doing?"

Emma's heart almost leaped out of her. "What? What is happening?" Her head was trapped so she turned her eyes to Podor. "What's going on?"

"Whoops," said Corala. "Easy mistake. There, I've fixed it."

"What?" said Emma. "What did she do?"

Leidar pushed Corala aside. "She had the machine set to extract, not return memories." He glared at Corala. "Go into the other room," he said. "I'll do this from here." Leidar tapped again on the computer. Emma's heart was in her throat and she wanted to cry, but she told herself to be strong.

"I'm here," said Podor. "We're all here."

Emma nodded.

Leidar tapped a few more commands into the computer, and then there was a click as he flipped the switch.

The sensation Emma felt was unlike anything she'd felt before. She could feel knowledge seeping into her brain cells, like hot lava on an ice field, melting away all the snow and leaving behind nothing but clarity. Images of the past flooded her brain, moving so fast she couldn't keep up. A truck under the stars. A lighthouse. A planet full of ghosts. An infinite void. A world of octopuses. A house underwater. Eve's home planet. World after world after world. And then home.

When she opened her eyes again, she felt like she'd been been in a room with half the oxygen she'd needed, and now she was breathing crisp, cool, oxygen-rich air for the first time. All the memories of the last several months, of adventures with her brother and these friends who were there with her, came back. With the memories came a deep sense of gratitude, for everyone who had been by her side. For survival.

She looked at Leidar with tears in her eyes. "Thank you," she said.

Leidar nodded softly. "I'm sorry," he said. He removed the equipment from Emma's head, and gave her a towel to wipe away the gel.

Podor helped Emma out of her chair. "All good?" he asked, his eyes hopeful.

"All good, she said. She gave him a hug and walked out of the room.

As she passed the mysterious hallway again, she gasped. "Ohhh," she said under her breath.

"Next!" Leidar called out. "Chuck, you're next."

Chuck headed into the glass room.

As Emma passed Dr. Waldo, a memory hit her. "Rupert," she said. "The elephant in the room." She smiled broadly. "Dr. Waldo, you are a funny man."

Dr. Waldo clapped with glee.

Chuck underwent the same process Emma had gone through. On his way back out of the room, he passed the hallway and his head snapped toward it. He looked at Emma. She put a finger to her lips. "Not now," she whispered to him. He nodded.

Next, Leidar called Corala back into the glass room. "You know you must," he said, staring intently into her eyes. She said nothing, but sat in the chair and let Leidar hook her up to the machine. Leidar quickly extracted Charlie's and Ree's memories from Corala, then returned the memories to their rightful owners. When Leidar was done and Charlie and Ree confirmed that all was normal again, he powered down the computer.

"That's it," said Leidar.

"Thank you," said Charlie. "Thanks for doing the right thing. I know it's not going to be easy going forward. You guys are doing the right thing."

"We will be with you," said Podor to Leidar and Corala. "You won't go through this alone."

Corala nodded, and she and Leidar left the Tower.

Once she was sure they were gone, Emma turned to the others. "That hallway," she said.

Chuck nodded. "I felt it, too."

"What?" said Eve. Having not gone into the glass room, she hadn't passed by the hallway herself. "You felt what?"

"Podor," Emma said. "You've said you feel a lot of energy in this Tower. I think you're right. When I walked down the hallway the first time, I felt something funny. Once I had my memories back, I knew why." She looked at Eve. "I think there's an elevator down that hall."

"An elevator!" Podor exclaimed. "You mean like the one in your lighthouse? The one that takes you to all the universes?" He rushed toward the hallway, but looking down it, he saw nothing remarkable.

"You'll need a key," Emma said, holding up the wishing rock pendant she wore around her neck. She walked slowly down the extra hallway, holding her hands out slightly at her side, as though they were antennae to help her find what she was looking for. The others all followed. "Getting closer," she said, shuffling along. She walked a few feet more, and suddenly a doorway that had not been there before slid open, revealing a small room inside. "Podor, may I present: your elevator," Emma said.

Podor's grin was the biggest grin they'd ever seen; he was almost in tears with joy. "An elevator! Here on Maluket! Will this one go to your Hub? Will I be able to visit you? Can I … oh my. So many questions."

Dr. Waldo patted Podor on the back. "All in good time, young man. All in good time."

Podor's smile faded slightly. "Should we tell Corala and Leidar? After all, we would not be here but for them."

Emma looked at the others and knew they all felt the same. "I don't think so. Not yet, anyway. I think they need to build up some trust first. You can decide when that is, Podor. I have high hopes for them, but trust is something that comes in small steps, over time. This is big. Start by seeing how they do on the outside world. And then, when they're ready …" She pulled the necklace from around her neck and gave it to their new friend from Maluket. "You, however, you saved us, Podor. We would not be here without you. Here is a key to the universes. And tell Akala, too. Be sure to visit us."

chapter twenty-three

"I got a message from Podor," Emma said. She, Charlie, Chuck, Ben, and Eve were gathered in their lounge at the Hub. Eve and Ben were finished working for the day. It was Friday—on Earth, anyway—and they were looking forward to a weekend for relaxing and resting. And, in the case of Charlie and Chuck, for looking into more destinations for their newly named Unparalleled Travel Company.

"Yay, Podor!" said Eve. She moved from her chair to squeeze into the seat next to Emma. "What does it say?"

Emma quickly scanned the message. "He says that everyone in the colony has agreed to help them sort through all the memories in the Tower, and they will return as many as they can to their rightful owners or their families. And he says Akala is leading the whole charge. She's got a completely new outlook on life, she's told him. Many of the people in the colony do, she says. Now that they've found a purpose. Something outside their own little world." Emma smiled. "I'm so glad. And he also wants to come visit soon. Especially to talk to Dr. Waldo and you guys about, well, everything."

"Write him back," said Eve. "Tell him to come anytime. We would love to see him, too!"

"So do you think you'll put Maluket on your travel list?" Ben asked Chuck and Charlie. "It was looking a bit sketchy there for a while, but I think, in the end, you've made some good friends."

Charlie looked at Chuck and answered for both of them. "Definitely," he said. "I think some of the people from the colony are interested in helping us, too. Which is amazing. But we'll need your help, Ben, in testing the planet. I want to make sure it's safe for us to breathe there. In case … well, if there are ever rogue memory thieves there who steal people's brains *and* bracelets."

Ben laughed. "Wow. Never an end to the excitement in the universes, is there? Completely unpredictable. You just never know what's going to be behind the next door."

As he spoke, the Hub door opened, and Ree and Ben stepped out.

Emma saw them walk in, then turned back to look at Ben, to see if he'd magically jumped from the couch next to Chuck, over to the door that led to the lighthouse. He hadn't.

"Ben," she said. "It's you." She stared at the Ben with Ree. "It's you with Ree."

Ben's eyes were already on the other Ben. "It must be the Ben from Ree's Earth," he said with a look of wonder and excitement on his face.

"Have you met before?" Chuck asked. "Met your doppelgänger?"

Ben shook his head. "No." By this time, the other Ben had spotted him as well, and their eyes were locked on each other. Ben stood as Ree and the other Ben walked over. As Ben neared Ben, Ree's Ben reached out his hand.

The two Bens shook hands, each with a growing smile as his eyes scanned over the other.

"Amazing," they said in unison, and then they laughed.

"I'm taking Ben to go see the Emergence on Maluket," Ree said to Ben, her hand in this other Ben's elbow, "and I thought you might like to come too, since you haven't seen it either."

"Um, yes!" Ben said immediately. "I'll go pack up. Just in case. Can't be too careful." His ear-to-ear smile never faded as he ran off to get a travel pack and an excess of pigeons.

Ree turned to Eve. "You should come, Eve. You don't get out enough. You work all the time."

Eve's gaze traveled back to her workstation, and a struggle crossed her face. "I mean, I would like to, but …"

"Work is *done* for the weekend. No excuses. And I will have you back in no time," Ree winked.

Eve laughed. "Well, then, yes! The way you guys described the Emergence, I definitely want to see that!" Beaming with happiness, she ran off after Ben.

"Anyone else?" Ree said to Chuck, Charlie, and Emma. "You're all welcome, of course."

"I'll come!" Chuck said, jumping up. "I'd like to see that again. It was incredible. I'll take notes for the company!" He hesitated, then ran off after Eve. "And I'm taking lots of pigeons! Just in case!" he said over his shoulder.

"Charlie and Emma?" asked Ree.

Emma looked at Charlie and read on his face that his answer was the same as hers. "Not this time, Ree, but thanks. You guys have fun."

"I think I've had enough of Maluket for now. But ask me again next time," Charlie said.

"Okay," said Ree. She waved at her Ben, who was running back toward her with a look of complete joy and excitement.

Emma was fascinated by how Ree interacted with her Ben, how she looked at him and how he looked back at her with a spark in his eyes. It was different, clearly, from how Emma interacted with the

Ben from Emma's Earth. There was an ease and a connection there that she didn't yet have. She decided that for now, that was okay.

Ben, Eve, and Chuck returned quickly, ready to go off on their mini-adventure.

"Do you have pigeons in your shoes?" Emma asked. She wondered how long it would be before she wasn't nervous again about leaving the safety of Earth and the Hub. If ever.

"Of course, Mom," said Chuck, rolling his eyes.

"Lots of pigeons," said Ben. "Smart to double check." He winked at Emma, and her heart fluttered just a bit. Hmmm, she thought. Maybe.

"Okay. Be safe, you guys," she said, but the group that was headed to Maluket was already racing to the Hub door.

Emma smiled as she watched them go. She would like to see the Emergence again, too, one day, but for now, all she wanted was to be here.

"I think I'll make some chocolate chip cookies," she said, jumping up to head to the little kitchen.

"That is a master plan, missy," said Charlie. "You don't want to just intention them into existence? We are, after all, in the Hub."

"No," said Emma. "I think I'd like to do it the old fashioned way right now.."

"Walnuts?" said Charlie, plastering on an endearing grin intended to convince her to add the nuts to the mix. Charlie liked walnuts in his chocolate chip cookies. Emma did not.

"Tell you what, I'll put them in half," Emma said, smiling.

In the kitchen, she savored the making of the cookies. She beat the butter into the sugar by hand, taking her time and enjoying the slight feel of fatigue in her muscles by the end. She measured the flour carefully, almost meditatively. After adding the chocolate chips, she meticulously split the dough into halves, adding perfectly chopped walnuts to one portion. As the cookies baked in the oven, she closed her eyes and deeply inhaled the sweet, warm smell. It was fun, she thought, to be able to jump from one place to the next without a moment's thought. It was fun to create things in the Hub with just the power of their minds. But giving time and effort to something, well, that made a person appreciate the end result all the more, she thought. If there was no work involved, you maybe didn't value it as much. You didn't know its worth. Work and effort and even failing sometimes, that made you grateful for things in a way that just having them never could.

Once the cookies were finished baking, Emma plated them up and carried them back to the lounge, where Charlie was sitting and reading a book he'd found.

"I've been thinking," she said, handing Charlie a plate of warm chocolate chip cookies with walnuts. She sat herself down on the couch next to him and picked up a cookie without walnuts, closing her eyes with joy as she took a bite.

"Trying something new?" joked Charlie. He put his book down, bit into one of his cookies with walnuts, and gave her a thumbs up.

She punched him in the shoulder. "Dork," she said through her mouthful of cookie. She finished chewing and swallowed. "No, seriously. You know how when I was in danger before, when all these adventures started, and you wanted to save me but I ended up having to save myself?" she said.

"Way to rub it in, Em, no worries, I'm good," said Charlie.

"I'm not trying to be mean. I'm trying to make a point. When I was in danger, I had to save me. But then when you were in danger, I tried to save you, but you had to save yourself," Emma said.

"Yeah, thanks a lot. If it weren't for me I'd be brain soup right now."

"We all would be. Ree and I just made it worse when we tried to fix it, really. I'm just thinking. Maybe, ultimately, maybe we can't save everyone else. Maybe each of us can only save ourselves."

Charlie chewed on this thought for a while. "I don't know about that," he said. "But whenever you're in trouble, you won't stop me from trying."

"Me either," said Emma. She leaned her head on Charlie's shoulder.

He reached an arm around his sister and gave her a squeeze. "Dork," he said.

Emma smiled. "I love you, too," she said.

connect

The Planet of the Memory Thieves is the third book in the Balky Point Adventures young adult science fiction/science fantasy series. If you loved this book, tell your friends and let Pam know! Leave a review online, send a tweet to @pamstucky, and/or drop Pam a note at facebook.com/pamstuckyauthor. Thank you!

Stay tuned for more Balky Point Adventures! Be among the first to know when a new story is coming out by signing up for Pam's mailing list at pamstucky.com!

Visit pamstucky.com to find out more about Pam and her other fiction and non-fiction books.

Made in the USA
San Bernardino, CA
16 March 2020